ADVENTURES
IN
VANGOLAND

The Rise Against Evil

SONNY WALEBOWA

ISBN: 1450590810
ISBN 13: 9781450590815

Library of Congress Control Number: 2010916228
CreateSpace Independent Publishing Platform
North Charleston, South Carolina

Cover Illustration by Erik Hodson
Edited by S. E. Walebowa
Final Editing by Mariah Lichtenstern

CHAPTERS

THE YOUNG HEART THAT HATES EVIL

During their usual early breakfast of saucy meatballs and scrambled eggs, the lanky Richard Dichaba leaned over the wooden kitchen table and kissed his wife, Victoria, with tenderness, and the smoldering embers at their lips burst into flames. With her tender fingers, she caressed his corporate tie that matched his gray suit and softly uttered the soulful words, "I love you, baby."

"I love you, sweetie," Richard said, bubbling with a smile.

Looking at her beaming face, one would never know that Victoria was fighting the biggest fight of her life, a debilitating brain cancer. Before, she was a banker, but her employer released her with severance after a long absence from work. Both she and Richard agreed that she would stay home until she had recovered.

Richard rose from the table and stepped into their only child's room. They named him Moabi, and his nickname was none other than Mo. His asthma inhaler was on the wooden bedside table—it was never too far from him, for his asthma attacks could be acute and enfeebling at times. A video game gadget lay on the floor, connected to an old Sony TV sitting on a wooden table at the back of the room.

On either side of the TV set, dozens of movies on DVDs were jaggedly stacked. Most were animated movies with animal characters. Mo loved animals. In one of his boxes perched in the corner, he had at least a thousand assorted animal toys. One of the activities that he liked to do with his father was going to the zoo, and it was not uncommon to see him watching the Discovery Channel.

One day Moabi was playing in the rain in front of their apartment when a lightning bolt struck him across his right hand. Finding him unconscious, his father rushed him to the hospital, and when he woke up, he was asthma-stricken. From that time, he became easily irritable. At school, he preferred to be alone, reading and drawing.

At home, his parents never really encouraged him to go out and play. This was especially true after he got into a fight with one of the boys in the neighborhood who called him Big Brows because of his thick eyebrows that curved in and connected almost in the middle of his eyes. However, his father would tell him that not all boys were bad but to never shy away from defending himself. Twice or thrice, he fought two older boys who threatened to take his football by force if he did not let them play with it. Gradually, he avoided socializing with others, and walking in his neighborhood became a rarity.

His father was his best friend—his hero. He took him to the parks and movies. They played football together. He once witnessed him chasing a vicious snake and snatching it by the tail before it could disappear into a nearby hole. Then he pulled it out and grabbed it by the neck when it charged. With a group of boys following him, his father marched down Hope Street to their apartment and threw the snake into an ice chest. He sat on it and convinced his scared wife to call the animal control department. From that day, Moabi believed that his father was the bravest person ever.

Normally Moabi would still be asleep when his father left for work, but this morning, he was fully awake. He grinned as his father bent over him, his tie touching the blanket as he kissed him on the cheek.

"Are you coming home early today, Dad?" asked Moabi enthusiastically, turning his entire body to face his father.

"Yes, today is Tuesday, Son. Remember, I told you I would get off early today? I was thinking maybe you and

I could catch a movie," said Richard, tapping Moabi's shoulder.

"Okay, Dad. Sounds like a plan," said Moabi, smiling. Oh wait, Dad, I wanted to give this to you before you go to work." Moabi reached for his sketchbook, which had fallen on the other side of the skinny bed. He carefully ripped the page off and gave it to his father. "Tell me what you think."

"Thanks, Son, I'll check it out," said Richard, carefully slipping the page into his ostrich-leather briefcase. "Love you," he called over his shoulder, dashing to the door and disappearing into the corridor.

"Love you too," said Moabi, throwing a blanket over his head.

• • •

Looking through the glass wall of the seventy-fourth floor, Richard could see an airplane in the distance flying toward the Hudson River. He was used to being up in the clouds among them. He plunged into his black leather executive chair to face the magnificent view of the city. With its sprawling skyscrapers, New York was a far cry from Gaborone, the capital of Botswana, where Richard grew up. He couldn't say that he loved one more than he loved the other, but he missed home. He dreamed of taking Moabi once Victoria recovered. Now nostalgic, he pulled the paper Moabi had given him out of his briefcase.

In the middle of the page was a picture of a strong male lion with a hefty mane locking his deep black eyes on a charging black mamba. The snake was flashing green spiky fangs. Below the drawing, Moabi had written:

> In the Rise against Evil, The king,
> a bold LION, fights the evil SNAKE.
> The snake wants to rule the jungle.
> Now they are in a fiery fight.

Although Richard was shocked by the image, an easy smile gradually formed at the corners of his mustached mouth. "That's my boy. He knows about good and evil." With the tip of his finger, he rolled a silver pen toward him to write some comments. But he decided to make a quick call to his son.

"Hi, baby," Victoria answered the phone.

"Hi, hon, can I speak to Moabi if he's up, please?"

"Hold on for him."

Mo, your dad wants to talk to you," Victoria called.

Still in pajamas, Moabi rushed to the phone. "Hi, Daddy!"

"Hey, Mo, what prompted you to write your story?" Richard asked, tapping the page with a pen.

It was quiet for about five seconds. "I hate evil with all my heart," the boy said.

Although Richard was surprised at the words that came out of his boy's mouth, he couldn't disagree with him at all. He continued to write on the drawing:

Good job, Mo. I like the story very much. Keep writing. I think it will be a great story once it is finished. You are going to be an excellent writer. Keep it up.

Love you, Son.

A rapidly increasing roar prompted Richard to look up suddenly. All he could see was the shining belly of a jet as its engines rumbled and whistled. His hand froze. His heart began to race. The pen plummeted on Moabi's story paper. "Me, too, son. I love you...goodbye," Richard said with a trembling voice before dropping the phone. Before he knew it, the plane whooshed into the building, sending pieces of debris blasting into his office. Irrationally, he thought about tossing himself through the window. *But that would not save me*, he thought. He burst through the door, rammed past the wailing people crammed around the jammed elevator and joined those scrambling to the stairway where darkness escorted them to the mouth of death. The smell of gas intensified. Smoke surged, causing an intense outburst of coughing. Suffocating and trapped, many pleaded with God, noses and mouths covered by either hands or clothes. Somewhere close and in the distance, Richard could hear the rupture of pipes, the bursting of glass, and a growing cacophony of terror.

When the skyscraper could not withstand pressure anymore, it crumbled into a heap of burning iron. Like many of those beautiful souls, Richard never made it home to his wife and son. Up to this point, Moabi had believed in God and trusted that He would heal his mother. Now, he could not understand why the Almighty had let evil prevail and take his father from him. His mother encouraged him to trust in God's magnificent grace, but secretly, Moabi had abandoned his faith.

•   •   •

It was early in the afternoon of the eleventh day after the tragedy hit when Moabi finally fell in deep sleep. Immediately, he began to dream. In the dream, a powerful pressure hit his father's office, blasting everything into pieces. He watched as a page from the story he'd given his father wafted through the shattering window and disappeared in the billowing soot. But as the debris hurtled, the paper shot through the billows, flew further up and drifted north. At some point, it looked like it had wings, which startled him. But as it soared over Battery Park, those things that looked like wings disappeared, and he could now see soot all over it. The paper descended through the lingering dust that enveloped Battery Park and landed under an iron bench. He woke up sweating as if he had been running.

He snatched his asthma inhaler from the bedside table and then tiptoed out of the apartment without being noticed. Outside and across the street, a tall man wearing a white shirt was walking on the sidewalk holding his son's hand. He reminded him of his father quite a bit, especially his easy stride. He watched them until they disappeared around the corner, and that was when he heard the bus roaring down the street. Without wasting time, he burst through the gate and rushed to the bus stop. By the time, he turned the last corner, the bus was already in motion, but he continued to run as fast as he could until he arrived at the bus stop. The driver slowly applied the brakes. Moabi was shocked because the local bus drivers never stopped for anybody arriving late. He noticed huge "We Love NY" words on the side of the bus as he rushed to the door. "Thanks," said Moabi stepping onto the bus, his forehead shining with beads of perspiration.

Looking at him in the rearview mirror, the bus driver nodded and winked at him. The mood inside the bus was rather somber yet colorful and rich, for most commuters were wearing T-shirts of different colors with comforting words such as, "In God We Trust." He sat opposite an elderly man wearing "Our New York—the Beloved Apple" T-shirt, whose eyes glared as though overwhelmed by the spirit of patriotism. The old man looked at him and smiled. From bus to bus to train, until he arrived at Battery Park, felt the same mood. He sensed the power of unity.

He scampered through the thick dust hanging in the park, and he rummaged under the grimy benches one by one until his fingers landed on a sheet of paper. Something inside convinced him that he was in the right place. Gasping for air, he reached into the back pocket of his trousers, pulled out the inhaler, placed it on his dry lips, and sprayed the medication into his lungs. As he pulled the paper out from under the bench, his heart began to beat fast. He couldn't see anything on the paper until he shook off the dust. He began to cry when he saw his father's handwriting.

When Moabi returned home and told his mother about his dream and subsequent discovery, she did not say anything to him about going to Battery Park without. All she could say was, "Are you sure you gave it to your father?"

Moabi replied, "Believe me, Mom, I gave it to him that morning. Look at this. He even wrote here encouraging me."

Left dumbfounded, with tears streaming down her cheeks, she ran her fingers over her husband's handwriting, proof of the dream that her son had just recounted. She'd heard about dreams that served as premonitions, but those that exposed the past were news to her. The closest phenomena she could think of were the stories of prophets who could see someone's past. Now she wondered if her son had that sort of gift. "Son, have you ever dreamed like this before?" she asked, looking Moabi straight in the eye.

"Nope, my first time," said Moabi, sharply shaking his head.

For Moabi, his father's encouraging words on the story paper became a treasure. He etched them in his heart. Although they did not actually alleviate the pain, they took the edges off and became a source of Inspiration—maybe even hope for hope higher power.

•   •   •

Every Thursday afternoon Moabi would go uptown for counseling. Victoria struggled with not only grief, but also her own mortality. She did her best to take care of herself with their limited means, while providing for Moabi too. She used Brook's life insurance to pay off the mortgage refinance they took out when she became sick. She put aside what was left in an equity-indexed account for Mo's college fund. They survived on Social Security and Disability checks until, after surgeries and aggressive treatment, Victoria went into an unlikely remission and returned to work in a position far removed from her previous career.

Seeing his mother in the predicament, she was in only pushed Moabi to become the man of the house at his young age. At fifteen, Moabi won prizes in high school for penning two powerful papers, *The Call to Rise Against Poachers and Water for Wild Animals During Drought.*

With part of his award money, he and Victoria formed a nonprofit organization called Surviving Cancer, which published stories about families affected by the disease along with education pieces on early detection. Every November, he ran the New York City Marathon to raise money for the cause.

He was not always successful as far as raising money was concerned, but the money he did raise helped patients who could not afford treatment. He knew he could do more if he had a team to help him. Unfortunately, he was a loner at heart, a young man who did not like to interact. Not because he was shy, but because conversation was something that overwhelmed him at times.

He preferred to work online, where he could ask people to support his vision without talking to them face-to-face. But in the back of his mind, he knew his vision could not bloom if he did not cultivate relationships. He sometimes longed for someone to call a friend.

"Always trust in God," the words often uttered by his mother, were quickly fading because there was something on the inside that bothered him. Every day now, he doubted the existence of God, if in fact He was there, how could he allow such evil things to happen? His mother read the Bible and prayed three times a day, but her situation was getting worse.

He thought about his father and the thousands of other good people who died at the hands of terrorists, about tornadoes that obliterated everything in their paths and kill the innocent, and about hurricanes that blew hardened walls of water on people. He didn't think a holy God would allow innocent people to be victimized by wars or by poverty.

His concept of God meant truth, justice, provision, and protection. When he didn't see his image of God, he ruled out that there was any—concluding that evil was an ever-present threat. He did not buy the idea that God was out there neglecting humanity on earth, because again, a true God would not be compassionate. One thing he believed and hoped for was to see good people coming together and building things that could prevent disasters, to see good nations becoming stronger than their enemies and taking care of those who could not take care of themselves.

As time progressed and Victoria's health deteriorated, they decided to look for a caregiver. Moabi convinced her to bring his cousin Gloria from California, noting that Gloria would truly love Victoria, unlike a caregiver who would just administer service for money. At first, Victoria was not comfortable with the idea because she knew she was not an easy person to deal with. She did not want to create a rift with any of her relatives. After a long period of emotional discussion, she grudgingly agreed. That decision relieved Moabi quite a bit, subsequently allowing him to adequately prepare for college entrance exams.

After Moabi gained acceptance to several universities, Victoria announced that she was sending him on Safari as a graduation gift. Bubbling with joy, he hugged his mother and kissed her all over her head, "Where, Mom? Where?"

Calmly, Victoria smiled. "Okavango Delta. That is where you wanted to go to be inspired to write a book, right?"

"Right, Mom! Right! Will I be able to meet anyone from Dad's family? I don't remember anyone from when I was little! How long is the trip? Talk to me, Mom."

"I was able to get in touch with your father's cousin. You'll depart to Maun from Gaborone, and he will pick you up when you return. You'll have three weeks to enjoy," exclaimed Victoria.

Moabi sucked his lips and shook his head in disbelief. Overwhelmed by emotion, he kissed his mother repeatedly. "I hope you didn't empty your reserves mom."

"No baby, I sold the diamond ring that your dad bought me. I thought it was fitting to use it for a Botswana trip since the diamond itself was from Botswana. I even have a couple of hundreds left to put in my bank," said Victoria.

Moabi released his hug, sighing, and said, "I thought that represented the forever love from father? Are you sure it is the right move?"

Victoria nodded, closed her eyes, looked to the ceiling, and touched her heart with her right hand. She was thinking about that she wouldn't have sold the ring if she thought she wouldn't die soon. Death was on her mind and wanted to see his son happy before it happened. "I am sharing your father's love with you, Mo. Trust me, this would make your father happy."

Across the living room, an old bookshelf filled with books stood against the blue wall. On top, a globe had been catching dust for many years. Moabi extended his arm and spun the globe before grabbing it. He placed it gently on the table and then blew the dust off. "Look at Botswana!" he marveled.

"I know my baby will write an inspiring book. I am going to love it, and the whole world will love it too," said Victoria from the couch.

"Thanks, Mom. It will make a lot of money, and we will wipe out cancer. Trust me on that one."

"That will be nice, Mo, but remember, money is just a tool, and God is the one who gives you the ability to make it. I trust you because I trust in God first."

The smile on Moabi's face faded when his mother mentioned God. Why do we have to give God a credit while he is not taking care of people? he thought. He wouldn't voice it loud because he did not want to make his mother sad. That would spoil the moment. "All I can say is that life is going to be better, Mom."

"With God, things are always possible," Victoria said. "I know cousin Gloria is going to take care of you, Mom," said Moabi, eying Gloria with a smile.

"Of course, I will," said Gloria, smiling and opening her arms to hug Moabi. "I know you are going to have fun."

"Thank you, Gloria," Moabi said as he wrapped his arms around her.

"You are welcome," said Gloria.

Moabi released the hug from Gloria and sat next to his mother. "I love you, Mom."

"Oh, I love you too, Son."

"I wish we could go together, Mom," said Moabi, extending his arm over her shoulders, his eyes welling with tears of joy.

"This trip is just for you. I'm not fit to travel a long distance. But I'm sure we'll travel together when I get this tumor out of the way," said Victoria, sighing.

"I understand, Mom. I will bring you a story, a story that you will never forget. I promise," said Moabi, his eyes becoming glossy with tears. "I am going to fight for you, and I believe you will be healed."

"Thank you, baby," said Victoria rising from the sofa. "That is encouraging." She did not want to cry in front of her son. As soon as she disappeared into her room, Moabi also called it a night.

●　　●　　●

The week after graduation, Moabi was on a flight en route to Botswana. His cousin, Mogogi and four other family members, two women and two men, came to pick him up from Sir Seretse Khama International Airport. They were elated and eager to see him. Only Mogogi knew him because he visited them the year his father passed, the rest had never met him—they had only seen his pictures.

As soon as Moabi came through customs, they all rushed to meet him. He looked more like his father in person than in photographs, they proclaimed. He even walked and stood like him, according to his aunt. Hugs and tears abounded; tears because it was the first time they met him, tears because his father went to America and never came back – and now it was too late. But they also rejoiced, rejoicing because at least his father had left them with his son.

As they left the airport, driving on the left side caught Moabi by surprise. For a minute or so, he felt uncomfortable. But nonetheless, it didn't take him long to be at ease and embrace the rhythmic flow of the occasional roundabout. They cruised steadily towards downtown as the sun beamed through the clouds — it felt like heaven was welcoming him.

Moabi marveled at the architectural diversity, like the eleven story Orapa House, a two winged building with the short wing that looked like a stadium stand leaning into and against the tall one. This was where the country's diamonds were sorted and valued.

The city center wasn't dense at all, but strikingly unique. It included scattered government buildings, Main Mall and some prominent residential properties. New constructions were underway, suggesting not only the rise in skyscrapers but also in the economy and perhaps population. However, Moabi noticed a decline in the quality of buildings as they neared Mogogi's house in Bontleng (which means where beauty dwells). Mogogi lived in a modest house with four rooms. The outside walls were stucco, and the interior was immaculate with touch of traditional decor complimenting the blue walls and red accents.

That night, they had fun feasting, dancing, telling jokes and stories. Moabi's uncle, Lekoko, roasted a lamb he brought from the cattle-post. In their culture, they didn't just slaughter a lamb every day. It represented something special — a kind of honor. When Moabi learned that, he felt loved even though there were just a few of them and their friends. Most of the elders and many of his other relatives awaited his visit to the family compound in the village of Mahalapye, where they preserved a more traditional way of life.

The next morning, Mogogi drove Moabi around the city, seeing poverty stricken places and glamorous ones. He learned that the city was named after the chief of the Batlokwa called Gaborone. They visited the "Government Enclave" where the statue of the first president majestically faced the "National Assembly." Then they went by the "Three Chiefs Monument." Mogogi explained that the three chiefs had traveled to Britain to protest against the British South Africa Company which was threatening to take over their territories. He elaborated that before the chiefs' journey, the country was already made a protectorate by the British who were protecting and expanding their interests in Africa. Mogogi concluded with what Moabi already knew—that Botswana gained independence in 1966 with the election of Sir Seretse Khama.

At the famous Pop Inn, they grabbed some spongy Mangwinya (fried fat cakes), fish, and chips (the kind Moabi called "French fries" at home), then continued on to Kgale Hill. There, Mogogi showed him the preserved set of "*The No 1 Ladies Detective Agency*" television series based on novels by Alexander McCall Smith. They ended the day at Botswana Craft. There, they listened to some traditional music, fusion and poetry while Moabi perused intricately crafted jewelry, smooth wooden sculptures, exotic masks, painted ostrich eggs, various musical instruments, and sweet-smelling woven baskets. Picking up a few items as souvenirs, he couldn't resist a T-Shirt featuring a map of the country. In fact, he would wear it with pride the next day in Mahalapye.

When they arrived at Madiba Ward in Mahalapye, the family showered him with love. His heart pulsated with joy as he walked on the same ground his father grew up as a child. His auntie shared a story with him that his father was a wild kid, yet so loving that he could bring one to tears. Moabi marveled that his father, who was born in such a humble place, had come to the end of his life in the World Trade Center in New York City. *"Life is a mystery,"* he thought, as he choked back tears.

Standing by the Mulberry tree, he watched a hen stretching her wings outwards as she led her brand new clutch through the narrow gate into the compound. A little bit further, along the fence, a cackling brood mingled among roosters with pointy combs and baggy wattles. Over the compound fence, goats and sheep were grazing around the ruins of mud houses. *"I wonder what happened to the people who used to live there*?" thought Moabi. But while still engrossed, Mogogi tapped him on the shoulder, bringing him back to reality.

Sitting by his cool and collected grandmother, Moabi watched young kids shuffling their feet with remarkable cadence as they danced for him. Some older folks joined to show their moves. At the big gate, neighbors trickled in to partake in the celebration. By the time the sun melted into the horizon, Moabi was overwhelmed with inexplicable joy.

The next day he was on his way to the pristine North, where the splendiferous Okavango River meandered with grace before birthing the magical delta—Okavango Delta. Arriving at the delta, birds, lions, leopards, elephants, rhinos, giraffes, and other animals gathered to quench their thirst and eat at their leisure. Creepy creatures suck in to practice prey on the weaker ones.

In the eastern part of the delta was a fenced-in national park consisting of wet, grassy lands dotted with lagoons. There animals dwelled in liberty. Notorious hyenas and wolves took delight in ruffling those they could intimidate, but when they saw those of superior strength, their tails went between their legs.

The enchanted Moabi joined a group of tourists riding in stout Land Rovers and Land Cruisers. They took off from the Maun Hotel in Maun and headed to a place called Tsodilo Hills. Slung across Moabi's square shoulders were brown leather straps supporting a black backpack. It had four compartments, each loaded with something useful for the adventure. Whenever he jogged, a bundle of keys and other gadgets in the small outer compartment jingled. In the second-biggest compartment, he had his notebook and a myriad of travel documents. Tucked in the middle of the notebook was his story paper, the same one he traced to Battery Park after he saw it in his dream. In the large compartment, he had a video game an iPod, binoculars, a still digital camera, and a compact video camera, each wrapped in a blue wooly cloth for Protection. Stashed in the last compartment were blank video tapes and batteries for both cameras.

The Land Rovers roared among animals scattered in families. Mighty lions strolled with authority and dominion. Packs of wolves assembled like villains planning a coup, and leopards exhibited their beautiful spotted coats in their breathtaking parade. Moabi clicked, and the camera clacked, capturing Botswana's best scenes.

As they roared over the sand dune, the hills began to rise sharply against the silver horizon. Soon it was apparent that what they were seeing were four quartzite outcrops lined up like a necklace from the tallest to the smallest, clearly dominating the dry savanna. A tourist in front of Moabi whispered to his enchanted wife, "Look at them. How beautiful. The City of Rock Art."

"They are also called the Louvre of the Desert," Moabi added politely as they disembarked from the vehicle. He had read about the local people, known as the San, who gave each of the hills a name according to their size and spiritual significance. The tallest, known as "The Male," was approximately 450 meters high, making it the highest point in Botswana. The second-tallest was referred to as "The Female." The next one in line was simply named "The

Child," while the little knoll was known as "The Divorcee," (for The Male was now married to The Female).

There were about 4,500 paintings on the rocks of the Tsodilo Hills, some of which dated back as far as twenty thousand years. Images of animals and naked humans were quite visible on the face of The Male, and there was a large concentration on The Female. Most of these paintings were the work of the San, although other groups, such as the Hambukushu, were believed to have contributed.

The spiritual aura of the site was so dense that tourists could feel a great peace. Despite the influx of visitors, the Tsodilo Hills remained a place of worship and reverence to the locals. The San believed that the most sacred place was at the tip of The Male and that the caves of The Female were the dwelling places of the spirits of deceased gods. All that the local people asked was that the hills be respected, that their gods not be disturbed. Moabi took out his camera and notebook, jotting some thoughts about the cave paintings for his story.

When he was done taking pictures of the tall hill, Moabi followed a narrow, rocky path that turned toward the next hill—The Female. The radiance and beauty of the paintings lured him to come nigh, while the rest of the tourists took the straight path, their conversations fading as they walked beyond the scattered bushes. As soon as Moabi passed by a boulder, he felt warm air brushing his neck, propelling him to turn around. He realized he was alone. Suddenly, the air became gusty, blowing his notebook open and whisking away the loose story sheet. He scrambled after it. Twice he tried to snatch it while on the run but, alas, to no avail. He did not anticipate that his life was about to take a turn. The path dead-ended into the dark entrance of the cave. Before he could grab the flying page, he tripped and fell on sharp, protruding stones. Blood speckled his palms as he watched his paper disappear into the dark cave.

It was completely quiet around The Female, and the wind that had caught him off guard had since passed. The cave entrance was pitch-black. He panicked for a brief moment but then quickly squashed the budding fear.

He remembered that he had a tiny silver flashlight. He rummaged through the backpack, pulled it out, only to realize that the batteries were dead. If the paper meant the whole world to him, then he had no choice but to go after it. He resolved to do it quickly because other tourists were probably waiting—if not looking—for him by now. He reached for his inhaler, taking two quick puffs before he began to crawl into the cave, groping for the paper. He felt the dry sand with his bare hands, and imagined the horror a trapped miner endured when the shafts collapsed. He thought about being stung by a black mamba or a scorpion and that he might not survive it.

About five feet into the dismal cave, a ball of light appeared in front of him. Shocked and amazed, he stared at the light, seemingly unrestrained by the walls of the cave. His eyes ballooned. He was not scared, but rather hypnotized, as he marveled at the ever-increasing light that now illuminated his face. Suddenly he was enveloped in the wool of a soft, bright cloud. While he struggled to comprehend the situation, the fogginess dissolved into an open bright world. He was shocked to be standing in a dry, sandy riverbed. Many aging, leafless trees stood still on the banks. Snatching up the story page that rested gently on the sand, he quickly turned around, hoping to find the Tsodilo Hills. Alas, there were no hills to be found—only the dry riverbed snaking into the gray wood. Confusion rose as he panicked. He had no choice but to make a decision: he went in the direction opposite of the way he was facing when fogginess dissolved, with the hope of getting back to the Tsodilo Hills. The hills never came.

The Morning was transformed into a hot day. Beads of perspiration formed on his face. On the banks of the river, the leafless, dry trees dropped branches that were decayed on the ground. Patches of lifeless, dry, brown grass studded the banks and beyond. Far in the sublime beauty of the blue sky, a white object like a kite flew in slow motion. "I wonder if that is a bird," Moabi mumbled, squinting his eyes. He watched the object until he could no longer see it. Then he sat down against the river wall, hoping that someone would come to his rescue.

He did not know that life was about to become uncertain and that he was no longer in his own world but in Vangoland, where evil was rampant.

WELCOME TO
VANGOLAND

Beelz, the snake, snatched a fly from the air and then muttered to himself, "For me to rule this Vangoland, I must kill King Tauza. I really mean it. This land belongs to me." He grinned as he emerged from his secret hole across the River Vango.

The River Vango divided Vangoland into two asymmetrical parts, East and West. Not too far from the river, in western Vangoland, dwelled the animals Vango Kingdom.

The Animal Kingdom was under the rule of King Tauza, the mighty lion. His bushy mane swept the ground when he strode by on his great paws of pride. His brown eyes twinkled like water in deep boreholes. As they would for any other revered king, the animals of the kingdom would all rise from their favorite spots to greet him with respect and humility.

Angelix, the white dove, was the king's spiritual adviser. Her nest rested in the tree in the heart of the compound. Angelix had the gift of heavenly wisdom, and her main task was to deliver it to the king every morning. She was the king's daily source of knowledge and wisdom.

As time went by, the king developed a special relationship with Beelz, the snake, straining his relationship with Angelix. He avoided here whenever he could. He would begrudgingly meet with her every morning, but the meetings were not longer fruitful. Instead, the king opted to work closely with the flamboyant, charismatic Beelz, who trivialized holy wisdom. Beelz argued that every animal had a bit of wisdom to share with the kingdom and that those who were more intelligent than others should be in the inner circle of the king.

One day, after a meeting with his wife, the king called for Beelz and told him to form a think tank of intellectuals.

They would meet once a week and Beelz would present the results of their discussions to the king.

The king seemed to enjoy the ideas and advice of Beelz's team more than the advice he received from Angelix alone. He liked the variety of ideas, especially the fact that he was now able to choose the ones he liked. Eventually, the king would no longer meet with Angelix every morning but once a week instead.

As time went by, sadness filled Angelix's heart, for her wisdom was now replaced by Beelz's worldly ideas. Consequently, she resented the new establishment and prayed for its annulment. Many changes took place as Angelix's wisdom was ignored. Storytelling and jokes re-placed Angelix's evening prayer with the animals. Her once-a-week presentation, Defending the Creator and His Creation languished. Her class for young animals, Hear and Obey was no more and eventually Angelix found her-self on the edge of citizenry, grieving.

CATASTROPHE ON MOUNT CONIC

Because of the king's rejection of wisdom, a curse fell upon the kingdom. Evil things gradually crept into the land. First, the human giants of the North or of Giantland invaded the kingdom.

The king of Giantland was looking for new territories to occupy, mainly for hunting. The number of animals in Giantland dwindled to a handful as the human population had exploded, and meat was one of their staple foods. Vangoland became a target for their meat supply.

After the animals managed to drive them back twice, Beelz proposed two ideas: constructing a compound for protection and building the royal family a hut for greater security. Without consulting Angelix, King Tauza started the projects.

First, they built the compound. The bottom half of the wall consisted of layers of flat stones. To erect it further, they piled tree trunks on top, making the wall at least five feet tall. For maximum protection, they girded the outer side of the wall with thorny bushes. A tall tree with a thick trunk and long branches marked the center of the compound. The animals gathered there when the king called a meeting. To the south of the compound, stood a wide gate, at least the size of two elephants walking side by side. The royal hut was ugly, with a roof that hung heavily on one side. It stood vulnerably at the far end of the compound.

After the projects were finished, Beelz secretly visited Giantland. He wheedled the giants, convincing them to attack the animals while they slept in the compound. He told them that the best thing to do was to make sure that they killed King Tauza and the other lions first. Doing that would weaken the kingdom. If the kingdom was weakened, the giants could come at any time, he explained. Beelz's plan was to get King Tauza killed so he could take over. He believed that if King Tauza was killed, he could actually make the kingdom stronger than ever before, and the animals would destroy the giants in the event they attacked.

Soon after they met with Beelz, the giants launched an attack on Vangoland in the midnight hours. Switching off the stealth engines of their electric speedboats, they cruised along without a sound for about a mile or so. They came to a halt by a giant, fruitful tree (the Movena tree), quietly hopped out, armed with swords, bows and arrows strung across their shoulders. Although they were technological people, they did not have guns. Their king forbade the production of guns and had destroyed the ones already made after overwhelming violence disrupted their kingdom. Those who refused to turn in their weapons were harshly punished.

With her great vision, Clips, the old black-and-white eagle, spotted them from afar. She immediately reported to the king that a gang of armed poachers was headed their way. Every animal was dispatched at once. In a short time, they were positioned to defend themselves against ambush.

As the giants tiptoed single file on a dusty path in the dark, King Tauza swiftly jumped on the two leaders. Their weapons tumbled to the ground. The angry beasts pinned some of the giants against tree trunks. Dazed and dizzy, others hobbled away. A herd of angry buffalo caught a couple of them and stampeded them before they let them escape. The uninjured poachers hurled their wounded comrades their boats.

Fleeing and scrambling, they unleashed their arrows haphazardly. Many of them flew over the animals, but one, driven by fate, hit its target. It cut through the king's leg. The wound developed an infection and the leg had to be amputated between the knee and ankle. Those who delighted in lawlessness called him King Three-and-a-Half, but this clowning stopped after one of the notorious wolves was punished with harsh labor on a summer day.

After that, the giants' leaders realized that Beelz was just trying to lure them to their demise. They declared that, if he reared his head again, they would hang him on a tree. They gave up on attacking the Vango Kingdom and decided to head to Mount Conic, where many animals dwelled. The animal kingdom called it Conic because it was shaped like a cone with beautiful but dangerous slopes.

On the mountain, the giants found animals galore, mostly mountain goats, antelope, and black bears. Their exploration of the mountain as even more rewarding after they found fruits as sweet as honey hanging very low on trees that resembled grape vines. Fruits similar to berries in Moabi's world—hesperidiums, pepos, and drupes—were also abundant.

At the very top of the mountain, they discovered a cave with a pond inside of it, prompting them to invite their king so he could come and see the beauty of nature. The king of Giantland loved it and immediately made it his special place. There, he began to worship his gods and throw lavish parties.

With the wealth of gold in Giantland, they built the road from the Vango River through the saltpan up to the foothills of Mount Conic with pure gold. This magnificent road was mostly used by the king's entourage while the king himself and some of his security travelled in a flying hovercraft.

It did not take them a long time to slaughter all the animals on the mountain, leading them to seek out more meat elsewhere.

THE DRAGON AND
THE GIANTLANDERS

Meanwhile, a black storm was sweeping across the Mabara Forest, a region two hundred kilometers North of Giantland. Three fierce gargantuan dragons dwelled in that forest along with black bees and flesh-eating silver beetles. The dragons had long terrorized all animals in the area. The storm put an end to that, and when it finally passed, the two old dragons, the parents of the third one, dangled headlong among branches of thorny trees, dead. The young dragon, Bubbles, survived with the silver beetles and black bees. However, the storm had scooped them on its wings and swooshed them away. As it soared into high altitudes, way far from the ground, a velvety voice uttered this message:

> Bubbles, there is a place in this world that is over-flowing with evil and needs to be purged of it. Listen carefully. Your assignment is to get rid of the Giants and their gods from the place that I am taking you to. You will remain there until further notice. However, you will face the same fate as your parents if you pursue evil.

The storm's lightning bolts flashed through the sky, exposing its force as it swirled vigorously. At the compound, the startled animals shuddered when they heard its thunder rumble like a chorus of roaring lions. This was no an ordinary storm. When it reached Mount Conic, it disgorged Bubbles, the silver beetles and the black bees right into the mouth of the cave. Then, just like that, it was gone!

The silver beetles were fashioned for war. They had hard bodies that looked like galvanized zinc and reflected light. When they attacked, their minuscule teeth were razor sharp cutting the flesh and leaving gashes on the enemy.

The pitch-black, shiny bees produced honey. They were almost the same as other African bees, except they were bigger—more than twice the size of the silver beetles. They had no stripes on their fuzzy, bulbous bodies.

Bubbles had short, bulky legs, and her head was bigger than a Boer goat's. She could not walk straight but waddled with an eerie slither. Like a chameleon, her color changed according to her surroundings. Black appendages that looked like a composite of worn-out ostrich wings and pectoral fins protruded on the sides of her saggy belly and swept the ground whenever she moved. When agitated, balls of fire flew from her mouth.

Inside the cave, the giant king and some of his high-ranking men were deep in worship, affectionately staring at their two gods, a male and a female—which were carved stones plated with gold. They had huge heads and big, glistening eyes that actually looked alive. They were at least seven feet tall and had easy smiles that never withered.

While this was taking place, Bubbles whirled into the cave with her entourage of silver beetles and black launching a brutal attack on the giants. With the narrow exit, many of them were trapped as the silver beetles attacked them everywhere, sucking their blood and mincing their flesh. Outside the cave, some fell down the sharp cliffs and suffered broken necks and limbs.

Among those who escaped was the king. He was unscathed but terribly scared. Down at the foothills, trembling, they managed to jump into their vehicles and sped away. They came to the Vango River, transitioned into their boats and zipped away. Nearby, animals that stood their ground ready to fight, and marveled when the giants fled without attacking. They realized that they must have experienced something terrifying on Mount Conic.

For this reason, the Animal Kingdom changed their name for Mount Conic to Mount Fear and dared not climb it.

• • •

Back at the cave, Bubbles took a liking to one of the statues, perhaps because of its stature and elegance or for its remarkable resemblance to a human being. It was the statue of the king of the giants. It was not as huge as the other two, and it was not gold-plated but just plain stone. It had huge eyes with protruding eyeballs and strong hands clenched into fists.

With her long tail, Bubbles whipped the heads of the two golden gods repeatedly, boisterously laughing. Then she wrapped her tail around their necks and pulled hard. As they tumbled, the statues broke into pieces of gold. Some sharp pieces fell into the sparkling pond and stabbed Ozca, the fish, who was hiding flat at the bottom. Ozca was a beautiful green and golden nembwe fish with a shimmering turquoise tail. He was five feet long and a hundred years old or more. One could not tell his age just by looking at him. Bubbles noticed the water was slightly turning red as she marveled at the nature of the pond. She wondered where the water was coming from. In a short time, she concluded that it was rainwater falling through the opening at the top of the gorgeous cave. Actually, the water came mostly from underground springs. The floor had tiny openings that allowed water to fill the pond. Minute cracks in the walls allowed water to flow out. In that way, the pond was ever replenished. When Bubbles saw Ozca, she was moved with compassion. After Bubbles coaxed him out from hiding, Ozca convinced her that he was a seer and that he would be able to inform her about what was really happening in places like Vangoland and Giantland.

BEELZ AND BUBBLES

At the end of the salt pan, Beelz, the snake, began to climb Mount Fear. However, this was not the first time Beelz visited the mountain. It all started with the thought that perhaps he could collaborate with the creature that had terrified the fleeing giants. If things went well, they could launch an attack on King Tauza and take over Vangoland together. With his sly charm, he was able to befriend Bubbles, the, dragon, and even developed a close relationship with her.

Beelz entered a dark, rocky tunnel and emerged in a space filled with beautiful light spilling through the open tip of the mountain. The bees swarmed in their nearby hives. When Bubbles started shouting at Beelz, her voice filling the whole cave, the beetles woke up and began to fly back and forth. "Bubbles, calm down," Beelz said softly.

"Calm down? You are calming me down?" said Bubbles, shaking her hefty head in disbelief.

"You don't understand," Beelz said as he came closer to Bubbles. "If you help me overthrow King Tauza, then you and I will rule the whole of Vangoland for life!"

"I do not need all that. I told you that you could come live with us, Beelz. Stop being selfish," Bubbles screamed. "Let them rule themselves."

"It has never been about me, never. I am doing it for the animals that suffer under King Tauza. I am doing it for you and me—so we can build the real kingdom, Bubbles. This cave is too small for us, especially if we are going to have a family together," said Beelz, looking at their red egg, which was the size of a watermelon. In fact, the egg also had faded stripes like a watermelon's, except that they were black and unnoticeable from more than a few steps away.

It was quiet for a while. Bubbles' green eyes were not moving at all, as Beelz's words resonated.

"I don't think you love me," Beelz muttered softly.

"What?" asked Bubbles.

"Because let's face it, if you did, you would help me," said Beelz, eyes glistening as if he was about to cry.

"Beelz, let me be clear. I do love you, okay, but that does not mean I want to be part of your sinister agenda. I fear the storm!" Bubbles exclaimed.

"The storm? That's the most ridiculous thing I have ever heard!" Beelz blurted out.

"Yes, the storm, Beelz. You know the problem with you? You don't listen, and you are selfish. You care only about what you want. You forgot about the storm, or you did not listen at all. What did I tell you about the storm, Beelz?"

Beelz lifted his head to look at the moon that was now in the center of the blue sky. "Ummm...the storm brought you here."

"And then what else?"

"That's all."

"See, you don't listen, or maybe I should say you are ignorant. For your own good, Beelz, listen. If I do evil, the storm will kill me. I was sent here to purge evil and do good."

"Well, I've got bad news for you, Bubbles. King Tauza has been planning to invade this place. What are you going to do then? Let the animals kill our little one? Think about it, Bubbles."

"I thought you had stopped lying, Beelz," said Bubbles. "I really do not believe you."

"What I am telling you right now is the real truth," Beelz shouted back, then paused. "Bubbles, listen, we have to oust King Tauza right now before it is too late."

Bubbles was pretty sure that Beelz was lying, not because he seemed to be smiling as he was talking but because she knew that King Tauza would not attempt to invade the mountain. "I am not afraid of King Tauza. If he attacks me, the beetles and I will devour him in a split second," said Bubbles, boasting and laughing. "As long as I don't attack first, I will be okay. Trust me."

"Well, don't say I did not warn you," giving her a stern look. "Tell me, what are you going to do when they block the entrance of this place and set you on fire from above?"

Beelz had gotten Bubbles thinking. What if Beelz is telling the truth? she thought. She then turned around to look at Ozca, whose head was resting on the edge of the pond, listening.

"Ozca, what can you tell us about what is going on in Vangoland?" Bubbles demanded.

Without wasting time, from his wide mouth, Ozca spit four little precious diamond stones. They fell on the floor, forming a trapezium shape if one drew lines between them. One stone revealed the past, another the present, the third the future. The last one, well, Ozca claimed that he could hear from the Creator with it.

"Well, well, well." Ozca scanned his stones thoroughly, eyes moving from stone to stone.

They both trusted Ozca's revelations. Many a time, he had shocked Bubbles by telling her what was in her mind moments before they saw each other. He had also left Beelz appalled by revealing to him exactly what he was doing before coming to see Bubbles. Knowing that, Beelz knew the truth was going to embarrass him, but he hoped Ozca would say something close to what he had just told Bubbles so he could still argue his point.

"Presently, I do not see anything dangerous." He whistled, shaking his head and blinking. He then fixed his eyes on the stone that revealed the future. "I see the young hare, Madonzi's son, holding a spear. Wait, and there is fire on both ends of the spear."

"It sounds like there is a lot to say about the young hare with a spear," said Bubbles.

"The spear means the young hare will be a mighty warrior and fearless," said Ozca, nodding.

"What about fire?" Bubbles asked.

"That he will fight with fire," said Ozca.

"There you go, Bubbles," said Beelz. "Remember when I told you that they might burn you from above?"

"Like I told you, as long as I do not attack first, we should be able to defend ourselves. I am not afraid of King Tauza and his little warrior. Ozca, what else do you see?" asked Bubbles, panning her head to Ozca.

"I see a human being walking around Vangoland, perhaps lost. He is not there yet, but soon he will be."

"Beelz, maybe you could use his help," said Bubbles, smiling.

"Maybe he is from Giantland sent to kill me," Beelz said.

"I don't think he is coming from Giantland. He does not look anything like a giant. He is a bit small in stature whereas the giants, as we know, are huge. I can tell you this though; King Tauza really hates human beings because the giants nearly killed him. But he will not rush to harm this human being. Somehow, this human being will involve himself in some of the kingdom's affairs. His involvement could be the catalyst to the reunion of Angelix and the king. If the reunion takes place, the kingdom will unite behind the king again. Even your followers will turn against you, Beelz," Ozca paused as Beelz interrupted him.

"One thing I know for sure, soon King Tauza will be no more," said Beelz.

"What else Ozca?" Bubbles asked.

"Do you want to hear the real secret of Vangoland?" Ozca asked.

"Oh, is there a secret in Vangoland? Go ahead," said Bubbles looking at Beelz.

"Well, according to the custom of Vangoland, Angelix is the only one who can anoint a new king. She has done that since the beginning of the Vango Kingdom." Ozca paused, coughing. "When she anoints a new king, she collects the blood of the dying king and sprinkles it on the forehead of the one being crowned. All previous kings died in her presence. However, the dying king must be in good standing with Angelix or her Creator. If King Tauza dies right now, it makes it impossible for Angelix to anoint a new king because King Tauza's blood is poisoned by his disobedience. However, if Angelix does not anoint anyone, she would not live with the Vango animals, leaving the kingdom vulnerable and likely to fall apart."

"See, the best chance is now. Bubbles, please help me to crush King Tauza before the human being arrives," cried Ozca.

"You crush him alone. That is your business," Bubbles yelled, turning to Ozca, his eyes ballooning red with fury. "Ozca, how are you going to help Beelz? He is getting on my nerves now. I already told him that I can't help him."

Ozca remained silent for about a minute or so while Beelz unrolled, as if afraid that Bubbles could punch his face.

"Speak!" Bubbles shouted to Ozca.

Ozca opened his eyes. "Seers don't just speak for the sake of speaking. We speak after we get the revelation first, then we can open our mouths."

"Remember that I am the ruler of this cave, so you should also be sensitive to how I want things done," said Bubbles widening her scary eyes.

Ozca had never really trusted Bubbles. Deep down, he did not like her at all, and not only that, he feared her. That belt of ragged teeth that protruded from her upper jaw scared him to death. She reminded him of the big, ancient, gluttonous shark that devoured the fish community in the Vango River. Because of that, he trembled at her raucous voice. "A transverse lobe of a human being, you know, from the ear, can help. Crush it to make a powder and bring it to me. The moment I spit on it, it will become a spell. Sprinkle it around where the king and his family sleep. Immediately they will become deranged and they will be forced to abdicate Vangoland." Ozca shook his head, hating what he had just said. His only silent wish was for Beelz to fail.

"Did you hear that, Beelz?" Bubbles asked.

"It is up to you. I don't want to continue this conversation anymore."

"I don't know when that human being is going to show up, so I can't wait for him, and if he shows up, he might be armed. I will continue to fight with my venom, and I know I will get what I want," said Beelz, leaving abruptly.

"You know my doors are always open for you," Bubbles called as Beelz curved and swerved into the dark tunnel.

●　　●　　●

As soon as Beelz arrived at the animal compound, he purposed in his heart to talk to King Tauza. Swinging his great length, he hissed vehemently and caught up with the king just before sunset. Beelz was a senior advisor to the king by this time. "I have something very important to discuss with you, my lord, exclaimed Beelz," lowering his eyes and grinning.

The king loved to hear from Beelz, especially when he talked about plans to help the kingdom during these hard times. However, this very day the king was not enthusiastic at all about talking to Beelz. This very day he was troubled by growing despair and frailty.

"Can we talk tomorrow, Beelz? I am tired right now," said the king politely.

"I will be very quick. Here is the scenario, my lord," said Beelz, eyes sparkling and his green fangs protruding from his rubbery mouth. "I think those giants of the North are going to kill us all one of these days, my king. In my dream last night, they were shooting at us. I mean, it was horrendous and a total mess."

The king looked at him and shook his head. "No, Beelz, you are wrong. They will never kill us."

Beelz's eyes darkened in disbelief. *How dare you say that*? he thought. The king had never disagreed with him like that before. He had always entertained Beelz's ideas.

King Tauza began to take a step toward his hut but stopped when Beelz followed and uttered in a low, desperate tone, "My king, when I brought up the idea of building the compound in order to bring us closer as a family, you delighted in the idea, right? He paused, his eyes teary. "Yes, because you saw it was good," he went on, answering his own question. "And by the way, it turned out to be a very good thing, right? When I came up with a plan to build your hut, you found it necessary because your privacy would not be intruded upon, right? When I introduced the drying and the cooking of Movena fruits, you loved the new taste. In fact, everybody loved it, right?"

The king interrupted with an irritated voice, pounding his paw on the ground, "Okay, okay! What do you have to say today, Beelz?"

"Think about this, my lord. The time has arrived for us to secure our surroundings. We should embark upon it sooner than later."

As soon as Beelz finished talking, out of nowhere swooped Angelix, the dove. She landed between them, her blue eyes as round as marbles. "Do not listen to Beelz, my lord. Security without the Creator is futile. If we obey him, he will keep us safe."

"Just shut up, Angelix. Why don't you just fly away to your nasty nest?" Beelz snapped. He then eyed the king, arrogantly grinning. "I apologize for that, my lord, but hear me: soon the giants are going to retaliate."

The king remained quiet, not even blinking.

"We must do something about our security right now. Securing our boundaries is a must," said Beelz, eyes wide and glaring with exasperation.

The king looked away toward the sky, as if seeking wisdom from above. He was actually caught up between two worlds—the world of Angelix and of Beelz—although for years he had ignored Angelix. This day, he was clearly indecisive.

All of a sudden, the king opened his mouth. "Okay, okay, okay, if what you are saying is true, Beelz, how do you think we should prevent them from attacking us?"

"My lord, please do not listen to him. He is lying," Angelix interrupted again.

"I said shut up, Angelix. How many times must I tell you?" Beelz hissed harshly.

Angelix reluctantly stepped back, frustrated.

Beelz eyed the king, shaking his head and expecting him to excuse Angelix.

"I am not going anywhere, Beelz," Angelix interrupted with confidence.

Beelz gathered himself. "I think we should send some of our animals to the outskirts of the Northeastern Vangoland where the giants are likely to come from in the event they attack."

Angelix shook her head violently. "No, my lord. First of all, we were not supposed to build the compound and your hut. When we did that, you distanced yourself from the Trust Law and the Law of Hear and Obey that our

Creator bestowed upon us. That completely opened the door to evil in our land. Deploying some of our animals to the outskirts will only make matters worse," Angelix paused to allow her words to resonate.

Other animals began to inch toward the heated conversation. They all knew how eloquent Beelz, was but were also aware of the brilliant arguments Angelix could make. This was a debate they could not miss.

Before Beelz could utter a word, Angelix continued where she left off. "We must change. By that, I mean we must truly turn our hearts back to our Creator, and when we do that—hear me now!—we will purge that mind-set of fear." Angelix sighed. "We must stop listening to those who think like Beelz does. They pollute our environment."

Many of the animals cheered and whistled for Angelix while a few booed her. Beelz kept a wide smile, his tail curling and uncurling. As for the king, he was now walking around in circles as Angelix's words found room in his heart.

Beelz's eyes dropped to the ground when he noticed that Angelix might have stolen the moment. He realized that his plan was in jeopardy. He would not be able to dethrone King Tauza if his loyalists were not sent to the boundaries. At this point, he had nothing to say. His fangs were all out, his mouth dry. He was even having a hard time forcing a fake smile.

Angelix cleared her throat and continued, "My lord, remember that before we built all these walls around us, we never had any trouble. It all started with Beelz lying and instilling a sense of insecurity and fear in some of our animals. I believe that once we put our Creator first, there will be no drought, and there will be peace and joy once again. Like in the past, love among us will reign supreme." Angelix gestured with her leg. "No, no, no, my lord, I disagree with Beelz. We cannot jump into the outskirts ignoring our own disobedience here in the midst of us. I pray that we are not sleeping with the enemy."

After listening attentively to Angelix, the king seemed to take into consideration all that she had said. "Beelz, I am not disregarding your advice or warning, but I must think deeply about what the two of you have just said."

"Well, that's fine with me, but remember that if you delay, you will be endangering the lives of innocent animals who might be killed by the giants of the North," Beelz warned as he retreated.

As the king turned to leave, Angelix jumped in front of him abruptly. She looked up into the king's eyes and whispered, "Are you going to stop listening to Beelz, my king?"

"I heard what you said, Angelix, but right now just leave me alone," said the king as he walked away.

"I think you have allowed evil into your heart."

"What?"

Angelix's words hit him like a rock. "Allowing what?" He turned sharply.

"You heard what I said, but let me repeat myself. I said, I think you have allowed evil into your heart."

"Off with you, Angelix!" shouted the king, waving his amputated leg at her. Hurriedly, he disappeared into his hut.

Angelix flew off to her nest, untangled it, and scattered the pieces. Some fell on the ground and some dangled loose from branches. Then she took off and landed on a tree a little bit far from the compound. There, she built a new nest overnight. Although she did not want to talk to the king because of his stubbornness, she still prayed for him.

From that point, the relationship between the king and Angelix soured and seemed irreconcilable. At the same time, River Vango started to dry up. Soon, all that was left was a dwindling pool not too far from the evergreen Movena tree. The king believed things would turn around, but his behavior became hostile to those who wanted to see Angelix return.

• • •

Once Angelix was no longer a threat, Beelz became increasingly belligerent. He was constantly complaining, lying, and refusing to attend meetings. He would disappear for days with no explanation or remorse. After many attempts to get Beelz and his two sons to comply with the rules, the king expelled them from the kingdom. As they departed, the indignant Beelz had the audacity to say "I will be back to rule this land. Believe me!"

Nothing would stop him from pursuing his ultimate dream—to take over the kingdom.

MOABI'S FIRST ENCOUNTER

Now Moabi treaded the hot sand of Vango River under the scorching sun, sweating profusely until sweat became scarce, leaving his lips crystallized with salt. He dragged his feet as weariness took its toll. He wished he could find shade, but the woods on the sides of the river looked haunted and extremely dry. He remembered reading about haunted woods, where skeletons came out of nowhere and haunted people who were lost. For the most part, he avoided looking at the woods because they gave him chills. He kept on going, and yet there was no sign of the Tsodilo Hills. Eventually, it occurred to him that he was likely in another world.

He reached into the backpack and pulled out a bottle of water, which was almost empty. When he shook it, it barely splashed. He emptied the remaining contents of the bottle on his dry tongue. He wished he had brought at least two bottles.

The sun had just slipped into the golden horizon when Moabi spotted the Movena Tree on the right side of the river—the only lively and animated tree left in Vangoland. It had a tall, broad, and bulky trunk with long branches bending down and touching the ground. Fruits glimmered like ornaments in the tree while others lay scattered on the ground. The swelling, shiny veins on the spongy green leaves were fascinating. Beads of clear liquid sparkled at the tip of every leaf. Nests resembling miniature baskets dangled from branches as bright yellow weaver birds darted in and out, in various stages of constructing and deconstructing their creations. Moabi knew then that there was something special about the tree since everything else around looked deathly. "There is life here," he mumbled.

For the very first time since his arrival in Vangoland, he felt compelled to step out of the dormant riverbed. As he climbed the gray clay wall onto the bank, holding his camera, he salivated at the sight of the tree's succulent white and brown fruits. It reminded him of the bacciferous tree across from his apartment building. The woman who owned the tree was always seated on the stairs guarding it. When she was not around, kids jumped the fence and helped themselves. This prompted her to purchase a dog with a big flabby mouth to scare the young thieves. It proved to be an effective deterrent.

Moabi dropped his backpack, plucked the white fruit and sank his teeth into it. Clear juices shot out. Immediately his mouth went sour. He spat and rubbed his tongue on his palm. Hesitant but determined, he picked a brown fruit from the branch. The brown fruit was tasty like a sweet potato or yam. However, he realized one thing: the bitter fruit quenched his thirst even though it had left his lips burning. It was a different story for the animals though.

For animals, all fruits made them very thirsty. When eating them fresh, they tasted sour and sometimes bitter, but when dried and cooked, they sure tasted delicious. White fruits were not as flavorful, so the brown ones were reserved for the royal family as a token of honor. The fruits would not have bothered the animals with their bitterness had it not been for Beelz, who introduced them to the drying and the cooking. Before then, bitterness was not a problem at all.

No one was allowed to loiter around the Movena Tree. That was part of the animals' traditional beliefs. Besides, they did not want to disturb the tree, for it was their primary fruitful resource. If it died, they would be in peril.

While resting under the Movena Tree, Moabi heard hooves pounding and galloping nearby. He frantically crawled around the trunk and found an opening. It was dark inside and rather scary. But as soon as he saw the large trunk of Zingi, the elephant, and the dangling mane of Sanza, the lion, emerging from the woods, he scrambled into the trunk. "My bag!" he lamented softly as he cupped his camera by the lens with one hand and patted frantically around him with the other. He'd left his backpack outside of the tree!

Behind Sanza and Zingi came a buffalo bull with cloven hooves and thick horns that pointed toward each other, pulling a wooden Y-shaped sleigh. Its undersurface was worn smooth by numerous trips to and from the Movena Tree. Fastened on top of the sleigh was a large, woven basket—at least five feet wide, six feet long, and made of intertwined blades of grass, small branches, and tree bark. It was very similar in technique to the nests in the Movena Tree. In fact, the same weaver birds made it.

They came to a stop. The buffalo stood still, yawning—perhaps in boredom, but mostly because of fatigue. Immediately Sanza noticed the backpack. Curious, he stepped closer, sniffed the backpack, then gestured for Zingi to come and take a look. "I think human beings were here."

"Maybe stealing our fruits," said Zingi pushing the bag with his trunk. "We should take the bag to the king."

"I agree," said Sanza, taking a walk to search around the tree.

Zingi strategically picked fruits with his barky proboscis and dropped them into the basket. Simultaneously, Sanza snatched fruits with his paws, skillfully flipping them into the basket. One thing that intrigued Moabi was the excellence and the uniqueness of their beastly utterances.

They grumbled in their tonality, and their loudness depended on the size of the animal. The bigger the animal, the louder the voice. Their locutions were somehow different from humans'. That fascinated Moabi, and instead of totally cringing back into the trunk cave, he poked his head out and listened.

• • •

Moabi would learn later how the animals began to speak. It was during a summer night—the full moon shining bright amidst the twinkling stars as Angelix was praying for the congregated animals. Their heads were bowed in anticipation of heavenly manifestations. It was common for miracles to happen when she was in such reverent prayer. Her voice changed dramatically from cooing to twittering with an embellishment of sporadic ululation. Then, all of a sudden, words began to roll out of her mouth accompanied by rings of clouds. The rest of the animals began to shout instead of bellowing, growling, yodeling, chirping, screaming, trumpeting, barking, squeaking, howling, growling, and so forth. Meanwhile, the rings of clouds compounded, becoming one big blanket of cloud that spread over the whole compound. When the cloud dissipated, the animals were shocked as words began to proceed out of their mouths.

In the end, they found joy in speaking rather than making mere noises as a means of communication. However, those animals that were not present remained dumb, and most of them drifted away from the kingdom, feeling out of place among the speaking animals. Other small animals, such as rats, mice, lizards, and some birds that were nearby when the language was released caught the language too. But because they were not using it among members of the kingdom, some of them ended up losing it.

• • •

When Zingi, Sanza, and the buffalo departed with a basket full of Movena fruits on their sleigh, Moabi crawled out from the trunk. He watched in disbelief as his backpack dangled from Zingi's trunk. As the animals disappeared into the woods, he followed. He hid behind the bushes when he thought he was getting too close. Then he would run to catch up so he would not lose sight of them. The bushes began to dwindle as they got closer to the compound, and he could now hear many voices. As soon as he saw the compound, he stopped, amazed at the multitudes of animals in packs, some roving, some playing, and some just reposing or not moving at all. "I can't go over there now, but I *must* find a way to get my backpack. There is no way I can leave without it. My father's note is in there, with all of my story notes," he mumbled, quietly retreating and retracing his steps. He made it back to the tree without any struggle, for the tree was so big it was hard to miss. He crept furtively into the coolness of the trunk cave, overwhelmed and sad. He didn't stay there for too long; he feared they could come back and look for the owner of the backpack. He pulled a couple of both brown and white fruits and ran across the river to the dry shrubs. They surrounded a tall tree that looked like it could fall anytime.

•   •   •

Moabi was right. At the compound, the king became angry and distressed when he saw the backpack. "I think the human beings are stealing our fruits! I know they would like to see us all dead," the king bellowed. "Keep that bag safe, I will look at it later." Then he ordered two young lions to go and guard the Movena Tree.

THE DEMISE OF MADONZI

A day after Moabi arrived in Vangoland, something mysterious and heartbreaking happened. Madonzi, the old hare, had just finished performing her weekly magic and poetry show that took place every Sunday at noontime, before feasting. Everyone was laughing as they enjoyed her flamboyant and breathtaking performance. Since she was the permanent assistant to the king, she joined the royal family in the hut to eat. After that, she then went behind the king's hut, to catch up with her son, Hero, who was impatiently waiting.

There, behind the hut, Madonzi shared wisdom with her son, Hero, whose long white ears stood up to receive every word. His two oversized front teeth protruded from his chubby whiskered mouth even when listening.

"Mom, can I ask you three questions?" Hero's mind had been reeling. This day, he was determined to find answers. Although his mother was rather secretive, he still trusted her to provide answers. Besides, his mother was his best friend. Unlike other animals, she would not mock him and call him an idiot for asking questions. Hero knew that there were certain things that were taboo. Even his own mother would not discuss to discuss those topics liberally. However, sometimes she would reveal glimpses of truth.

"We do not have much time for questions, Hero. We have to be at the meeting soon," said Madonzi.

"What meeting? There are just too many meetings nowadays," said Hero, grumbling.

"Yes, Hero, stop complaining. The king just called the meeting, and everyone has to be there," reiterated Madonzi, her voice betraying agitation.

"Okay, Mom, I understand. I heard Beelz, the snake, used to be your friend. Is that true? Where is Giantland? And where did you get this beautiful sword that you perform magic with?" asked Hero, tilting his head to the side as if begging.

Madonzi coughed, clearing her throat, "Beelz was never my friend. Why are you asking?"

"Because you never talk about him," said Hero. "Okay, how about Giantland and your sword?"

Madonzi was a great storyteller. Her eyes twinkled as she eased into her comfort zone, at least for a short time.

She definitely preferred talking about the sword than about Beelz.

"Beyond the great thorns and rocky valleys lies the land of the human giants. They call themselves the Giantlanders. They live in a beautiful city of magnificent lights with tall buildings that seem to pierce the sky. There is a lot of gold in that city, and all roads are paved with gold. Among the tall structures, there is one taller than them all. It is also built with gold. There, they gather to worship their gods. From childhood, they work hard day and night. Meat is their staple food, so they are active hunters. Another reason they kill animals is for ivory—"

"They kill animals? I don't want to hear about them anymore!" exclaimed Hero. "So what about the sword?"

"Going back home after we fought the giants, we picked up some weapons they left behind. That is when I found my sword, perfectly sized, as you can see. I picked it up because I loved the lavish leather sheath." Immediately after saying that, Madonzi collapsed, hitting the ground harshly. "They killed me, be careful!" she gasped before falling silent.

Fear struck Hero. For a second or two, everything went blank. Then tears began to stream down his cheeks. He could not make sense out of what was happening. "Mom? Mom!" He yelled. There was no answer. Not knowing what to do, he threw himself on top of his mother. "You can't leave me! No, you can't leave me! Wake up, Mom!"

• • •

Meanwhile, under the big tree in the compound, the meeting was commencing, for the situation in the kingdom was not getting any better; indeed it was growing worse. The pool in the river had gone dry. Where would they get water now?

Well, the new senior advisor to the king, Madingi, the pig, had met with some of the pigs and wolves to discuss the problem the previous night. Madingi brought up the idea of digging a water hole in the river where the puddle was, especially since the place was still wet. In the end, the group agreed that Madingi, the pig, must take the motion to the king first thing in the morning.

It took time for her to face the king, not knowing how he would react. She practiced her posture and cleaned up her nose so that she would look presentable and believable. Then she ventured to see the king. The king came out of the hut and angrily said, "What do you want, Madingi?"

"My lord, I have an idea that you are going to love," Madingi said.

"What is it?" asked the king.

Madingi looked down, but she quickly remembered that if she was to convince the king, she must exude confidence. Otherwise, her words would mean nothing. She looked the king in his eyes and said, "I think we should pause the construction work at the dam and chase the water by digging a well where the puddle was."

"You can't be serious," said the king, shaking his big head. "Madingi, the water did not slump but evaporated."

"My lord, I believe that there is a lot of water in the river," said Madingi sucking her surging mucus. "We just have to dig, my king."

"Are you trying to waste my time, Madingi?"

"No, my lord, I will never dishonor you. See, there are layers below the riverbed such as clay soil or bars of rocks that prevent water from being totally drained down. If we get to those layers, we will have plenty of water."

The king shook his head. Squinting his eyes, he questioned, "Are these layers everywhere in the river, Madingi?"

"I can't say everywhere for sure. But because the puddle sustained us for a long time, I am convinced that there are layers beneath," Madingi explained.

"Okay. I will see what I can do," said the king as he turned around to his hut.

Now, they had assembled under the tree with reverence. King Tauza and his wife, Queen Mambo, sat with authority, facing the rest of the animals. When present, Angelix, the dove, would sit with meekness between the king and his wife. Behind the king's wife was Madingi, the pig. Since replacing Beelz as the senior advisor to the king, Madingi thought highly of herself. She was a pompous, dirty creature. Her dark eyes glared nothing but pride. She was able to get Beelz's position because she came up with the plan to construct the dam by the river. Gazing into the blue sky with lazy brown eyes, Zambi, the spoiled son of the king, sprawled idly in front of his mother. He was born with a dangerous disease, which, when it struck, caused him to convulse with seizures. Only Angelix had a remedy: a prayer. However, the disease subsided after Zambi crossed the age of one year, and Angelix's service was no longer needed.

Out of nowhere, a colony of black bees buzzed, roaring in a V-shaped array. In a split second, a hullabaloo erupted among the animals. The bees were swift and exacting. By the time they finished, the royal family and those in the leadership were skipping around in pain. It seemed as though the bees had a target as they attacked with precision. One thing the animals had noticed was that these ill-famed bees had shown up when the drought escalated. Of late, they would come and harass the animals, especially when they were toiling at the dam. The king did not wait for the commotion to subside; he called on everyone to calm down so the meeting could go on.

With a deep, husky voice, he inquired, "Where is my Permanent Assistant Madonzi and her dear son, Hero?"

There was no answer as the animals looked around trying to locate Madonzi.

"I don't see them anywhere. Anyone seen them?" the king inquired.

There was no clear answer, but some shared that the last time they saw her was when she came out of the king's hut. Some said they saw Hero rushing through the gate not too long ago.

Hero finally burst forth, sobbing. "My mother cannot speak to me. She is not breathing."

"What?" the king asked. "What are you saying?"

"My lord, she can't speak. She is behind the hut," said Hero, now crying loudly. His mother's last words were still reverberating in his head.

One of the wolves shouted, "He is crying crocodile tears, my king."

A mocking voice could also be heard.

They all followed the king to the scene. Indeed, Madonzi was dead. It was the saddest moment in a long time—a time when they really needed each other, a time when they were expecting a breakthrough; a time when they hoped for the best. Immediately, they laid Madingi to rest behind the compound.

• • •

The following day the king resumed the meeting where he announced the digging of the water hole in the river. "We drank all the water that was in the pool," the king said. "But the good news is that we can find more water. By that I mean, we have to start digging a water hole in the river to get to the water hidden beneath. We will continue with the dam project as soon as we get the water." The king paused again and scanned the crowd.

A hum of dissent arose at the back of the crowd where the wolves congregated.

"The water should sustain us until it rains. We shall waste no time. We must move immediately and swiftly.

Zingi is your supervisor, and Madingi will be the director of this project," the king declared.

Undoubtedly, Madingi had earned the directorship because once again, she had come up with the idea.

"Chi, the tiger, and I will follow later to check on the progress of the water hole. My cousin, Sanza, will remain home to prepare dinner for all of us," said the king.

All the animals followed Zingi to the place of future waters. It was only about a hundred feet from the ever-fruitful Movena Tree. Of course, they could not just leave work and go nibble.

Still grieving and reluctant to go, Hero walked slowly behind others, but before he could go through the gate, the king called him back. "Tell me quickly, son. We need to know what went wrong. She died in your presence, right?"

Hero winced. Tears sprang from his puffy eyes. "My mother said something like 'they killed her,' and now I am scared, my lord."

The king shook his head in disbelief. "Who killed her?"

Hero rubbed his eyes. "She did not explain. She just passed away after that. She could not finish the last sentence. I don't know if she meant to say they will kill me too. I don't know. I am scared, my lord."

"Then why did you wait for me to come to you?" shouted the king.

Hero cringed.

"You are supposed to come to me if there is any problem. You hear me? Come see me when you are ready to tell the truth." The king's mane above his forehead stood up, frightening Hero even further. "I do not want to come after you again. Am I clear? Now go and work with others."

Hero kept quiet, his heart throbbing as tears sprang from his eyes. The king turned his back on him and walked away. Traumatized, Hero hopelessly hopped into the wilderness, wishing he could find someone who actually cared.

CHASING WATER

Delving deep, the animals grappled with some damp sand. With the wetness came the promise that they would have to keep on dredging and grinding. They all took turns plunging their feet into the wet pile of sand to cool off. When everyone was getting fatigued, Zingi, the elephant broke into the national anthem to inspire courage.

God is for us,
Oh come, you sweet grace,
And let us drink from the river of peace.
God is our provider.
For with love we multiply.

King Tauza is our king,
Whose authoritative voice thunders.
The jungle trembles at his breath
As he calls our names,
To receive orders of the day.

• • •

As for Hero, he was hiding under the bushes very close to the work site so that now he could watch them as they toiled under the scorching sun. He watched them sweating and withering like flowers. That ignited his conscience. He developed compassion for his comrades, but he hated the idea of facing the king. The thought of seeing the king sparked rage within him. "That was mean for him to accuse me of not telling him right away about what my mother said before she died. I was grieving and he did not care. He is a selfish king," he mumbled. Yet he was aware that, by not showing up, he was actually digging himself into a deeper hole. Knowing the king, there would be no mercy.

HERO MEETS MOABI
AND BEELZ

While they sang, their voices eventually got on Hero's nerves and he hopped into the wilderness. He hoped that no one was watching. Emotions ruled over him, and immaturity added its sting as he wandered like a vagabond.

Finally, he got tired and very thirsty. His mouth was crusty and his face wore sadness. At this point, he couldn't wait to find a cool spot. He remembered the Movena Tree and longed to go under its leafy branches. That would not work because it was too close to the other animals. Besides, no one was allowed to linger there. The penalty for that was very stiff.

It did not matter anymore to Hero. He was done with traditions and culture. So, he dashed toward the tree where Moabi was hiding. In his mind, he vowed never again to live under King Tauza.

As soon as he was about to duck under the nearby shrubs, his eyes collided with Moabi's. He jumped back, exclaiming, "Who are you?" He gazed at Moabi's frozen face, and then he darted away as fast as he could run. It was the first time Hero had seen a human being. He remembered the story his mom had told him about the cruel giants of the North.

Quickly, Moabi panned his camera toward the escaping Hero until he disappeared behind the dry wood.

As Hero passed by a big, old, fallen trunk, he spotted a hole covered with a spider's web. He immediately came to a stop. He liked spiders and often was fascinated by their architectural skills. He sniffed the web and could barely see through it. The hole was dark, but there was a sense of peace coming out of it. Peace was precisely what he was looking for. His little paw ripped the web and landed in the hollowness. The soil broke under his feet, sending him sliding into the deep.

Cool darkness welcomed him, and he could feel it in his body. Then, stories of darkness he'd heard from his mother popped up in his mind. The strong sense of meeting some strange living things haunted him, amplified by the fact that he had just unexpectedly collided with a human being. Gradually, the sliding came to an end. Without moving, he listened. It was as silent as a grave.

Attempting to move forward, he bumped his head against a wall. He couldn't go left, as there was no room. Before he could attempt a step to the right, he heard a soft whooshing sound. His fur stood up, and a chill ran down his spine. He thought of going back, but confusion confined him. His mother sometimes said, "A double-minded creature never wins. It is lack of wisdom that causes confusion."

After a long pause, during which he listened intently he decided to take a chance and proceed into the unknown. He had been in a couple of holes before, but he had never been as nervous as he was in this hole. *Certainly there is something about this one*, he thought. Holes had never been his favorite spots anyway, for he didn't like extreme darkness; normally he preferred small bushes. His mother had warned him about holes and other pockets of darkness; explaining that sometimes they harbored danger.

This turned out to be the longest hole Hero had ever explored. As the tunnel curved, he brushed against a cool, soft body that left the feeling of a whimsical breeze. He liked the feeling, and he decided to sit down and enjoy the moment. It smelled good too. As he was bending his legs to rest on his belly, a thin, sweet voice interrupted his thoughts.

"Welcome home, Hero, my dear. I have being waiting for you."

Hero jumped up, shocked.

"Don't be scared, I have good news for you. Just before your mother was killed, she told me that you would be coming to stay with me."

77

"What?" Surprised, Hero said, ears perking.

"They do not like you over there. Tauza, the so-called king...ha ha ha." Beelz laughed out loud. "He is determined to get rid of you."

This was unbelievable to Hero, a shift in his mind. This creature was confirming his mother's last words. He immediately believed this soft, unique voice that seemed to have turned darkness into light. After all, his mother had told him almost the same thing. This world he was now in was more than what he expected.

Beelz moved his tail. "Excuse me, my Hero, you are sitting on my tail. Do you mind if...?"

Hero panicked and jumped to the other side of the darkness, slamming into the wall.

"Just relax and make yourself comfortable. There is plenty of room here. My fear is that they might be waiting for you outside, and by the way, you are more than welcome to stay with me here."

Hero was interested in knowing how his mother had been killed more than anything.

"Hey, Hero, are you hungry?" Beelz offered.

"Just a little bit, but I would prefer water, sir," Hero answered. Gazing into the distance, he started to see some forms and shapes. He saw glittering, shining spots right about where the voice was coming from. Beelz opened his marble eyes wide; they sparkled, and his mouth glowed red.

By this time, Hero was sure that he was talking to a snake. "Well, Mr. Snake, your skin looks beautiful and silky," Hero exclaimed.

"Call me Beelz, please," Beelz corrected.

"Beelz, hah! So this is where you live now?"

"For now, but let me tell you something, they are jealous of my beauty over there. Look at your king—he is so ugly. He is like a monster. He cannot comprehend my elegance, you know. My skin is so smooth, and his is rough. He cannot think, and I am an incredible thinker. But you know what? They should blame God for that, not me," Beelz exclaimed.

After listening to him carefully, Hero had something to ask. "Do you ever get out of your beautiful house?"

"Let me set you straight, this is not a house, but a mansion. Back to your question, I only go out during the night to enjoy the land of my ancestors. King Tauza does not like me because I have expressed to him that I want to rule Vangoland, and believe me—I said *believe me*," said Beelz, banging his tail against the wall, "I can do a better job than he does. He is not capable of doing anything constructive by himself, yet he is very stubborn. Having said that, I shall rule Vangoland."

Hero was shocked to hear this. He had never heard anybody criticize the king like that before. *How could that be*? he thought. Nor had he heard anyone dreaming or claiming that he could be a king. This was a totally new scenario to him. He began pondering the idea and wondering why Vangoland had to be ruled by the Tauza family only. He started to ask himself deep questions and found himself more inclined to move toward Beelz, who seemed more honest and warmer than the king was toward him. For a brief moment, he actually thought about Beelz's expulsion from the kingdom, but that did not bother him anymore.

"Tauza does not want to listen and accommodate new ideas. Now he thinks I am interfering with his rule too much, but I am the one who liberated him from the laws of Angelix. Look at the situation now. There is no water. Way before the drought, I proposed that we build a dam. Later he asked Madingi to design it, but it was too late. He rejected my counsel. There would be water in the dam right now, but he never thought of Vangoland drying up. Tauza has no discernment at all. A good king cares about the future and the next generation, not only about his dominion. A king should be the one with the right judgment and direction. That is why I resent the idea of monarchy because there will be stupid king after stupid king," Beelz said with eloquence. "Right now, the whole land is on the brink of being invaded by the giants of the North, and I tried to advise him with some security ideas, but he opted to be confused."

Hero listened attentively, simultaneously engrossed in thoughts that made him even thirstier. "Do you have some water, please?"

"Yes, I have honey and water. In a minute, I will give you a tour of my mansion, and you will have a good time enjoying what I have here for you, okay?"

With this sort of warm hospitality, Hero found himself comfortable. He told the story of how his mother died in his arms and how King Tauza was mad at him. "I was in shock; I still am..." Hero lamented about his mother.

Beelz sympathized with Hero. He promised that he would help him avenge his mother's death. "Now follow me," Beelz said, unrolling his body.

They crossed a slice of light spilling through a crack in the roof. Hero was astonished by the snake's length and the way he elongated gracefully as he uncoiled. He saw Beelz's glossy colors as he crossed the light. Purple, yellow, orange, and green striped elegantly on his jelly body. Hero was stunned by Beelz's beauty. Indeed, one could say he is a beautiful creature, Hero thought. He could understand why some could be jealous of him.

"I have a question," Hero said. "Do you live by yourself here?"

Beelz turned his head back to Hero as he made a loop with his body, extending his head straight up. Pain flushed his face before saying, "I used to live with...my sons, Binz and Gaz. It was on a beautiful morning when they left for the river," he paused, getting emotional. "But they never came back. I suspect your king ambushed them."

"I am sorry about that, Beelz," said Hero solemnly.

"Thanks, Hero. I am coping with it better now. It does not make me weak anymore but strong and courageous."

"That sounds good. Maybe that is how I should look at it myself in regard to my mother," said Hero.

"That's right. This should make you strong and not break you. You have to know who your real enemies are so you can stay away from them," Beelz said.

"I like that," said Hero, sighing.

"And like I said, you are more than welcome to stay here with me if you wish," said Beelz, his eyes glinting and his body glistening as he ventured forward. Another crack above allowed the light to spill through, which revealed the gleaming honey and a sheet of water that streamed down the wall like an indoor fountain.

Hero's eyes opened wide in awe as he traced the honey up the wall, which was at least three feet high. But he quit salivating as soon as he saw a colony of black bees nesting there. He stepped back, remembering the sharp pain inflicted by a raging bee while he drank water in the river.

"Those things sting badly," said Hero, shaking his head.

"Don't be afraid of the bees. They are very friendly unless they are being attacked," said Beelz, smiling. "And they basically take care of me."

"I can see that they make a lot of honey for you. Lucky you, Mr. Snake."

"Let me tell you something, Hero, when you treat others nicely, they will in turn do the same. Your king and some of his followers do not practice that," said Beelz.

"That's very true, Beelz. We all deserve to be treated right, you know," Hero said.

"Look on your far left, opposite the honey. There is water there." Beelz gestured, swinging his neck in the direction of the water.

From the fountain, a shimmering spring ran easily into a stony oval basin. Hero was astonished by the little fountain in the hole. He watched the water spreading seamlessly over the smooth gray concave stone that stuck out of the wall a few inches. Hero quickly jumped into the basin to help himself, gulping for a long time. He had never tasted water as pure as the water he was now enjoying. It tasted almost like sweetened rainwater. He wished all of the animals could come and drink, but he smiled when he thought that not all of them could enter the hole.

"Is this water a miracle, Beelz? Where does it come from?" Hero asked.

"Well, yes and no. It is a mystery because it tastes so good, and it is a fountain in a hole. But it is not a miracle as far as the source is concerned because somewhere underground there is always water. These kinds of places are rare though," Beelz said, grinning. "Does it make sense?"

"Kind of makes sense," said Hero, his mouth going back to the water.

Beelz panned his head toward Hero, and his eyes lightened with pomposity. "Listen, Hero. You know who gave them the idea to dig in the river?"

"I wouldn't know, trust me," said Hero calmly.

"Well, that idea came from me," said Beelz, smiling and searching Hero's eyes to see how he was reacting.

Hero tilted his head up, squinting and confused. "I don't get it, Beelz. How?"

"I can't go into details, Hero, because I still have to trust you to divulge specifics."

"I understand that. I thought we were friends though," said Hero.

"Not friends yet. However, you might become one. Friendship is won and is not instant. Just because I like you does not mean we are friends. Friendship is the result of trust."

"I see," said Hero, seemingly respecting and appreciating Beelz's wisdom and protocol. "Hopefully we can become friends."

"I hope so too," said Beelz, smiling.

"I have to share one more thing with you. It is really bothering me."

"What is it?"

"When I passed by the tall tree—the one across from the Movena Tree —I saw a human being. As I ran away, he pointed something at me."

"A human being? At first, Beelz seemed to be appalled, but his face quickly lit up, raising his head.

"Are you sure?"

"Yes, I saw him."

That means Ozca was right. All I need to do is capture that human being and cancel the possibility of Tauza and

Angelix reconciling, Beelz thought. Out loud, he asked, "You said he pointed something at you?"

"Yes, a black thing," said Hero.

Beelz wondered if the black thing was a gun. *If it was indeed a gun, I will have to devise a strategy*, he thought. "Make yourself at home. I will be back," Beelz said as he rushed out.

He could shoot me, Beelz thought. "I have to make sure Pinches, my queen bee, locates him. I must act swiftly now," he mumbled, making a quick turn.

HERO SNEAKS INTO
THE WATER HOLE

The moon was shining bright as a day when King Tauza and Chi, the tiger arrived at the water hole. Whinnying, Busta, the wild horse, pounded and scooped out the sand. It was as if the presence of the king was giving him more strength. After some time, finally the sand came out mixed with wet, gray mud. All of a sudden, Busta neighed and stood on his hind legs, pawing at the air with his front legs. Then there was a big roar. Clear water began to spring up through the muddy sand.

• • •

After climbing half way to the top of the tall bark-less tree, Moabi sat on the bare branch. There, he watched the animals as they lapped water one by one, two by two, and some in groups, depending on their sizes. He thought of walking over there to introduce himself and tell them how happy he was for them, but at the same time he was fearful of how they would react. *They might listen to me and be merciful if I show up rather than be found hiding or sneaking up on them*, he thought.

● ● ●

As soon as everyone was done drinking, Bizwax, the tortoise, crept to the king and reported, "My lord, I saw Hero disappearing in the bush when we started digging, and he never showed up again."

"Well, we have to make sure that he does not come and drink our water," King Tauza said. "We do not play games here. He must learn a lesson."

They were all silent as the king paced around and fumed. His brown eyes searched the crowd and landed on Woozy. "Tomorrow we will come back to build a wall around the well. In the meantime, Woozy, listen. I want you to guard this well tonight and make sure you catch Hero. Do not let him escape," the king ordered.

Woozy bragged about how he was going to do it. "If I see him, he should say goodbye because I will swing him around by those long ears. I will break his neck, you understand." Woozy was not usually merciful, and he probably meant what he said. He meant business. Once, he'd had an argument with one of the pigs. He resented the way that particular pig mocked him. The pig continued to ridicule him with his rhetoric, but soon the sorry pig found himself dangling from a tree. Woozy was no joke; he was quick to take decisive action.

· · ·

During the night, Hero showed up. He ran quickly in front of Woozy to check whether he was awake. Woozy was quick to get up, but wobbled as he galloped after Hero. He followed him out of the river. Hero took a swift turn around a nearby tree, and Woozy plummeted down as he attempted to stop. He lost track of Hero and ended up running around like a mad dog chasing wind. By the time he decided to go back to the well, it was too late. The notorious Hero had not only reached the well, but also urinating in the water. If Woozy was really smart, he would have gone back to the well immediately.

· · ·

Moabi had contemplated checking out the well, but instead stayed under the tree. Laying down on his back, his head on the dry protruding root, he marveled at the star-studded sky. Captivated by stunning clusters of constellations, the thoughts of his mother faded into a fretful sleep until he was rudely awakened by bird poop splattering on his forehead. He stayed up the rest of the night, his back against the trunk, wondering resentfully where the bird had come from.

$$\bullet \quad \bullet \quad \bullet$$

Early in the morning, the king sent his cousin, Sanza, with food to feed Woozy and to see if he had made a catch. As soon as he arrived, strange things caught his eyes. Surprise, surprise! Threads of Hero's hair were floating on the water and drifting to the edges. That enraged the king.

Adding to his shame and disappointment, Woozy was told to bail out the dirty and fuzzy water until clean water resurfaced.

The next day, the king asked for volunteers to guard the well. All of the animals remained silent. Many were afraid of the responsibility and did not want to be embarrassed.

"Can anybody catch this fool?" the king asked impatiently.

"I can, my lord," said Bizwax, shocking them all.

They all broke into laughter, literally booing her. Even the king tried to hide a condescending smile.

"Give her a chance, my king. She can do it," the king's wife insisted.

Pigs and wolves shouted, "Oweee oweee oweee. What can she do? She is as slow as a snail!"

"I don't know about that. We do not want to waste time, dear," said the king, eyeing his wife. "It would take the tortoise years to catch the young hare."

Everybody laughed.

Of course, Bizwax was the slowest animal of them all, but at least she was not dumb, contrary to popular belief.

"Be quiet, please. None of you has the guts to catch Hero, so why make fun of Biz?" asked the king with authority.

"Trust me, my lord, it would not take me a long time. I have a solid plan," Bizwax convinced calmly.

"I know you can do it, Bizwax," said the king's wife, patting Bizwax on her shell.

"How you will do it, I really don't know. My wife says you can do it, and so I say, go for it, Biz! Catch him!" encouraged the king.

Many were astonished and left speechless by the king's decision. Bizwax knew a certain place of beehives and of decaying hollow trunks not too far from the river. She liked honey so much that she would not let anybody else know about the honeyed place. When she was not working, she would pass time by looking for hives. She would bring home honey and share with others. She would also bring home wax that she used to build animal toys. Whenever there was a newborn in the kingdom, she would present a gift.

The honeyed place became her very next stop on her unpopular mission to catch Hero. For a tortoise, it wasn't a quick trip, but she didn't dawdle either. She believed in the saying: "Strategy is better than mere speed."

Despite being attacked by a mob of angry bees, with her strong forelimbs, she clobbered the honey trunks until the beehives were laid bare in the open. She drank some honey, but not so much as to make her thirsty. She forcefully extracted a lot of wax from the beehives, stacking it in one place where it became a huge ball. Then with her elephantine hind leg, she rolled the ball to the river, maneuvering it between thorn bushes and over patches of gray, dry grass.

As soon as the wax became too soft and threatened to melt in the heat of the late afternoon, she halted in the fragmented shade of a deciduous tree.

Right before sunset, as she sipped water at the water hole, she marveled at the wall that had been completed that very afternoon. Now the only gap left was what she had to guard.

• • •

A bit farther away, Moabi stood up and stretched his arms. He had made up his mind. The day had cooled off, but it was still warm. Knowing that the animals had already gone to the compound, he walked toward the river.

•   •   •

Now Bizwax had embarked on kneading the wax, mixing it with clay soil on the shore. After an hour of molding, a shape that resembled a human head emerged. In another hour or so, she had molded a human statue. Then, with her stocky legs, she rolled it into the river.

•   •   •

Standing on the bank, Moabi watched the beaming sun slipping behind the gray wood and marveled at how magically it was withdrawing its precious rays. The thought of spending another night alone in the strange land made him miserable. He fought off tears. After sunset dissolved into the looming darkness, he jumped into the river and began to walk.

Beelz had been waiting. As soon as Moabi started walking toward the waterhole, he contemplated striking Moabi from behind. Moabi looked back, sensing something. Beelz decided to cross the river quickly.

That was when Moabi caught a fleeting glance of Beelz, his head up and his tongue flicking. Moabi took a deep breath. He had never seen a snake as long as this before. He watched Beelz as he disappeared in the thickening darkness. One thing in particular he disliked about snakes was their scaly, uncannily supple bodies. He feared their venomous fangs, too. Like a flood, all those fears rushed to his mind. The thought of Beelz attacking him while sleeping flashed in his mind. He kept going to the direction of the waterhole.

•   •   •

Bizwax forced her head under the head of the statue, her hind legs gripping the ground as she pushed it up in an attempt to erect it in between the two poles of the gap. Alas, the statue wouldn't completely stand. As soon as it was halfway up, it just slid on her shell and plunged to the side. After a couple of unsuccessful attempts, she thought of crawling to the compound to ask for assistance, but she feared that the king would deem her a waster of time. Also, if she went, she would not make it back in time to catch Hero, and so she was stuck, trying to come up with a new plan. She helplessly remained in between the two poles with her head on top of the statue, gazing straight along the river. With distress mounting, she began to wipe the sand off the statue, glazing it with her smooth gular horn. Then she positioned it horizontally in the gap, where it fit well, leaving no space from pole to pole. Although Hero could easily jump over it, Bizwax still expected him to be curious enough to play some silly antics with it.

Then Bizwax watched the moon rising and the stars populating the sky. She marveled at the splendiferous light illuminating the fast-aging wood on the banks of the dormant river. The freshness of the night reminded her of old golden days when lack and despair couldn't be found in Vangoland. She began to sing one of her favorite songs.

Blessed to live in the land devoid of evil
As peaceful as heavenly place
With ethereal nights
Of celestial designs
Moon and shining stars
Dancing openly on the peaceful blue sky
Thanks to the Creator for His mastery
Who keeps misery far away from us
Lalalalaa...mhmhmhu...

While Bizwax was still humming and dreaming about what their land used to be, she saw a figure approaching. "That isn't Hero, for sure. That's a human being."

The figure slowly kept coming closer.

"I hope that is not a ghost," she murmured, cringing and retracting into her shell until her head touched the ground. "If that is a human being, it surely is not a giant from the North." She retreated until her rear legs were submerged in the water hole. Then she extended her head over the statue, only to find out that the person was closer than before. She plopped back into the water.

"I saw you, tortoise," said Moabi. "You do not have to hide. I will not harm you."

Bizwax remained quiet and still.

"I watched you earlier when you were crafting this statue," he said as he pointed to it. "I know you can't stand it up."

After about two minutes or so, Bizwax emerged, her red eyes blinking as she gasped for air.

"Who are you?" Bizwax asked nervously.

"My name is Moabi, and I came here from the Tsodilo Hills in Botswana, but I live in America."

"I have never heard of those places," said Bizwax, talking fast. Are you lost?"

"Yes, I am. I thought you could help, but you said you have never heard of the places I just mentioned. I guess I am doomed," said Moabi.

"It sounds like you are sounds," said Bizwax flippantly, trying to mask her fear.

"I watched you struggling with your statue, and if you like, I can help you stand it up," Moabi said, kicking the statue gently.

Bizwax kept quiet for a while, wondering if she would be doing the right thing to agree. "*Amph*. Well, go ahead... I need to catch this little notorious hare."

Moabi bowed down, bending his knees. "I saw the little hare with very long ears the other day by the fruit tree, and he burst into high-speed as soon as we locked eyes," said Moabi, grabbing the statue around its waist. He stood it up and positioned it to face the river.

"That was quick, short man," said Bizwax. The only reason she called Moabi "short man" was because the only human she had ever seen was a giant of the North.

Moabi laughed. He thought it was comical to be called "short" by a tortoise. "You are a funny tortoise. Moabi is my name, not 'short man.' Guess what? I know yours."

"You know my name? Don't lie. You don't know my name. What is it?" Bizwax asked curiously.

"Your name is Bizwax."

"How do you know my name? Are you a prophet?"

"No, I am not a prophet, but I have been in this place for quite some time now." Moabi paused, looking straight at Bizwax, whose eyes ballooned in awe.

"And..." said Bizwax.

"And so I kind of know what is going on in this place since I have followed you animals since I got here. I have been to the compound and at the dam site, and I watched all of you laboring here," Moabi explained.

"Are you a spy?" asked Bizwax, shaking her head in disbelief.

"No, I am not."

"Why are you interested in our lives?" Bizwax enquired.

"To tell the truth, besides being fascinated by talking animals, I am lost. "I didn't know how to face you all, so I hid under the big fruit tree over there," pointing at the Movena Tree. "Some of your animals took my backpack.

I left the tree for another just across the river because I feared being discovered, but I couldn't leave this place without my backpack."

"Your what?" Bizwax asked.

"My bag. A small back with straps," Moabi clarified.

"Oh, that was yours. Well, King Tauza has it. Okay, okay. I understand. Can you please spread the legs so that its feet touch the poles?" she requested, gesturing with her head.

Moabi pulled one foot at a time.

"Make sure they adhere. Sort of press them hard on the poles to prevent the statue from falling when the hare tries to push it," Bizwax added assertively.

"Maybe I should be the one who is guarding this place," Moabi joked.

"You might be able to guard it, but you might not be able to catch him. See, he will run away as soon as he sees a real person, but with this," said Bizwax, tilting her head toward the statue, "he will be curious enough to come close, and he will be tempted to touch it or play with it."

"I see," Moabi nodded. "Just wanted to help!"

"We must get out of here and maybe wait under that tree," said Bizwax, gesturing to a tree that was surrounded by bushes on the bank.

It was quiet for a long time until Bizwax broke the silence. "I know someone who might know your places."

"Really, who is that?" Moabi asked, his eyes widening with hope.

"Her name is Angelix. She is a wise dove and claims to have been to distant places and other worlds. Basically, she knows everything," said Bizwax, speaking under her breath.

"I have not seen her. She lives with you all?" asked Moabi.

"Yes, she is the leading spiritual being in the kingdom, but right now she has a contention with the king and has chosen to stay away," said Bizwax, sighing. "She hates evil."

"What kind of conflict are they having?" asked Moabi.

Bizwax shook her head. "I didn't know you would ask me a lot of questions. I shouldn't have started this conversation." She paused, sighing again, "Well, listen; the king is supposed to be getting the Creator's wisdom and counsel only from her, but he decided not to listen to her at all. So after a long time of frustration, she finally gave up and left."

"Do you all believe in God?" Moabi inquired.

Bizwax answered quickly, "We believe in the God who created us."

"Does he take care of the animals?" Moabi asked.

"Well...now, we have a draught, probably because of lawlessness in the kingdom. The king's new practice of openly belittling Angelix has caused a curse to fall upon us. Many animals do not even obey him anymore, mostly because he has resorted to fear mongering. Ungodly leadership yields bad fruits," Bizwax said.

Moabi added, "I personally believe that a just God cannot be influenced by evil. A good God would not neglect the innocent." He paused, and then continued, "I was struck by a lightning that nearly killed me, and my father was killed by evil men and my mother who loves God dearly is dying of cancer."

"So you don't believe in the Creator?" Bizwax asked.

"Right now I'm doubtful of his existence. If there is one...I have not found him," Moabi answered and then sighed. "By the way, do you know where Angelix is now?"

"Yes, she lives on an old tall tree not too far from the compound. She is always in her nest, praying. She is probably working on something to defeat evil. I know she has not given up on us. Otherwise, she would be gone by now. Some of us tried to go there and talk to her, but she does not come out. Not too long ago, the king warned that nobody should try to go there, or they will be in trouble."

"That really makes me want to see that dove right now," said Moabi. "Can you take me to her?"

Bizwax looked at Moabi with her mouth wide open, appalled. "Are you serious? I can't just take you to see Angelix. I am already in trouble by entertaining a stranger. I already told you that the king forbids anybody to go there because he has issues with Angelix, and he wants everyone to have a problem with her. I mean, that is just a protocol right now. You got it? Even if I could, I don't think Angelix would help someone who does not believe in the Creator."

"We both hate evil. Maybe you could introduce me to the king, then," Moabi suggested.

"Well, let's catch Hero first. Then we will talk about that," said Bizwax, winking at Moabi. "I think we should keep quiet now because we don't want to scare Hero."

THE TRIUMPH OF BIZWAX

Hero woke up in the middle of the night after a long dream. He was mumbling and groaning. As soon as he woke up, Beelz was right there talking to him.

"What's wrong, Hero?" asked Beelz.

"I had a dream."

"What was the dream about?" Beelz asked.

"Well, I dreamed about many animals gathered together on a land floating in the river."

"I like that dream. Before I can interpret it, can I ask a question?"

"Yes, you may," Hero nodded.

"Was I in the dream?"

Hero paused for a second before he could answer. "I cannot remember very well because there were so many animals, even some that I have never seen."

"Was King Tauza there?" Beelz asked.

"Like I said, there were just too many of us in that dream. I couldn't tell who was who," answered Hero.

"If I was in your dream, I would say it resembled freedom and peace. Gathering together means unity. But if I was not there, hmmm, probably those animals were on the brink of plunging into extinction because I am the one bringing peace and harmony."

"Maybe you were there," said Hero, trying to cut the conversation short.

"I know I was," said Beelz, smiling.

"Well, look Beelz, I don't mean to disrespect you. I will be back. I must go outside and stretch," said Hero.

Beelz shook his head and remained quiet for a short while. Then he said, "Be back, and don't bring me problems."

"Don't worry about that, I am very careful and considerate, you know," said Hero smiling.

●　●　●

"*Sh*," said Bizwax, alerting Moabi to what was happening down at the water hole.

Hero stopped and perked up his long ears as if he'd just heard something. Hearing nothing else, he ventured on, deciding first to circle the wall around the well to make sure he was alone. He was aware that the animals were trying to arrest him. He did not find anything threatening until he arrived in front of the statue. Panicking, he tripped as he tried to escape, but he gathered himself quickly and sprang for about twenty meters on the sandy riverbed. Then he turned sharply to see if anybody was chasing him. There was no one.

Hero trotted back to the water hole. He wanted to see if what he'd seen was what he thought it was. *How come that thing did not chase me? I've got to be careful here*, he thought. When he saw the statue, he began to chuckle and giggle. He danced until he tripped, falling on his back and laughing hysterically. Fueled by bravado, he approached the statue. "Who are you?" he asked. "Are you going to fight me or catch me?"

There was no reply.

"I am talking to you, stupid little...are you deaf?"

The statue remained quiet.

Hero started to perform some boxing moves, punching a fist into his palm. If the animals thought this silly little creature would deter him, he was going to show them otherwise.

Bizwax and Moabi were enjoying the moment. Bizwax's head was resting lightly on a piece of fallen wood, holding his laughter. She had tested her figurine and knew it would work. She was just waiting for Hero's curiosity to land him in the hands of her sticky statue.

"You are not the smartest, Hero," Bizwax whispered. "You are just a baby. You cannot fool us. I might be slow, but I know what I am doing. Besides, I have been around for too long. What separates me from you is wisdom."

Moabi nodded, hoping that Bizwax's plan would work; although, he was a little bit doubtful.

Hero unleashed a fiery punch, catching the sticky, Remove this word figure between its blank eyes. His tiny fist sank and he could not pull it back out. "Leave me alone," Hero yelled.

The statue did not say a thing. Hero began to crank the other fist to gather more power. Would it hurt the statue? With the intent of knocking the statue out, he exerted more energy than before; but alas, his other paw became stuck as well. Realizing that the little creature had him firmly in its grasp, he became nervous. Fear crept in. "Let me go, please. I promise I will never come back. Let us make a deal, please."

A subtle laughter erupted beyond the banks of the river. Hero froze. By now, he knew he was in trouble. He was shocked when he heard Bizwax's laughter. For a second he'd thought he was dreaming. Realizing he was trapped and was now being ridiculed, he tried to fight back. He had no choice but to use his legs. "Maybe I could push this stupid thing down," he mumbled. But how was he going to detach himself from the statue if he did that?

The situation got worse when he slammed his head into the statue. *Pang!* His head sank into the wax. He wailed with pain and frustration. The fight was over for Hero. He was now glued to the statue, goofed up, and miserable. He couldn't even think right.

Bizwax slid down the river wall and enthusiastically crawled to the water hole, this time laughing out loud. Moabi followed calmly.

"I have good news, Hero," Bizwax said. "Not for you but for my king. For you, it's all bad news. You are done."

When King Tauza and the rest of the animals arrived at the well to witness what the king later called called, "The Triumph of Bizwax," they found Bizwax waiting by her trembling catch. She had advised Moabi to stay away until the time was ripe to mention him.

Madingi, the pig, could not believe her eyes. All of a sudden, she looked spiteful. She fumed, her forehead crumpling. Jealousy filled her dark eyes and she disturbed instead of being happy that Bizwax had caught Hero.

When Hero was questioned, he prattled through a murky confession. "My mother told me that I have demons," he explained. "It is the reason I am causing so much trouble...I...I...I wish I had stopped earlier. My mother told me to tell you that I should be tossed up in the air, and upon hitting the ground, the impact will absolutely exorcize the demons out of me."

The king nodded. "Hmm, that sounds like a good idea. I know your mother was good at discerning problems and coming up with solutions, but you still need to pay for your notorious deeds. I am going to punish you, regardless. No wickedness goes unpunished in Vangoland." The king grabbed Hero by his tail and tossed him up. Hero sprang in the air and landed far from the rest of the animals. Speedo, the cheetah, did not give him a chance. He ran after him and grabbed him by his scrawny leg.

Hero shouted, "This is not fair, my lord! Why is Speedo hurting me like this? I am not trying to run away. He hates me!"

The king shook his mane in disagreement, not trusting Hero anymore. "I see you are full of silly jokes. Zingi, take him home, and we shall punish him until his ears grow short."

"My lord, let me show you something before you punish me," begged Hero.

"What are you talking about? If you waste my time, you'll be sorry you understand?" the king shouted.

Given a chance, but surrounded by all of the animals, Hero picked up a tiny stone with his paw and tossed it into his mouth. He closed his eyes. After gurgling, he spat, surprising them because what came out was a shiny, precious stone that looked like a diamond. Everyone was stunned, and while they were still mesmerized, he picked up the precious stone, threw it back into his mouth, and spat out the little brown stone he'd initially tossed into his mouth. The king was astonished to see Hero performing magic.

Hero knew that the king liked magic. His hope was to be pardoned. "Now, my lord, since I am free of demons, I will be able to perform magic whenever you want, just as my mother entertained you."

Some wolves and pigs booed him, but the king was happy to know that there was still going to be someone to perform magic for him.

"Get him, Zingi," ordered the king.

Zingi scooped Hero up with his trunk.

It was at this point that Bizwax raised her head and moved toward the king. "My lord, I have something special to tell you. Maybe I should do so while the rest of the animals are still here."

"What is it?" asked the king.

"There is a stranger who helped me catch Hero. He says he is lost, and he was just roaming around and found me struggling, so he offered me a hand," Bizwax explained. "Also, he said some animals took his bag from under Movena Tree and that's why he couldn't leave."

"Did you say a stranger?" inquired the king.

"He is a human being, but definitely not a giant. I think he might be an alien or something of that sort."

"Come back!" shouted the king to the departing animals. Then he turned around to face Bizwax again. "I was really wondering how you did this by yourself."

At once, the animals that were already climbing onto the riverbank turned around. Many were wondering what was next. "I hope this is not about a new project. I am tired of projects that take all of our energy," said one of the wolves, gagging. As usual, some laughed.

"Are you ready, Biz?" asked the king.

"I am ready, my lord," said Bizwax.

"Well, Bizwax says she killed two birds with one stone last night. She says she also caught an alien," said the king, jokingly.

Moabi's heart skipped, and for a second or two, his legs trembled.

"Bring him in," the king commanded.

The animals looked at one another with confusion.

"Bring the alien!" the king shouted.

Bizwax gave a high-pitched whistle that sounded like a young elephant crying.

Moabi flinched, his legs shaking as he walked. He had never been this scared. Normally for him, fear would go away immediately but not this time. It was as if he had been sentenced to death as he neared those deep eyes of the king.

King Tauza rose from the middle of the circle to meet him, and Moabi wished he could vanish.

"Open a space for him," said the king to the young buffalos.

The young buffalos shifted to the side to allow Moabi to enter the circle. All of the animals gasped and whispered to one another as he entered.

"Come," said the king with a warm tone and a smile.

Moabi stepped forward and faced the king. "Who are you, and where do you come from?" asked the king.

"I...I...my name is Moabi. Before I got lost, I was touring the Tsodilo Hills in Botswana, but really I live New York in America," Moabi explained.

"I have never heard of those places. Are they in another world?" the king asked.

"Perhaps, your majesty. I was chasing a paper on which I had written a story into a cave, and all of a sudden, there was a pool of light. Before I knew it, I could not find my way back. I found myself walking along this river, not knowing the direction where I came from. I could not even see the Tsodilo Hills anywhere, and eventually I just ended up roaming around, hoping for a miracle."

"I told him that Angelix might be able to help him," Bizwax jumped in.

"I don't want to hear anything about Angelix right now, Bizwax," the king interrupted harshly. "Don't ever mention her name again."

"I am sorry, my lord," Bizwax apologized, cringing.

"Have you ever heard of the giants of the North?" asked the king.

"Not at all, your majesty," answered Moabi.

The king looked around, scanning the eyes of the curious animals before he said to Moabi, "So what do you want to do now? Stay with us until you find a way to go back or...?"

Moabi shook his head, biting his lower lip as he tapped the sand with his shoe. "If you permit, hopefully I can dwell in your kingdom as I continue to seek help to get home," he said.

"Okay, hopefully we can learn more about you and your places," agreed the king. "This is what I want you to do: as long as you are here, I want you to report to the compound every morning. If you do not report and you are still in Vangoland, you will be breaking my law and the rules of this land. You understand that?"

"I understand," said Moabi, looking around to see the reactions of the other animals. "And my backpack?"

"You will have your bag back," assured the king.

Most did not seem to approve of the king's decision. They hoped it was not one of those decisions that would lead them deeper into trouble. Angelix's loyalists could only hope that the king would not make this person his god since it seemed he had fallen in love with him almost instantly.

"It is now time to go," said the king. "Zingi, bring Hero with you. The rest must work at the dam site, and Chi will supervise until Zingi is back. Sanza must come with me so he can start preparing food."

Bizwax gazed at everyone leaving and wondered whether the king would say something to her, and as she was still in wonderment, the king turned around swiftly, his dense mane swaying, and spoke. "Bizwax, stay here and continue to guard our water."

"Yes, my lord, I shall do my best," said Bizwax.

"And by the way, your friend can stay with you since you two seem to do a better job together," said the king.

"Yes, your majesty, I will be okay here with Bizwax," said Moabi.

He was glad to stay with Bizwax, as he perceived her to be humble and kind.

In a short time, Sanza, the lion, came galloping with Moabi's backpack hanging from his teeth. Moabi stepped back as Sanza dropped the bag in front of him and returned without saying a word.

"*He* looks scary," mumbled Moabi looking into his backpack.

•　•　•

Moabi tried to get a little bit more relaxed among the animals. However, he sensed that the king's deep eyes and stern face were not welcoming at all. Woozy, the buffalo's tense and angry-looking face made him uncomfortable. For some reason, Moabi did not like Madingi, the pig. Besides her dirty face, he noticed that every time he looked at her, she would look away or drop her face to the ground. That reminded him of some people he knew. Despite all of this, he was quickly getting comfortable and acquainted with Biz.

He listened attentively as Bizwax painted the animals' history with colorful words. She described a rich kingdom that lacked nothing, where unity was their strength and the fullness of grace purified their hearts. In a rhapsodic manner, Bizwax talked about the perennial river with green banks and the silver morning dew that spread on the blades of the ever-springing grass.

"We could feel a sense of peace in us and in others— I mean real happiness," Bizwax claimed as her eyes became teary. She looked up to the sky so the tears would not trickle down her face.

"Did you say the main reason why you are now having all these problems is because of the dove?" asked Moabi.

Bizwax shook her head, her face becoming grotesquely ugly. "Is it the nature of human beings not to listen?" asked Bizwax, still shaking her head. "By the way, this is between us. Otherwise, you will get me in trouble. I did not say the dove is the cause of our problems. I said, the problem started because of the conflict between her and the king. Don't ask me about the dove again."

"Well, I apologize for my insensitivity. Please do forgive me. It is not my intention to make you angry," Moabi said with a sincere tone.

Bizwax shook her head. "See, there you go again. Who said I am angry?"

"I thought you were," said Moabi, speaking calmly and carefully to make sure he did not rub Bizwax the wrong way.

"I am not angry with you. I was just being nostalgic, thinking about our soothing past. I miss those days when Angelix was happy and respected by everyone. Gone are those days. How I wish they could come back again!" cried Bizwax.

Moabi bent his knees and slid his hand back and forth on Bizwax's rough head. "Things will be okay."

"I hope so," said Bizwax, choking back tears and a smile wrinkling the edges of her mouth.

THE ROOF

As was their routine, king and his wife were taking their late-afternoon walk with their son, whom they were training. Taking a walk was also part of harmonizing their marriage. Sometimes they would walk around the Movena tree and kneel down in reverence but truth be told, this came as a result of fear—fear that the Movena tree would go barren and not bear fruits. So the king and his family would visit the tree and plead with it to remain fruitful and not be like the river.

"Make sure you fix my Movena fruits right, Sanza. I want them delicious. Yum, yum, yum!" said the king as he and his family approached the compound exit. "And keep an eye on the boy," he said regarding Hero.

In addition to cooking, Sanza was ordered to take Hero up on the roof of the hut to fasten some of the loose strings binding the grass. That was part of Hero's punishment. Sanza stood behind Hero as they mounted the crooked ladder. As they were climbing, Hero floundered but managed to get to the top without falling.

Now, while dried brown and white Movena fruits were cooking and smelling good, a naughty little thought manifested itself in Hero's mind. His mother used to advise him against temptation, saying, "When temptation is full blown, it leads to decision-making, and ultimately, actions are taken."

Hero looked at Sanza's eyes and realized that Sanza was now pretty comfortable with him. He was whistling a song and enjoying the work of his skillful paws. As leaned over to stitch the grass, Hero noticed some ticks were jammed under Sanza's tail.

"Hey, Sanza, let me help you."

"Help me with what?" Sanza replied with a deep, harsh voice and not really paying attention.

"Well, these ticks must be feasting on you. They are sucking your blood for sure."

"They have been there for a long time, Hero. They are just part of my life now," said Sanza, fastening a string. He used to climb a tall tree where no one could see him and would find a strong branch, and then he would swipe the crack of his buttocks on it. He gave up after many unsuccessful and painful attempts to get rid of the ticks, especially that winter day when the whole experience resulted in an excruciating hemorrhoid.

"Do you think they should be there at all? I don't think so," said Hero.

"Stop asking me stupid questions as if you are capable of doing something about it. I tried to remove them, Hero. It was a nightmare," said Sanza dismissively.

Hero's eyes kept darting towards the cooking pots on the ground. In his mind, he already saw himself eating the king's food.

Sanza turned around and looked at Hero. Hero looked at him. Sanza noticed that Hero was serious and seemed somehow believable.

"Well, I think I can help you right now, Sanza. I mean, I can remove them without hurting you. I used to remove ticks from my mother," Hero explained. "I can do it, Sanza. Let me rescue you," he continued in a sweet voice.

Sanza turned around so that his buttocks faced Hero. "Go ahead, but don't hurt me."

Hero got hold of a twined strand of fibers of the Movena tree—the same strings they were using for roofing. He passed it through the eye of a wooden needle and carefully began to poke Sanza's tail. Sanza jumped. "It will hurt a little bit, Sanza, but surely I will yank them out. You know they have been sucking you for a long time, and so they went deep, so please be patient with me," he said, biting his lower lip. "I have to prick a little bit deeper."

"Ush," cried Sanza, looking up as the bees buzzed by above them.

"Oh, come on now. You are strong, Sanza. Why cry like a baby? Be patient, and I will be done in a second," Hero said.

"Go ahead. Don't hurt me though. Otherwise, I will eat you alive. You understand?" warned Sanza.

Hero jabbed the tail about five times, searching for a soft spot. When Sanza complained again about the pain, Hero explained that he was not trying to hurt him but genuinely trying to help him. "I am only trying to help you, Sanza. Ticks are not healthy for you. You really need this."

After continuous piercing, Sanza seemed to have adapted to the pain. "I feel good, Hero. You must be doing a good job back there. You know what it feels like now?"

"Like what?" asked Hero.

"It feels like a massage—a really good one, by the way."

"Well, that's even better," said Hero, smiling.

"I feel good, o-o-owo-owo, I feel good." Sanza was starting to believe that Hero was not really that bad, and maybe one day he could trust him like he had trusted Hero's mother, Madonzi. "I want you to grow up to be smart like your mother," encouraged Sanza. "I worked with her for a long time. Just follow the rules of the kingdom, and you will be okay. The king will delight in you."

All of a sudden, Hero pierced through the delicate part of the tail, the soft part.

Sanza howled.

"Sanza, I found two big ticks deeply sunk into your tail. They are sucking your blood, eating you really badly," gasped Hero, speaking fast and as though he was deeply concerned. "You have to be patient."

"Okay," Sanza responded.

Quickly, Hero tied a rope around one of the roof timbers and immediately asked Sanza if he could take a short break to relieve himself.

"Are you done?" Sanza inquired.

"Not yet, so do not move because I am still working on one of the ticks," said Hero.

Sanza didn't mind at all Hero taking a break from picking his tail. He wanted the ticks to be gone. "Do not be too long, Hero. We need to finish this before the king comes back," said Sanza, patting the grass.

Hero dashed straight to the cooking area and kicked the lid off the king's pot. The lid hit the ground. He could not believe what he was seeing. Brown Movena fruits were simmering in thick brown soup. Hero salivated as the steam rose from the pot. "They smell good. I just have to taste now," he said, giggling.

Hero had never tasted the king's food before. Those who claimed to have tasted it had testified that it was the most delicious food in the kingdom. This was what kept Madingi very close to the cook, Sanza. Against the escaping steam, Hero yanked a piece of fruit out with a wooden fork and threw it on the wood pile to cool down. He picked it up again and then chuckled as he brought it close to his nose. Chuckling, he pointed at the restrained Sanza with it.

"Put that back unless you want your paws cut off!" Sanza ordered.

Hero sank his front teeth into the juicy chunk until his upper lip was fully buried. Sanza tried to leap, only to discover that he was sewn to the roof.

"I'm going to find out who killed my mother," Hero called up to him. "You work it out with King Tauza, and if I come back, you can tell me all about it. I don't need any of the nonsense around here, and please don't think you can catch me with that stupid statue Bizwax planted at the well. By the way, tell her she owes me big time." He laughed as he turned around. Then he trotted through the gate and disappeared among the dry bushes that surrounded the compound. "I am going to see my real friend now," shouted Hero as he hopped away.

Sanza didn't even hear him as his emotions took control.

●　●　●

At the water hole, where Moabi was listening to Bizwax telling Vangoland stories, Sanza's roar arrived in rolling waves.

"I am wondering if everything is okay at the compound. I've never heard Sanza howling like that," said Bizwax.

"How do you know that was Sanza? I thought all lions sounded the same," Moabi asked.

"Once you hear the yowling a couple of times, you will know who is who," explained Bizwax.

Sanza thundered again.

Bizwax knew that there was something wrong. "Maybe you should run over there and find out."

"You think the king will not be mad at me? Remember that I am still new here, and as far as I know, he told me to stay with you," Moabi said, shaking his head.

"I honestly think the king likes you," Bizwax said. "If he didn't, you would know. You would probably be in custody. Besides, we are a team, aren't we?" Bizwax asked.

"We are," said Moabi.

"You know the other thing? Whatever is taking place there might add value to your story," Bizwax said persuasively.

Although Moabi did not feel right about the whole situation, he finally agreed, and as always, he picked up his backpack and disappeared through the aged wood.

At the dam construction, the animals could hear Sanza's urgent cry.

"Let's go! Let's go! Something is wrong!" Zingi ordered the working animals to leave the construction site and hurry to the compound.

Everyone was shocked to see Sanza sprawled on the roof like a thief before punishment. Some surrounded the hut, while others searched for the perpetrator. Wolves and pigs seemed to be enjoying this moment as they howled and snorted, laughing obnoxiously at the helpless Sanza.

"I am going to get you. Keep on laughing!" Sanza shouted to the pigs and wolves. He was deeply humiliated, disgraced and ashamed that he'd let Hero get away. He felt like Hero had stripped him of his dignity.

The king, his wife, and their son heard the roaring and returned to the compound too. In disbelief, the king shook his head when he saw Sanza looking foolish on the roof. Instead of being angry, he laughed. *How can a beast like Sanza be tied on the roof by a tiny animal such as Hero?* he thought. "Well anyone can be deceived, I understand that. But rarely like this," the king said to himself. He then ordered Chi to climb up on the roof to free Sanza.

Even though Sanza was determined to see Hero brought to justice, facing the king was a greater challenge. He had been tricked. He had to explain what had happened. Where there is no discernment, one is bound to fall in the pit, he thought.

Contrary to the king's recent temperament, Sanza was granted mercy. The king did not think Hero was posing danger to the kingdom, so this was not a serious situation. He even smiled at Sanza. "He taught you a lesson, ha! Without wisdom, you will always be deceived. You must wake up, Sanza."

"Yes, my lord, I understand," said Sanza, humiliated.

After Sanza unfastened, Moabi returned to his friend, Bizwax. He was disappointed that he had not been able to shoot a video because he did not want to offend the king. It would not have been easy anyway because he was standing behind the rowdy wolves and the prideful pigs. The pigs wore supercilious smiles and stared at him with annoyance and disdain. He could hear their grunting and muttering as they mocked him. Then they would look at each other, grinning widely with dingy, dirty teeth.

HERO IS CAUGHT AGAIN

The following day, the king launched a massive hunt for Hero. His conscience gnawed at him that Hero was not his main problem. There was a growing concern of disunity in the kingdom, and he feared that his partially amputated leg made him vulnerable. His son was far from ready to govern Vangoland. He fought to suppress those thoughts and instead of repairing his relationship with Angelix, he went after Hero so as not to focus on his errors or endure the pain of thinking about them. Focusing his fury on Hero was his way of escaping from reality. Without a doubt, was the easy target?

Speedo, the Cheetah, swore upon her dead mother that Hero would not slip between her claws. Clips, an eagle, soared into the sky. Despite her aged eyes, she could still see farther than any other animal in the kingdom. Surging, she remembered the great tragedy that befell her years ago. Her two little ones, newly hatched and whom she was training to fly, flew toward Mount Fear, and she watched helplessly as they vanished in the dusty cloud above the conical mountain. On that day, she had guided them twice, intersecting them with her motherly wings and warning them not to go too far. The third time she let them fly by themselves. By the time she realized they had gone too far, it was too late. Now Speedo eyed Mount Fear with disdain.

●　●　●

Days passed by without catching Hero. What the animals did not know was that Hero had been visiting the outskirts of the animal compound. One afternoon, he ventured out of Beelz's underground mansion to play in the well as he had done before, determined that he would be evade Bizwax's wit.

While Beelz was busy sipping his honey, Hero secretly tiptoed up the hole and stopped right before exiting. Cautious, rested his head on the edge of the opening of the hole. He had never felt nervous like this before. He glanced at the scorching sun that hung beneath the light-blue sky. Then he looked side to side. When satisfied, he sprang out of the hole and headed for a nearby tree. Sitting on the pieces of decaying bark, his tiny body against a worn trunk, and his ears perked toward the sky like corn husks, he scanned the environment.

Dry, hot air swept across his face. In spite of the unbearable temperature, he felt unstoppable. He had become egocentric and pompous. Beelz had been mentoring him, especially on how to elude his enemies. Through this assimilation process, Hero had become a pathological liar. To some degree, Beelz's words had given him confidence and power. He had bought into Beelz's rhetoric, and now he totally believed that the king had killed his mother. Beelz's words played vividly in his head: *"Your mother tried to convince Tauza that I was valuable to the kingdom and not to expel me, and just by saying that, he got rid of her."*

Beelz also encouraged Hero to depend on the power of a free mind—the inner belief that anyone could do anything if his or her focus was unbreakable. He also stated that submitting to the rules of the Vango kingdom had enslaved "It is all about rules, rules, and rules. Now you are free from Tauza's oppressive rule, Hero."

One of the biggest and strongest animals in the kingdom was Big Rhino. He was a calm, relaxed beast. He did not like to engage himself in issues that did not pertain to his life. While other animals, including other rhinos, went around in groups, he kept to himself and stayed aloof. He was an introvert by nature. Although he was physically gifted, inside he was as weak as a dry leaf. He was very sensitive, and all his answers were defensive.

He was one of those who could not assume responsibility by themselves; he had to be directed. He was not a self-starter by any means. One of the insecurities that plagued him was the fear of talking in gatherings. He couldn't offer his opinion because he feared what others would think of him.

Now Big Rhino sluggishly made his way toward the tree where Hero was hiding. Hero's heart leaped as Big Rhino neared. He rushed to the bush that was on the right side of the tree. He hoped Big Rhino did not see him.

Slowly Big Rhino walked toward the bush not knowing Hero was hiding under it. But as he approached, his nose on the ground, Hero catapulted himself into the open space.

Big Rhino struggled pick up the speed to catch Hero. His hefty hooves tripped over a fallen branch and crashed to the ground with a loud noise. Speedo, the Cheetah, was not far off and saw what happened. He immediately ran after the scampering Hero. In a minute or two, Speedo had closed the gap. Hero saw a hole a couple of feet away and did not waste time. He painfully forced himself through the tiny opening. Speedo passed the hole—one of Speedo's flaws was that he couldn't stop immediately—but nonetheless, he quickly made a sharp turn.

After sliding a long distance into the hole, Hero was surprised to meet Beelz. Little did he know that Beelz's mansion had multiple openings.

"Where have you been? You don't just leave and come back here anytime you want," fumed a grumpy Beelz, charging. "What is wrong with you?"

Hero cringed. Beelz's eyes were as scary as an inferno. "They're coming after me! I hope they did not see where I went," Hero tried to explain.

"Why are you bringing the enemy to my sanctuary? Beelz shouted, lunging at Hero with his venomous, spiky fang.

Dodging, Hero jumped over Beelz. "At least I can survive outside. Here, Beelz is trying to kill me!" he muttered as he sped toward a skinny shaft of light ahead.

Hero emerged from the hole like a lightning bolt with Beelz's honeybees dispatched after him. They caught up to him before he could take cover. He rolled like a crumb on the ground, the pain penetrating his soul. Upon opening his eyes, he saw a thorny bush and, in a bid to escape, quickly plunged himself into it. He wished it was water, but alas, it added insult to injury. Merciless thorns pierced his body from head to toe. Meanwhile, the colony retreated to the hole.

Hero could now hear hooves and paws pounding not far away. He knew then that his fate had arrived. Escape wouldn't be easy. An inch of movement in the thorny bush brought on agonizing pain. So he jumped out quickly and headed in the direction of the well.

Meanwhile, Bizwax and Moabi had joined the hunt. Obviously, they knew they would have a hard time catching him, especially Biz because she was not gifted at all when it came to sprinting. But there was one idea that they thought was worth trying. They built four booby traps with sticks, and Moabi planted them in different places between the river and the compound. With high hopes and confidence, they returned to the river.

Hero was running as fast as he could, "They can't catch me now," he muttered, dashing toward a fallen tree. As soon as he jumped over the trunk, he landed on a trap. He cried for help, as pain pierced his paw and sunk his heart.

Within a short period, Clips spotted him and descended into the area.

Soon, Hero looked like a thief surrounded by a mob about to deal with him badly. He shrunk in guilt and shame. His heart thumped as the booby trap gripped him tightly. "Help me! Please help! This thing is killing me!" he cried out.

"Shut up, stupid," Zingi said harshly.

"But this is hurting me. Can't you see?" Hero cried.

"Well, you deserve it," Zingi said sarcastically, smiling and eyeing the onlookers whose expressions confirmed that Hero deserved the excruciating experience.

A pig shouted, "Let the little trickster die!"

Driven by compassion, Chi maneuvered through the vivacious throng, stepping toward the visibly shaken Hero. "Hero, what do you have to say about your rebellion?" Chi asked softly.

"I am so sorry, Chi. Please rescue me," Hero sobbed, yet words sticking in his throat.

Chi looked at Zingi, as if he was going to say, "Have mercy on him." Instead, he said sternly, "Release him from the trap before he dies, lest the king put the blame on you."

"Well, go ahead," Zingi replied. "I am not doing it, and if he escapes, I do not know how you will face the king."

As Chi carefully fiddled with the trap and loosened it from Hero's feet, blood shot out, splashing him on the forehead. Then he gestured for Zingi to take over. Harshly, the elephant coiled his trunk around Hero's body.

"Don't squeeze me, please. Ow! Oh that hurts," cried Hero.

"No, Hero, you need to be squeezed until we get to the king. I can guarantee you that you won't be treated lightly this time. I feel sorry for you, Hero," said Zingi, shaking his bulky head.

The king was happy when they arrived with the now unconscious Hero. He noticed that Hero had some wounds on his legs and neck and had swollen eyes. Like Chi, compassion stirred the king's heart, but he felt compelled to remain stern before the others. He ordered Sanza to gather some wood and build a cell for Hero. "Leave a space for air to come in."

There were plenty of thick sticks around the compound, so with the help of other lions, such as Dumie, the cell was constructed quickly. It was about half a meter long and half a meter in height. A little window was made to pass food and water. Sanza threw Hero inside. It was dark with just a tiny opening on the roof. The pigs and wolves strolled by and mocked him, telling him that he was going to rot in the cell.

$$\bullet \quad \bullet \quad \bullet$$

The next morning when Sanza brought Hero some water, he found him soaked in tears. Sanza asked, "What is wrong with you? You wanted this, right? You deserve to be punished. Forget about seeing the sun and the moon or the beautiful sky. Darkness is where you belong."

"I just want to be..." Hero tried to explain, but Sanza had vanished.

$$\bullet \quad \bullet \quad \bullet$$

On the third night, it was very, very dark when Angelix secretly landed on top of Hero's cell and started to pray in a low, soft voice. No one could see her, but Hero could hear her. "My God, I pray for your grace to work in Hero and for him to know your love. Amen."

Angelix flapped her wings quietly and crouched down to look through the crack in the roof. "Now listen, Hero, God hates everything that is of lawlessness. God created you, so you must obey him and the authority of this land. Now if you are genuinely willing, Hero, I want you to repeat after me. Remember, I am only helping you because God is using me to relay His message to you. Do you understand me, Hero?"

"Yes, yes," Hero said enthusiastically.

"Now repeat after me. God forgive me of my rebellion. I receive your truth in my heart. Moreover, I will love my family. Amen."

Submissively, Hero repeated the words after Angelix.

"Now listen to me. When Sanza comes to you, tell him that you want to see the king. When you get there, you must humble yourself. Tell him nothing but the truth. Good night, Hero." Invisible, Angelix took off and flew over the king's hut.

Hero was overjoyed. It was as if Angelix had removed the snare of fear away from him. As tears streamed down his face, he felt the thorn of sorrow subside. He started to walk around in his cell, energized.

• • •

The following day, Sanza found Hero in a rather peaceful state, "Hey, you look happy today, Hero. You like your cell, huh? Don't get too comfortable in there though. You still owe me big time," Sanza warned.

Hero opened his mouth with confidence. "I need to talk to the king. I have to tell him something - the truth, only the truth."

Sanza reported to the king that Hero was in a strangely blissful state and would like to speak the truth. "I think he may just want to escape though," warned a now skeptical Sanza.

"What kind of truth?" the king asked while chewing a lump of dry Movena fruits.

"I do not know, my lord. I think he is just lying," said Sanza.

"Bring him in then," said the king in a deep, husky voice.

Sanza dutifully retrieved Hero, with his strong front teeth carrying him by his ears to the king.

The king dismissed Sanza as soon as Hero was inside the royal hut. "Please make sure you close the door behind you," ordered the king. Dots of light spilling through the porous rooftop caught the king on his forehead, yet barely exposing the deep brown eyes.

"Hero," called the king.

"Yes, my lord, I am here," Hero answered.

"Before you can tell me your truth, what is it that has gotten into your small head? What is wrong with you?" the king asked. His bold belly sagged on the hard bed that occupied almost a quarter of the hut. The bed itself was low, a pile of branches and a layer of brown grass. As the king rose, the bed made a smashing sound. At the foot of this king-size bed, Queen Mambo was caressing the young prince, Zambi. Lately, Zambi had been going through rigorous grooming so that one day, he would assume the kingship.

Hero remained quiet.

Losing patience, the king shouted at Hero, "Answer me now!"

"My lord, after my mother's death I felt like I did not belong here. The pigs and wolves had always bullied me and I knew it was going to be worse." Hero paused. "I thought you did not like me," he said, casting his eyes downward. "Even though my mother told me to live by faith not by fear, I thought they were going to kill me too."

"Oh...really." The king's eyes widened. "That's not the case, Hero. Although I hate what you do, I do not hate you," said the king.

There was a long silence.

The king spoke again. "Well, you said 'they.' Who are 'they' who were going to kill you? The pigs and wolves?"

"I do not know, my lord. My mother died before she could tell me anything. She just said I should be careful."

There was yet another long silence that was broken by muffled laughter from outside. It was one of the nosy wolves pressed against the wall, soon to be run off by Sanza.

Hero started to sob bitterly. "I was confused, my lord. I did not know what I was doing, but now I realize that I cannot run away and be bad. I was scared of you. I had no faith. I learned a lesson. That I...I should respect, especially you, my lord. I apologize, my lord. I was wrong." Hero started to cry more loudly. "Please forgive me my lord," he begged.

"Hero, um, give me a reason why I should forgive you and why I should believe and trust you." The king's voice filled the room.

Hero rubbed his teary eyes with his little sore paws. "I can clean the whole compound today, just to show you I have changed."

The king remained quiet for some time. He looked at his wife and said, "Do you think we should let him do that? I mean, do you think we should even listen to his lies?"

"Give him a chance, sweetie. He will be all right." The king's wife nodded and smiled, but the look on Zambi's face signaled that he disagreed.

"Okay, okay, fine," said the king. "No one is going to supervise you, Hero. This is your last chance to prove we can trust you. Go ahead, start working, and report to me when you are done. Understand?" the king said.

"I do understand, my king."

LOOSED

Behind the compound, there grew some bushes with slim branches and dry leaves. With his paws, Hero wrenched a couple of them loose, then bundled them together to make a broom of his height. He wobbled as he hurled the broom over the wall into the compound. No one ridiculed him since they all left for the dam construction site except the royal family.

Standing on his hind legs, his front legs grappling with a branch, he began to sweep the compound wholeheartedly, despite the stinging of sweat that ran into his scabbed wounds. To forget the pain, he broke into a poem called "Blessings" that he learned from his mother.

Respect the elders
So blessings may shower you.
Delight in order
And to others remain true,
Unlike those who tread the path of disorder,
For theirs is darkness after death.

He grinned, and turned around feeling as though someone might be looking. The king was there, smiling. Hero quickly resumed work.

"You are doing well, Hero," the king encouraged him.

Hero was surprised at the king's sober and kind words. Smiling, he even felt more energized. At the end of the day when everyone showed up, the whole compound was clean and every animal was happy except the pigs and wolves, whose eyes glared jealousy.

Some of them derided him with their negative words. One wolf said, "You will never be forgiven for what you have done, Hero."

One pig had the audacity to say, "Don't think you are going to get away with it, Hero. Sanza is not done with you. He is going to cut your ears."

The pack of wolves began to circle and pace around him. They called him all sorts of names, labeling him the "evil agent." He felt rage building up in him, but he avoided conflict by darting in between their oppressive paws.

●   ●   ●

The fifth day on the Vangoland calendar was always a special day. It was a day of storytelling and reminiscing, when the king would brief the kingdom on matters of the week. Busta, the wild horse; Bizwax, the tortoise; and Clips, the eagle were called before all of the animals and congratulated on their recent achievements. They were then appointed to the advisory board.

As for Moabi, there was no honorary title bestowed upon him, but he was recognized for working diligently with Bizwax, especially in the design of the booby traps that nabbed Hero. That did not sit well with the pigs and the wolves. They would rather find joy in booing him. Their stinky demeanor never failed to show, and they were never easy to please.

Watching the king recognize Moabi and thinking about the pain, he endured when snared, Hero's heart skipped twice. Nodding, he winked and smiled at Moabi, acknowledging the fact that he, Moabi, and Biz had outwitted him.

As the event progressed, the king surprised many by summoning Hero to perform magic. Hero's heart leaped, and for a second or so, he did not move at all. The king had caught him off guard. "I can't do this," he muttered to himself.

Hero was seated along on the far right, behind everyone else. Now all eyes were on him. Slowly, he got to his feet, already enduring mockery. Without any option, he limped around the razzing crowd and stood before the king, trembling with nervousness. He took a deep breath as his throat dried up. Like a shy child asked to sing or pray, he looked confused. At that moment, the whole place was quiet with all eyes on him.

Someone from the king's row yelled, "You can do it, Hero."

Hero knew exactly where the sweet voice was coming from. It came from the king's wife, who sounded like a mother encouraging her son. He began to rock his body side to side, taking a step back and forth. Then he picked up a brownish little stone from the ground with his shaky little paw. Unlike his mother, who could graciously and marvelously stand on two legs, Hero could only stand on three - at best - unless he was holding onto something. His cheeks jiggled as he tactically juggled the stone in his mouth. "Are you ready?"

Only few shouted with excitement, "Yes, we are!" The rest were just sitting there, either perplexed or apathetic.

While all eyes were fixated on him, he spit a small shining stone that fell by the king's ashy paw. The king smiled and jabbed his wife with his beefy shoulder. A roar erupted among the elated animals, but those mired by jealousy hated it. With his tongue, he snatched the shining stone back into his mouth and jiggled his mouth again. Upon opening his mouth, the little brown stone fell on the ground and a roar exploded as the king's wife squealed with delight. To reach his mother's standard, whose tricks were sensational. Hero needed to be polished just a little, but the youngster showed potential and charisma. There was no doubt that soon he would become a legitimate illusionist.

The pigs, the wolves, and some of the young lions were flabbergasted, for it seemed that Hero was on the verge of winning the king's heart—if he had not won it already. They did not think the skinny Hero deserved any favor or trust because of his past reputation.

After the surprising event, Madingi approached the king. She said something to the king that nobody else heard, but everyone saw the king nod. Then Madingi rejoined her fellow pigs. The king bellowed, calling Sanza, the lion. In a hear-and-obey instinct, Sanza jumped up quickly and dashed to his most respected leader.

"Call the young man here, please," commanded the king.

The king stared at Moabi with a solemn face as he neared.

"What are those things in your bag," demanded the king.

Moabi wiped the sweat from his face and slid the straps off his shoulders, his eyes on the king. Then he unzipped the backpack and tilted it toward the king.

"Can you remove those things and one by one explain what they do, please?"

Moabi pulled the video camera out. "This one is a video camera—for making movies."

"Can you explain that to me, please," said the king, sitting down on his tail.

"What it means is, when I aim at something and push this button, it records what it sees on a recording device called a tape. Then, I can play it back and see it again."

"So, if you were to...record me, then you could see everything that I was doing during your recording, right?"

"Exactly," said Moabi. "This one here—" He was now holding the still camera. "This one shoots only stills."

"Okay. And what about the rest?" asked the king dismissively.

"This gadget here is my video game," said Moabi, brandishing the gadget. "It is powered by batteries and sunlight. Right now, all my batteries are gone, and I am actually relying on sunlight."

"What is a video game?" asked Zambi, the king's son, who seemed quite interested in the word game. As soon as Moabi said the word, his ears perked up.

"It is a game played on this little machine, and it is called Occupy Whole Screen. It is played by a built-in opponent, the little chunky man standing at the far end of the screen, and the person—in this case, me— playing the game. This game is about warring with words. You take the side of positive words against the side of negative words or vice versa. The person playing against the built-in opponent chooses a side. However, the built-in opponent always has the advantage of being the first to make a move. When I started playing this game, I used to alternate between the two sides. I did that because I wanted to learn vocabulary, especially as an aspiring writer. Nowadays, I like to war with positive words only because I am learning how to think and react positively against negative situations," Moabi explained. "I mean, that is just me, you know. Some people do it differently. I believe words have power.

If I can incorporate many positive words in my belief system, I can fare better against our negative world."

"Don't get too philosophical on us. We know how to react to life," said the king. "I am sure my son is interested in knowing whether there is a winner in your game." The king panned his eyes from Moabi to his son, who was gazing intently at the gadget as if to say, "Can I see that?"

"Am I right, Zambi?"

"Yes, Father, that's it. And how do you actually play the game?" asked Zambi hastily, sensing his father's impatience.

"Okay, if I am warring with positive words, my opponent's aim is to occupy or populate the whole screen with negative words. I oppose him by dismantling his negative words by typing or speaking the opposite of the word he unleashed. This is where I type my words," said Moabi, pointing at the small keypad with faded chrome letters below the glossy rectangular screen. "The little speaker here on the left transmits my words to be recognized," he said, touching it with his middle finger. "Once you press this green button, the game starts, and immediately my opponent spits out a word. I have to respond within three seconds. If I fail to respond, his negative word is retained and instantly changes into a tiny red ball that darts toward the corner on his side. The more words that are retained, the more red balls are lined up perfectly, row by row. If I fail to dismantle my opponent's words, then he will occupy the whole screen with tiny red balls, and he will be the winner. Likewise, if I manage to pull down my opponent's words one hundred times straight without failing, then my words would have turned into beautiful little shining stars occupying the whole screen and making me the winner. See?"

"So the screen can only hold one hundred red balls and/or shining stars?" asked Zambi.

"That's correct. By the way, this is not as easy as it sounds. If my opponent has retained some words and the next time he fails because I responded with the right opposite word, then his oldest red ball is dismantled. The same thing would apply to me: if I fail to dismantle his word, his score goes up, and so this game can take a long time to finish."

"Can you and the opponent have a draw?" asked Zambi, whisking his tail.

"Good question. I was actually about to explain that. No draw, son of the king. Either my opponent or I can win at fifty-one words. It is always nice when I win at 90 percent to 100 percent though. Unfortunately, my opponent always comes up with difficult words," Moabi explained.

"Are the words the same and come in the same manner every game? Is there any trick on how to win the game?" Zambi asked.

"All the words in the new game are different from the ones in couple of previous games. By the way, there are about six thousand words - all adjectives programmed in this machine and—"

"Six thousand! That's a lot of words," Zambi exclaimed.

"I know! Hah!" said Moabi.

Zambi shook his head, his eyes twinkling enthusiastically. "That was just too much information, but I kind of like it. Will you teach me?"

"If the king permits and I am still here, it is possible," Moabi answered.

"Give me an example," said the king, smiling.

"*Hmm*, well let's say my opponent comes up with the word *dismal*. Then I could respond by typing or say the word *cheerful*," Moabi explained.

"Okay, okay, sounds good. It sounds like it might waste a lot of time though," said the king, looking at Zambi.

Zambi's happy face changed to sadness upon hearing his father's negative utterance.

"It actually conserves time because it empowers me with an immense wealth of vocabulary and encourages me to think positively when I encounter negativity," said

Moabi, in response to the king. "Words are like seeds. You either sow negative words or positive words."

"Whatever. What about those papers?" asked the king.

"How can I start this?" Moabi paused, wiping his sweaty forehead with his palm. "I use these papers to write my story. Do you remember when I explained to you about how I arrived in Vangoland?

"Yes, I vaguely remember. Vaguely," replied the king. "What about it?"

A bit shaking, Moabi, pulled a loose paper out his coverless notebook. He looked at it and sighed. "Well, I could have neglected this paper if it was not that important. I chased it because it bears the story that I wrote to my father before he passed away."

"Oh really?" said the king.

"Yes, King," said Moabi, choking back tears. "My ambition is to write great stories."

"What are you writing about now?" asked the king, smiling.

"Well," Moabi paused, biting his lower lip. "I am glad you asked that. I'm actually writing the story of your kingdom. I think is fascinating—especially with what you are going through," he said almost solemnly.

"I cannot grant you that," the king said, shaking his head in disbelief. All of a sudden, the king's voice rose angrily. "Are you trying to spy on us? Here is what I am going to do. I am going to keep your bag until you are ready to leave this place," said the king, turning around and limping to his hut.

Hurt, Moabi walked dejectedly through the wooden gate as he followed Bizwax back to the water hole. He was beginning to doubt his safety in the kingdom and wondered if the king would not order his demise.

Later on that evening, the king called Hero to the hut. "It seems like your wounds are healed now, Hero?"

The king smiled at Hero as he asked. "I am healed, my king."

Then the king continued, "Good. Those bees did not play with you. Did you run into their hive or what? Tell me, what happened?"

"Well, my lord, I saw a hole and just went in, and this snake—he said his name was Beelz—he attacked me. Then as I ran away, he sent his bees, and they caught up with me."

The king's heart started to beat fast and his deep eyes widened. "Beelz, hmm, did you say Beelz?"

"Yes, he said his name was Beelz."

"Is that where you were all along when we were looking for you?"

Hero's eyes dropped to the floor. He felt a chill quickly traveling along his backbone. His two front teeth bit his lower lip. "My lord, allow me to tell you something..."

The king looked at him and said, "Go ahead."

"Well, my lord, when I was away, I stayed with that Beelz. He told me that he wanted to reign all over Vangoland."

The king pounded his bed and shook his head, with anger rising. "He will never rule this land."

There was a long pause as Hero cowered with fear. The king regained composer and softened his tone.

"Take us to Beelz's hole first thing in the morning?"

"I am ready, my lord," Hero said, trembling.

BEELZ RELOCATES

Beelz knew that the king would not waste time. As soon as his bee entourage returned from chasing Hero, he ordered them to be ready for migration. Pinches, the shiny black queen bee, was angry and dissatisfied at the untimely exodus. She was the leader of all the bees. Beelz had befriended Pinches and her bees immediately after he was expelled from the kingdom. Since then, they had been traveling with Beelz everywhere he went. But this time, Pinches expressed displeasure.

"This is a nice place, Beelz. There is water here. We have made it nice for you. We have been serving you in earnest and producing more than enough honey for you. It is going to take us a long time to build another home," Pinches reasoned

"I said let us go. We will find another nice place. Just follow me, darling. We do not have time to waste," urged Beelz as he tipped his head from side to side.

"Where are we going to find a safe place with pure water like this one here?" Pinches groaned, rolling her eyes.

Waving his tail, Beelz yelled, "Pinches, we have to leave right now! They are coming after us. If you stay behind, they are going to kill you."

"What about Gray?" asked Queen Pinches.

Beelz turned his head sharply toward the queen, who was buzzing above him. "Are you crazy, Pinches? Don't worry about that nasty mouse. Let's go!" shouted Beelz.

Gray, a fat mouse, had lived a peaceful life in this hole until Beelz showed up. Truth be told, he was now happy that Beelz was leaving.

● ● ●

Early in the morning, King Tauza; Queen Mambo; Zambi, their son; Sanza, the lion; Chi, the tiger; and Zingi, the elephant followed Hero to where he last saw Beelz. He showed them the two entrances to the hole.

The king said, "Chi, make fire and set it on the far exit." He divided them into two groups, making sure that both exits were guarded. The plan was to choke Beelz with smoke and force him to come out. Hero's stomach sank as Chi ignited a fagot of twigs. He thought of Gray, the innocent mouse, who also inhabited the hole, but was too afraid to contradict the king's plan.

Gray was alone in the hole, happy now that his oppressor, Beelz, was gone. He could no longer bear being forced to perform tasks that overruled his beliefs. This was what Gray had endured from Beelz—always tormented by thoughts of being annihilated on any given day. He had to scratch Beelz's itchy, peeling skin off of his body with his tiny, soft nails every morning. He could be summoned to do it at any time. And not only that, all his movements were guarded with threat of bee stings and bug bites. He had lived with fear since the arrival of Beelz.

When Hero came to live with them, Gray was distrustful and avoided him. When he overheard Hero and Beelz, he realized that the hare was not a friend of the evil snake, but a naive youth. He'd tried to warn Hero that Beelz was a pathological liar. Hero seemed ambivalent, so Gray left him alone.

Now alone in the hole, Gray frolicked back and forth as if practicing for a sprinting competition. He was laughing endlessly, marking a long-awaited freedom. He didn't anticipate what was about to happen.

As hot smoke rushed in, he tried to escape, but he could not see where he was going. Blindly, he plunged into Beelz's honey. Stuck, he cried out for help.

His subtle voice traveled through the tunnel and smoke to the outside world. This caught the attention of Chi, who was outside by himself next to the already extinguishing fire. He yelled to others, "Someone is in there. I heard a thin voice coming from the hole. Come and listen."

"You did?" Hero asked as he neared.

"Yes, just listen," said Chi. "Someone is in there."

Hero listened closely and could hear the distinct voice of Gray. Emboldened, he shouted, "Gray is in there! I am going in!" Hero exclaimed as he paced around.

Due to the scorching heat, the king and his family were sitting under a tree about twenty feet away from Chi and Hero.

Hero did not ask for permission from the king, nor did he think about whether Beelz could be well and ready to strike. Quickly he grabbed a stick, pushed aside the extinguishing fire and jumped in. He slid down the smoky hole until he crashed deep down at the bottom. He could hear Gray whimpering not too far to his left.

"Gray, Gray, where are you?"

"I am stuck in honey! Come rescue me, please!" cried Gray.

"Who are you with?"

"They left me by myself," said Gray.

"I am coming to get you," said Hero.

Hero turned left toward Gray, coughing and choking on the smoke.

Getting closer, he haphazardly tried to grab Gray but snatched nothingness. Hero's little paw plunged into honey, making it hard for him to make a move.

"Gray, where are you?"

"I am here."

"Where did Beelz go?"

"He moved out with all the bees after they chased you."

"Why did you stay behind?"

"He did not say a thing to me. They just left me, and I was happy he left me behind anyway," said Gray, sobbing.

Finally, after many attempts to get through the honey, Hero touched something like a soft tube. He pulled it.

Gray screamed. "You have torn my tail, Hero," cried Gray.

"I am sorry, Gray, but your tail is too soft," said Hero. He pushed through the honey until his paw was under Gray's body. With Gray in his grasp, Hero pulled with all his might, leaning back until he stumbled with Gray on top of him. Within seconds, he was darting through the light of the entrance. *Never dwell with the evil one; find a way to run away,* Hero thought.

Hero emerged at the exit, gasping for air. Upon noticing what he was holding, everyone was astonished.

"Did you jeopardize your life for this?" Madingi mocked, laughing as Hero dashed by.

"That voice," murmured Gray weakly, "I've heard it before. With Beelz..." he trailed off.

Perplexed, Hero ignored Madingi, and with little thought of what Gray said, he continued on to the king who was still waiting under the tree with his wife.

"Who is this now, Hero?" asked the king, staring at the sticky Gray.

"My lord, this is Gray. He was a captive of Beelz, but he says the snake left him and relocated with his swarms," explained Hero.

"Are you sure he is on our side?" asked the king.

"Yes, my king." Hero paused. "Hopefully, he will also reveal something."

Slowly, Hero knelt down and put Gray on the ground. With a stick, he gently scraped away honey from his trembling body. Gray blinked repeatedly as soon as the king started to interrogate him. Then there was no movement at all.

"Where is Beelz?"

There was no answer.

The king kept on staring at him, and after a brief silence, he said, "I think he is dead, Hero."

Hero ran his paw on Gray's back, tears trickling down his cheeks. "He was innocent." Then Hero dug a small hole with his paw and carefully rolled Gray inside.

"You must have loved this little animal, Hero," Madingi said sarcastically.

"Why don't you shut your snotty mouth? Hero said. His tear fell on Gray's body. "He was a good animal."

"A good animal? Really? Staying with Beelz? I guess Beelz is a good animal then."

Hero turned around and looked at Madingi with an angry face. "Beelz found him in that hole and forced him to stay with him. You understand?"

"Stop that conversation now," the king ordered at once.

Hero vaguely began to recall the mouse's final words when he saw Gray moving a tiny bit. "Oh my, oh my! He is alive!" he shrieked with hope.

Snorting, Madingi peeped in and then exploded with laughter. "You're hallucinating!"

Zingi also came by, looked into the shallow grave, and did not see any movement. "I think that is a figment of your imagination."

After feeling certain that Gray was dead, Hero covered the mouse's limp little body with dry grass.

"It is time to go now," said the king. Rising to his feet, grains of sand rolled down from his belly.

As the sun descended into the skyline, returning home was the only option, but first, they stopped by the water hole to quench their thirst. The rest of the animals that were not with the king were waiting with sadness since there was no water in the water hole. A little bit farther, on the riverside, Moabi sat with arms folded across his chest, staring sympathetically at the despairing animals. His thoughts drifted to memories of his ailing mother. He fought off the idea that she could die any time. He vowed that if he couldn't find anyone to help him out of the animal kingdom, soon he resume walking.

MOABI'S WATER HOLE

As soon as the king and his entourage descended into the river, the rest of the animals rose to their weary feet.

Before the king could enter the water hole, Bizwax coughed twice, clearing his voice. "We have big problem, my lord."

"What problem?" asked the king, passing Bizwax without even looking at her as he entered the gate.

"Well, as you can see, my lord, I really don't know how to explain this," lamented Bizwax. "There was a lot of water this morning, and there was no sign of the water hole drying up. This is weird."

The king shook his head in disbelief. He turned around and stepped outside. He looked his wife in the eye. "More trouble."

Queen Mambo looked calm, as if everything was okay. "Let us have Angelix pray for us," said the king's wife.

"No, Angelix is full of pride. She decided to move out of the compound without telling me. That is disrespect. I do not think I need someone like her, especially during these times."

The king's wife kept quiet, avoiding an argument.

The king hobbled back and forth, as some animals mingled around. "Madingi?" the king called.

The pig hurriedly appeared before the king. "Yes, my lord?"

"What do you think happened to the water hole?"

"The only scenario I can think of is that the water drained down; I think that is what happened."

"Everybody, listen," shouted the king. "We have to dig because the water drained down." He paused and looked around upon hearing some noise apparently negating the call to dig. "Zingi will supervise, and we will not be going home until the water surfaces. Understood?"

Overnight, they dug deeper and deeper, crushing little rocks and hammering through hardened clay soil. A hooray of victory broke out every time they reached a new layer. Soon they encountered their biggest challenge: a layer of hard rock. Hooves pounded and paws scraped until the early hours of morning, but to no avail. One by one, they came out of the empty hole discouraged and weary. The king had no clue what to do, and even when he realized that there was no way they were going to break or

crush the granite stone, he still ordered the fatigued buffalos to pound it.

They dug three other waterless holes. However, the king
would not give up. His orders become even more aggressive.
At the height of this ordeal, having discussed many ideas
with her friends, Madingi suggested to the king that they
must seek help among the giants of the North. If the king
agreed, they could bring their machinery and drill boreholes.

The king blasted her, saying, "Are you crazy? Those
greedy humans would come and take our land, and they
would not refrain from oppressing us. Do you want the
foreigners to take your land?"

Embarrassed and curling her tail up, Madingi returned
to her friends. Besides Madingi, only a few in the king's
inner circle could actually talk to the king directly. The rest
had no courage to do so.

At the crack of dawn, they began to rise to their feet,
stretching and barely hopeful. As the glorious light of the
sun quickly spread, Moabi slowly walked through the
worn-out animals. He was determined to confront the
king regardless of the outcome.

Moabi bowed his head before the king and then respectfully said, "I have an idea, your majesty."

"What is it?" the king asked.

"Instead of just digging haphazardly, maybe we can
use the method that I studied in school."

"I said, what is it?" repeated the king aggressively,
drawing attention.

"Well, I will try to explain this as quickly as possible—"

"Quickly, please," interrupted the king. "We don't have time to waste."

"We must locate certain plants on the shore that suggest the presence of water in the river. We will know those plants because they are not totally dry, or we can notice them by their types. After locating these plants, we plunge a long rod or sharply pointed stick in the river adjacent to those particular plants. If there is water, the sharply pointed stick will come out with wet soil when it is pulled out," Moabi explained.

The king looked at his wife and Zambi, who were now sitting close together and listening attentively to Moabi.

"Maybe we can dig by the Movena tree. I am sure there is plenty of water there," Moabi continued.

The rest of the animals wondered what Moabi could possibly be discussing that kept the king and his family so attentive. Some even came closer to listen.

"Forget about digging by the Movena tree. I am afraid that if we dig by it, it might stop producing fruits. We do not want to disturb its suction. Besides, that tree is an important source for us," said the king. "We do not want to make it angry."

"I understand. Well then, the next option is to locate certain plants that have roots reaching down into the water table."

"What kind of trees are you talking about?" the king inquired. "All I see is dead plants except the Movena and a few shrubs."

"I saw some plants that look like Vangueria and Grewia..."

"What?" the king asked, shrugging his shoulders and trying to understand what he just heard.

"Yes, your majesty, Vangueria and Grewia. You might be wondering what kind of trees those are. They are the types that have long roots, which means we would have to dig deeper and possibly for a long time," Moabi explained.

The king was quiet for a minute or so, ambivalent about whether to believe the young man or not. But there was a convincing inner voice that propelled him to buy into Moabi's idea.

"Let's take a chance. We have nothing to lose," said Queen Mambo.

Immediately, the king rallied everyone, and they all followed Moabi past the Movena tree and arrived by the two plants on the banks that he had spotted earlier on.

The animals knew these plants but did not know if they held any significance. Moabi climbed onto the riverbank, plucked a leaf, and smelled it. It did not smell anything like Vangueria or Grewia. He turned around holding the one that looked like Grewia and faced the king, "This is it."

"Are you sure that's the one? We call it Moemba here," said the king.

"This is not exactly Grewia, but I believe it is of the same family."

"Which means there is water somewhere here in the river?' the king asked hastily.

"Yes, your majesty, I believe there is water down there, but first we must drive in the stick to check if it is worth digging," said Moabi.

One of the elephants broke a branch from a nearby fallen tree, and about two hundred feet from the wall, he drove it into the sand. When he pulled it out with his trunk, the tip was moist. That sparked a slight enthusiasm. Immediately the animals began to dig, although some were resentful.

First, the paws scooped the sand away, and when it got a little bit harder, the hooves pounded. They traded off, scooping and pounding, until water burst from beneath a gray solid mud, as if there was a rupture in the pipeline. A jubilant roar broke out. There was so much water that it quickly filled a water hole of about one meter in depth and approximately two meters in diameter. After the royal family quenched their thirst, all lined up. Moabi watched them as they gulped. Despite the guzzling, the level of water kept on rising. Many passed by Moabi smiling, thanking him of the fruitful idea. The pigs passed by belching forcefully instead.

●　　●　　●

The next day when the king showed up at the new water hole to drink water, he brought Moabi's backpack with him. Moabi unzipped every compartment, and every piece of equipment was there.

"Can I use my materials to tell the story of this magnificent kingdom now?" Moabi asked.

"Yes, you may," said the king, smiling and nodding.

Bizwax was surprised at the kindness the king was showing to Moabi. "I wish he would talk to everybody like that," she muttered.

Moabi was officially part of the king's inner circle.

BEELZ'S PLAN WITH MADINGI, THE PIG

Beelz continued to evade and confound the animals. One of his skills was that he never left a track revealing his path. He avoided slithering on bare ground entirely. When he came to a bare patch, he would curl up and catapult himself onto the next patch of grass or go back to find a way to circumvent the grassless place.

Unlike the old place, Beelz's new hole had only one way in and one way out. It was hidden inside an old, hollow bending tree trunk. It descended through the roots then slanted sideways into the ground to an immediate dead end. This hole was twice Beelz's size in width and maybe a bit longer than he was. Even though the entrance was inconspicuous, he felt vulnerable. He would work his way into the hollow, and then he would turn around to face the entrance. That is how he slept, ready to strike.

During the day, Beelz would lay his head on the entrance so he could see the outside world and the "opportunities" that might pass by. Pinches, the queen bee, and the rest of the colony occupied the part of the trunk above the entrance. They had already made more than enough honey for Beelz. He needed only to reach his head up a little bit to lick it.

Every day, Pinches would meet with Beelz. The bees swarmed the animal's water hole, filled their abdomens, and split up. Some were deployed to Giantland to gather pollen. Others would buzz secretly over the compound to spy.

One the night of the full moon, under dazzling stars, Beelz hastily departed from his hiding place, the hollow tree, hissing and leaping on the way to the compound. Through thorns and thistles of the compound wall, he pushed and maneuvered, long patches of dry skin peeling off until his head appeared on the inside of the compound. "Hey, Madingi, I am here," he hiss-whispered.

Slowly, Madingi emerged, looking around cautiously to see if there was anyone in the vicinity. "I hear you, Beelz."

"Hey, I do not trust Hero anymore. I am sure he told the king where I was."

"Yes, he did. Immediately after you left, they went to your hole and burned it. Hero went inside the hole and came back with a little mouse called Gray."

"Where is Gray now?" asked Beelz.

"Dead."

"Did he tell them anything?"

"No, he came out of the hole on his last breath."

"Good. Now, what is going on with Hero?" Beelz impatiently asked.

Madingi was jealous of Hero because he had cultivated a good friendship with the king. "I think he is messing up our plans, Beelz."

"Yes, that is what I thought. We need to get rid of him, but first, we should carry out our original plans. We need to speed up the process," Beelz said. "We should target the king right away before we run out of time, and then we can deal with Hero."

Madingi explained to Beelz that there was no way they could reach the king's food to poison it.

"Well, this is what you have to do then," said Beelz. "As soon as Sanza takes the food to the king, put poison in Sanza's food."

Madingi shook her head.

Beelz rolled his eyes. "Because if we get rid of Sanza, then you can cook, and you can have control of the cooking procedure."

"It does not work like that, Beelz. Sanza does not fix his own plate until everyone has eaten," explained Madingi. "Secondly, your poison expires quickly if exposed for too long. And last, the king will never allow me to cook the food for him. However, I suggest that we eliminate Zingi. Then I can be an assistant to the king. As soon as I assume that position, I should be able to get rid of the king. Unlike

Zingi who stays by the king's door at mealtime because he cannot fit in the king's hut, I could be right next to the king during mealtime."

"Okay, that sounds like a solid plan. I will come back tomorrow night because right now I have a sore throat." Beelz coughed. "I can't secrete any poison, but tomorrow for sure, it will be done. I think we are close to taking over Vangoland. Oh - and you can be sure that we will get rid of the human being," Beelz assured Madingi as his head disappeared into the wall.

Getting rid of Zingi is the best thing to do. That would make me the king's assistant right away. If things don't work out with Beelz, at least I would have a high post in the kingdom. After all, even with Beelz as the king, I would still become his assistant, Madingi thought, smiling.

THE ENEMY STRIKES AGAIN

Indeed, Beelz made another heinous visit to Madingi. In the morning, Zingi was found sprawled on his side. He was unresponsive, his rubbery mouth dripping slimy fluid and his scruffy belly swelling fast like a huge balloon. Local flies signaled his demise and confirmed that the enemy had struck again.

Most of the animals thought Beelz would never dare to return, but they were utterly wrong. The king believed that as evil as Beelz was, God would not spare him. He pondered these things, and in the end, a convicting thought popped up: maybe he himself was the reason bad things were happening to them. If that was the case, he should seek Angelix's advice again. He knew Angelix was the messenger of God, yet what she offered he would not receive. His ego blocked that thought from flourishing; instead, he vowed that he would catch Beelz and cut him in pieces.

Zingi, the elephant, had been a humble servant. He was known for his loyalty and was highly trusted by the king.

The spirit of sadness took toll on the animals. A small group organized by leopards gathered just outside the compound and talked about departing Vangoland forever, as they no longer felt safe. Not only did they mourn the great Zingi, but they also longed to bring Angelix back into their midst. Many believed that her departure had worsened things and that the king had treated her badly.

The only way to protest against the king was by refusing to work at the dam. One of the young buffalo suggested that at the king's briefing, they should chant, "We want Angelix! Bring back Angelix! We want the holy dove of God!" They all agreed to do so.

THE DEFIANCE

Even Moabi and Bizwax had to leave the water hole to go listen to the king. A haze glowed around the moon that night, casting light on mournful faces. While they were eagerly waiting for the king to emerge from his hut, something happened to Dumie, the lion, something he had never experienced before. Blissful musical notes began to bubble in his heart. He rose like a peacock at sunrise. Then he broke into a beautiful melody.

God is stronger than alchemy.
Woe to our archenemy,
For God is ever here to assist.
Soon the enemy shall cease to exist.

The king and his family emerged from the hut and took their places before the rest. Then the king spoke majestically with sober eyes, "My kingdom, we are under attack, but I want to encourage you today to follow and believe in me. When we do that, I am telling you that nothing shall stop us. First, we shall all work hard. Loafers shall not reap good rewards. Those who work hard surely shall be handsomely rewarded. Therefore, we all must labor in love. Let us all stick to our unshakable principles based on love." The king paused at the sound of murmuring. Suddenly, the young lions roared, embracing the king's moving speech.

"By the Creator's grace, we will gather our strength, and together we shall defeat the enemy," the king paused. "We must step out of our own cells of fear, jealousy, and hatred. We must absolutely obey the law that says we should love one another, and only then will we be blessed forever. Let the Vango kingdom be blessed!"

There was a cheer as most embraced the king's words. Hero jumped around with great joy, but alas, this was not how the king's briefing would end. A group of leopards, young buffalos, zebras and some foxes would not allow the opportunity to slip away from them. "We want Angelix! Bring back Angelix! We want the holy dove of God!"

This chant surprised many, for leopards and buffalos were known for their loyalty to the king, which actually made the protest more compelling. The king was dumbfounded—before his anger became visible. However, the chanting inspired more voices.

As the situation was getting out of hand, Dumie, the lion, growled, charging toward those who were chanting. In a second or so, all of the lions had surrounded the protesters, allowing the king to address them.

"I am warning those who choose to disobey me and the rest of the kingdom, if you continue with that, you will reap what you sow. The meeting is dismissed," growled the king angrily.

Every animal went to his or her spot to sleep, and Moabi and Bizwax began their trip back to the river, enjoying the walk. On the way, they usually shared funny to pass the time. The pace wasn't actually bad because Bizwax could at least move faster than turtles and tortoises of Moabi's world. The only part that Moabi did not like much that Bizwax couldn't walk and laugh at the same time. This time, however, Bizwax seemed somber and deep in thought. "What seems to be troubling you, Biz?"

Bizwax stopped. Blinking, she looked up at Moabi. "I am thinking about what just transpired. I have never seen anyone disobey the king like that."

"They are frustrated. They said they want Angelix back," said Moabi. "In my world, we know that when people can no longer take the pain they are enduring, they express it loudly. But then, how the loudness is expressed matters."

"I totally understand what you are saying, but even if they are right about Angelix, I think they were wrong to interrupt our king," said Bizwax, taking a lazy step forward.

"To me, they looked pretty determined to continue with their protest. Don't be surprised if more animals join them. This I know, which could also be true here: when creatures revolt, something fundamental has been displaced or taken away from them. See, in my world, we despise anything that deprives us of freedom, and if the situation does not improve, we ultimately rebel."

"But then how do you bring the freedom back without causing problems?" asked Bizwax. "Or to be precise, how do we bring Angelix back? Because I believe she is the remedy of this pain that we are going through as a kingdom," said Bizwax.

"I am desperate to see Angelix myself because, like I said before, she might be able to help me go home," said Moabi, smiling. But to answer your question, I think someone should boldly and humbly talk to the king."

Bizwax stopped moving again and looked at Moabi. "You already know that the king does not want to talk about Angelix..." she trailed off. Then, hopefully, she suggested, "Perhaps because you are from outside, the king might actually listen to you. I think he trusts you now since you were able to locate water for us."

"You think he will listen to me?" asked Moabi, seeking confirmation.

"Yes, I see how he looks at you, like you are his son. He smiles at you and all that, you know," Bizwax pointed out thoughtfully.

"His son!" Moabi crouched down, laughing.

"You think you can do it?"

"I will have to think how I can do it without infuriating him. If I can successfully do it, that will be awesome because I believe Angelix will help me get home."

"There you go!" said Bizwax, venturing on. "Go for it."

MASTER CHI AND HERO

The thought of Beelz striking again kept Hero awake. When he couldn't sleep at all, he hopped to Chi's sleeping spot. He had great admiration for him and hoped he could offer some consolation.

"What is wrong, Hero?" asked the tiger.

"I don't want to be scared of that stupid snake anymore.

I want to defeat him."

Chi looked at Hero, shaking his head in disbelief. "Stop hallucinating, Hero. I don't even know if you understand what you are saying."

"Chi, let me be honest with you. I followed you yesterday and watched you training, and it fascinating. Can I join you tomorrow?"

"Let me be clear: I don't like that. Okay?" Chi said with a stern face.

"Well, I am so sorry," Hero paused, scratching his right ear with his little paw. "It is just that your sleeping spot is so close to and I had been wondering where you were going every morning. So I finally followed you and I'm interested in what you were doing."

"Again, I do not like to be disturbed when I am training. You should never follow me, and if I catch you, you will not like yourself," Chi warned.

"Okay, I will not follow you then. But may I ask humbly that you teach me to fight Beelz?"

"You are too weak to do what I do, and you can't fight a vicious snake like Beelz. All I can say is that you must be crazy. Now leave me alone and go back to sleep."

Hero stepped back, but before he turned around, he said, "That is why I want to train, to be strong. Please, Chi."

Chi looked at him dismissively. "Could you please leave me alone?"

Hero went back to his sleeping spot, discouraged and disappointed. He kept on looking back at Chi, hoping that Chi might call him back. Although he was disappointed, he did not give up. He hoped that Chi would change his mind.

The next day, early in the morning, Chi surprisingly passed by Hero's spot. "Let's go."

Hero jumped to his feet and looked at Chi, slightly confused. "I am ready."

As soon as they got out of the gate, Chi took off fast.
After a while, he stopped abruptly and looked back. Hero
was still following, trotting and already fatigued.

"You said you wanted to move fast, right?"

"Yes."

"You must run as fast as possible with me. I do not
want to train a sluggard. You understand? Wasting time is
not part of my nature," Chi shouted.

"I am ready, but I can't run as fast as you do."

"Yes, you can. You must focus. That is what matters."

"I guess focus is the word, not speed. Then I am with
you."

Chi eyed him with a stern look again. They took off fast,
Hero behind Chi's tail. By the time they arrived at the training spot, Hero was breathing as if something was blocking
his esophagus, his tongue hanging from his mouth.

"Good job," encouraged Chi.

"Thanks," said heaved Hero, leaning over to catch his
breath.

"Wake up, we do not have time to relax. We have only
one hour to do this."

At once, Chi balanced on his rear legs, front paws hanging
in the air, then moved back and forth as he punched air and
uttering words that sounded like his name, "Chi, chi, Chi."

Hero's head was moving with Chi's moves, his eyes
glued to the exhilarating action. Chi jumped up, rotating
his body three times before landing again on two feet.

About five meters above him, branches dangled from a slanted tree. He leaped toward the branches. With his jagged teeth, he ripped a little branch off a larger bending branch and threw it to the ground, leaving Hero aghast. Chi somersaulted over the ripped branch, landing on the other side.

"This is how you move—fast," said Chi. He then broke the same branch into many pieces and tossed them away. "Now, of course, that was a lifeless object, but that is how you win."

"That was amazing. How do you do that?"

"It is your turn," said Chi.

"Oh, okay. What do I have to do?"

"Stand on two like your mother used to do when performing magic."

"No, I can't do that, unless I am holding on to something."

Chi looked aside as he fought laughter. "Okay, no problem. I will assist you."

Chi grabbed Hero's front legs and raised them up. He then stepped backward, assisting Hero in moving forward on two. When Chi felt Hero could stand on his own, he left him alone, but Hero's front feet went right back to the ground. They did this a couple of times. Still, Hero failed to stand by himself.

"Look at me, Hero. Do not think about anything else, your mother, your king, or Beelz, okay? Just focus. Otherwise, it will take you years to do this."

Hero could not afford to spend years trying to do the same task over and over without mastering it. They tried again. As soon as Chi left him alone, Hero dropped the move.

"Let's try it again. You are doing well," Chi encouraged. Hero was amazed to see that Chi was not getting impatient with his sloppy attempts. He managed two steps before letting go.

"Come on—you can do this, Hero."

They moved together as Hero struggled, legs trembling. Hero managed four steps.

"All right. Good job," said Chi.

Hero smiled, encouraged.

"Before we go, let's try something new. Stay on two, don't move. Punch my palms with your little fists, like I was punching the air earlier. Go."

Hero shook his head, glanced up to Chi and bit his lower lip with nervousness. He stumbled forth, falling numerous times, yet Chi caught him before he touched the ground. Bit by bit, moment by moment, Hero's endurance yielded some success. As they were leaving, he remembered something that he'd thought about before starting training.

"Hey, Chi, you think you can also train me with that sword that my mother left me with?"

"Yes. Make sure you bring it tomorrow."

"Thank you! By the way, I have another small request. Would you tell me about where you were born? I had always thought we all originated here in Vangoland until my mother mentioned that you were from some animal park in a far place."

Chi slowly sat down as Hero continued talking.

"Despite my curiosity, she did not finish the story," Hero said.

"So, you still have interest in my story?" Chi asked.

"Of course, of course; otherwise I would not bother asking you!" said Hero, smiling enthusiastically.

Chi grinned, whisking his tail. Without a doubt, he was very pleased to share his story. He always delighted in a good conversation with someone who seemed to care about him. The only other animal he really socialized with was Magexie, the leopard. Rumor had spread that they were romantically involved, but they kept the relationship secret.

"Well, I am originally from a wonderful forest of the land of China, but I was taken to a small zoo by the big city where I met my wife, Cheng. One day, as we were basking in the sun, relaxing and scratching each other's backs on the summer grass, out of nowhere, needles went through our necks. I tried to stand up, but I fell, overwhelmed with dizziness. When I woke up, we were in a flying machine, caged." He choked back tears. "After many hours of travel, we landed in a place our captors—the officers, called Moremi Game Reserve...very beautiful place, indeed, with many magnificent animals. People around the world come to see that beautiful place. In China we lived in a zoo, but we felt a sense of freedom in Botswana."

"But how did you get here?" Hero asked.

Chi's eyes rose to the sky before he faced the curious Hero. "It was in the evening after sundown near the southwestern corner of the game reserve. We were the only two tigers there and we were still trying to get used to the region—to get to know other animals."

"Cheng and I preferred to spend evenings in solitary retreat. I was grooming her neck when all of a sudden I noticed her awkward stillness. Her mouth gaped open, drooling slimy fluids. Her tongue had turned blue, her eyes were wide open and dark. My heart pounded. I moved my ear to her heart, and there was neither beat nor breath. Cheng was dead. I cried like a baby. No one was watching except God. I looked up to the sky, asking heaven for help, but only the chorus of toads and crickets filled my ears. Emotions began to take control of me. Then I began to pace around, pondering her senseless demise. No clear answers came to me."

"That sounds horrendous!" Hero cried.

"Yes, and I know you can relate, but let me finish, please. I became overwhelmed with fear. There was a tall fence bordering the reserve, but I flew over the fence without even touching it and landed in a babbling brook. I ran like a wild dog on a rampage, as far as I could. There was a full moon, casting light over the delta. I felt as though it guided me as I crossed lagoons, splashing, and frightening the birds that congregated nearby. I was convinced that whoever had killed Cheng would be after me next and I wanted to get as far away as possible. My guess is that in the morning when wildlife officers detected what had happened, they began searching for me. I was near the main road leading to a small village when a truck loaded with armed men came roaring from the opposite direction. Before they could see me, I hid in the bushes nearby."

"What would they do to you if they caught you?" Hero asked.

"They would probably take me back. But after they passed, I lifted my eyes to the west. A line of bluish hills that reminded me of China stood visible on the horizon.

If I could only find a cave, I thought as I headed to those mountains."

"Whoa; it sounds like quite an adventure, Chi," said Hero.

"Let me finish the story, okay?" Chi said quickly, ignoring Hero.

"Now, there was another path that branched out and went directly to the hills so I chose to take it. The path dead-ended in a cave. This was what I was looking for: a place to rest in a peaceful environment. Inside the cave was total darkness. I stopped. All of a sudden, I heard a soft rustling sound that escalated into a growling, hypnotic whir. Instead of being scared, I felt rejuvenated. The air was cool and crisp as if it had just rained. Suddenly, I was engulfed in a great luminance that forced me to shut my eyes. When I tried to look again, behold, I could see the sun radiating down from the most brilliant, azure sky. I was no longer in a cave but in a different world. I walked alongside the Vango River until it snaked into the forest. Behind me, the hills were nowhere to be seen. This is how I found myself in Vangoland."

"Wow, what a great story," Hero said.

"I could tell that a great kingdom was here," Chi continued. "Unlike now, life was good here. I could smell peace. I found solace in the richness of the jungle,"

"Were you really scared? I can't imagine you being scared."

"Yeah, I was, but sometimes you can fall in love with scary things."

"Wow, that's...deep."

"I was taking a nap by the river when I awoke surrounded by Sanza, the lion; Speedo, the cheetah; Dumie, the lion; Magexie, the leopard; and Woozy, the buffalo. All eyes were on me. They were trying to talk to me, but couldn't understand what they were saying. At some point, I could tell they were making fun of my accent. I just looked at them, you know, hoping they wouldn't hurt me. Then, they escorted me to King Tauza. I couldn't say a word to him that he understood. He just laughed at me."

"I was wondering if the animals where you are from spoke like you," Hero interjected.

"No. They don't speak over there, but I heard some animals mimicking some words when human beings interacted with them. Not too long after my arrival here, Angelix prayed for me to receive the language and immediately I was able to speak. From then on, King Tauza loved me. He understood my situation and was even sympathetic. I became a trustee shortly after we defeated Beelz and his sons."

"Your story is touching. Can I ask you one more question?"

"What is it?" asked Chi.

"So you and Magexie, the leopard...?"

"What about her?"

"Is there anything between you two?"

Chi's face slowly melted into a youthful smile. He broke into a sprint, whisking his tail joyously. The sun was already coloring the sky pink and yellow. Chi looked at

Hero as they ran side by side. "Just friends Hero. We have a great relationship."

"That is awesome," said Hero, smiling. Chi and Hero continued to train together every day.

•   •   •

Moabi was disappointed when the king canceled their appointment at the last minute. As he walked towards the center of the compound, he bumped into Hero, who was excited about training with Chi and boasting about how he was going to destroy Beelz. The next morning, Moabi woke up very early and hid near the compound exit. As soon as he saw Chi and Hero exiting, he followed. He wished he still had some batteries so he could capture their training on tape. *My eyes will be the lens and my brain will retain the information and pictures,* he thought.

•   •   •

"Hero, I want to tell you something that is more important than just training physically," said Chi as they ended training with stretches.

Hero's eyes widened with curiosity. "I am listening, Master Chi."

"We have to go now, but quickly let me explain something to you. No matter how skilled you become, you must rely on the Creator not on yourself or external circumstances. Remaining humble before the creator will create in you an excellent character and, in turn, you will be better able to make good choices."

"Wow, that is powerful and profound," Hero remarked as they ran back to the compound.

OPERATION BEELZ

The king appointed Chi to lead and execute what they called "Operation Beelz." But before they could do that, some things needed to be taken care of. They all gathered by the meeting place, under the big tree. Without wasting time, Sanza jumped up on a wooden platform made of stacked-up tree trunks. They had recently put it together at the request of the king. When holding the meeting, the platform allowed him to see everyone, all the way to the compound wall. The king hoped to discourage dissenters. Sanza panned his deep-black eyes from right to left, and the animals grew silent. He spoke slowly with a deep voice. "We have one important goal right now. What is the goal? To catch the heinous Beelz. Can you all repeat after me?"

"To catch the heinous Beelz!" they shouted enthusi-astically.

"Good, now listen," said Sanza. "Not everyone here will go with Chi. The king has ordered that he must take only a third of you, and so two-thirds will remain here with me." He pounded the platform with his ashy paw. "Yes, the majority will remain here with me to work on the compound wall. We must fill all those little gaps to make sure that the enemy has no chance to make his way in."

A sarcastic laugh was heard from the back. Sanza angrily stared in the direction from which it had come. "Who is that?" he demanded.

There was no answer from where the laughter was heard, although, of course the pigs, hyenas, buffalos, and some leopards knew about who it was.

"If I catch you, you will not like it," Sanza said. Then he continued, "We do not want to miss even the small-est gap. I know some of you might be sleeping by those gaps, and maybe they are so small that you can't even see them, so please make sure we do not miss any. Protect yourselves against the enemy."

It was not long before there was an interruption, this time a serious one. The young buffalos and leopards, joined by pigs and wolves, shouted, "We want Angelix! Bring back Angelix! We want the holy dove of God!" In a minute or so, there were many voices stressing the same words.

Out of the king's hut came Zambi, the king's son, looking disturbed by the voices demeaning his father's rule. The noise became more disruptive as more voices joined the club.

Then Zambi whispered in Sanza's ear. Without wasting time, Sanza and the young lions jumped on everyone who was shouting and chanting, slapping, and smacking them hard. Soon only the angry lions could be heard growling.

"Are we ready now?" asked Sanza, furiously shaking his mane.

Most of them reluctantly nodded their heads in a quiet manner. The poor protesters were still wincing in pain. Then Sanza gestured for Chi to jump onto the platform as he stepped down. Many stood up to give Chi a standing ovation. Hero's cheeks swelled with a smile. Most animals liked Chi, except those who were jealous, like the mysterious Madingi and some other pigs.

"Thank you, thank you. Be quiet. Please sit," said Chi. They all sat and kept quiet.

"As Sanza stated, I will pick only a handful of you." He paused. "We must protect our kingdom. So now, as I call your name, go toward the gate and wait for me there. By the way, where is Madingi? I do not see her here," Chi asked, looking around.

"She is very, very sick," one of the pigs exclaimed with a husky voice.

"Oh, since when? I saw her last night visiting with the wolves," said Chi.

"Since past last night," one of the proud, boisterous pigs answered.

Madingi was prone to lying. Chi suspected that she was faking sickness to stay home.

"I will go and check on her," shouted Sanza, going in her direction.

Chi divided his squad into five groups, and each had a leader. One group was led by Speedo, the cheetah; one by Woozy, the buffalo "Mr. No-Nonsense" one by Clips, the eagle; and the last group by Dumie, the lion, whom the king really liked more than other lions. Dumie was fierce and bold, and many a time he had represented the king in meetings.

"Which group wants a human addition?" asked Chi.

An out of control laughter burst from the area where the hyenas were seated and another erupted from the pack of wolves. It was not a surprise; those two groups of animals could laugh at anything, at any time. However, Chi ignored them.

Moabi would not mind being part of Speedo's group. If he could fly, he definitely would have been delighted to join the eagle's group. He hoped that Dumie would not choose him. However, none of the leaders showed interest in him.

"Well, it seems like no one is interested in taking Moabi in, so I am adding him to my group," said Chi.

Speedo's group headed west, Woozy's went south along the river, Dumie's group headed east toward the salt pan, and Chi, paired with Hero and Moabi, headed north. Chi chose to go north because there was high possibility of meeting the human giants of the North, and he believed he could handle them.

All the holes they came across were empty, and they set fire in them or filled them with sand. They found no trace of Beelz anywhere. Every group worked very hard. By late afternoon, Dumie was engaged in an argument with the pigs who were lagging behind in deliberate disobedience. They were playing pig games, grating the soil off the ground, stuffing it in their mouths, and competing to see whose dust would go highest in the sky.

Most of the pigs were known for their intelligence, but they were too often obnoxious and pompous. The secret meetings they conducted with their leader, Madingi, were comedic, contrarian, and zealous. But since Hero started visiting with them and sharing what Angelix and Chi had taught him, the numbers of attendees had dwindled. Some pigs and wolves experienced a change of heart. They vowed to stop acting cynical and to renounce their support of Madingi's antics and underground rebellion.

Hero's message was that they must receive love in themselves in order to love others. Hero encouraged them to look at things in positive way— that to love is to live. Only then would they rise against evil. Hero called that *true change*.

During one of Hero's visits with the pigs, Madingi had the audacity to try to humiliate him. "Why are you wasting your time preaching foolishness?" Madingi snorted with a pronounced pause. She then continued, "I mean, do you really think you can change anyone?"

"I think if animals keep on hearing the message of love, their hearts will be changed. I know you are in denial, but that is what is happening to some of your friends. True change begins in the heart and flows into the environment," said Hero.

Madingi's eyes darkened as her heart puffed with fury. "Oh, is that right? Who are you to tell me about love?" She turned her face toward Hero and looked into his eyes. "You don't know anything about love, and you need to be taught about love, Hero. All I know is that you are still a danger and a pathological liar. Those who believe you are fools, Hero."

"I changed because I received love in me, Madingi," Hero responded humbly.

"This is ridiculous and a waste of my time." Madingi huffed as she turned around and left.

Now, as the defiant pigs continued to dawdle, Clips led a team of assorted birds searching and patrolling tenaciously from the sky. The black vultures could not wait to nibble on Beelz, should the chance present itself.

But, alas, there was no sight of him, even as the sun descended.

Normally, no animal could play games around Woozy especially when it was time to work. But with his guard down at the end of a laborious day, he found himself fighting laughter as hyenas cracked crazy jokes. His character was softened, and he was almost reduced to their level as he could no longer control his chuckling. When he broke into laughter that sounded like a dozen cackling hens, they just listened to him. After they absorbed his mirth, they all joined in as if he had anointed them with his laughter. He laughed until tears streamed down his face.

Dubie, the most notorious of the hyenas, had been holding back, but could not wait to incite the pack at Woozy's expense. With his short, funny-looking, ashy, hairless ears, Dubie was known for his provocative jokes. Most animals loved him for his crude humor but hated him for the same when a joke was directed at them.

"Hey, Woozy, tell us what happened at the well."

Abruptly ending his laughter, Woozy turned around to face Dubie, his eyes darkening with anger. "What do you mean, 'What happened?'" he demanded, tears of laughter evaporating from his face.

"Well, the whole kingdom knows."

"Knows what?" Woozy charged toward Dubie, who retreated into the rest of the group.

"Rumor has it that you were sleeping hard and snoring when you guarded the well. I heard that you rumbled like thunder in the distance as Hero played with your vibrating nose." Dubie inched back as he made his claims, but the group had formed a wall, playfully pushing him toward Woozy.

Woozy's emotions began to swell like yeast in dough as the laughter escalated.

"I am going to break his tiny neck," Woozy fumed, referring to Hero. He stormed away with anger, distorting his face. It was scary, as if he would attack anyone in his way. He had forgotten words of Chi: never let emotions rule you.

Just then, Chi and Hero arrived to consolidate the teams. Clips had just reported to them that the king was ordering the animals back to the watering hole. Beelz had not been found. Instead of responding in solidarity, the animals groaned and complained. Some cackled about the futility of the search.

"Is this what we are here for?" Hero asked with confidence, eyes wide open and ears sticking into the air.

"Shut up, you little twit," Woozy bellowed, his spits praying all over. Chi noticed the glare of anger in Woozy's black eyes.

"What is wrong, Woozy?" Chi asked calmly, stepping toward the buffalo.

"This little incompetent fool is spreading rumors that he was playing with my nose and that I rumbled like thunder in the distance. Why should I listen to you and this little liar?" He fumed, pacing back and forth as though he could ram Hero with his head.

Hero cringed, a shudder running through him.

"Tell me now, why? Why?" Woozy shouted. "Why, Hero?"

Hero thought of not saying anything, afraid of inflating the buffalo's wrath. But keeping quiet would not save him; it would make others think he was wrong.

"Why what?"

"Don't play with me, Hero. I will break your neck right now," said Woozy, chewing his lower lip.

"Hold on, who told you that?" asked Hero.

"Does it matter who told me?"

"I think it matters, because whoever told you could be lying about me," said Hero courageously.

"Dubie said it," said Woozy.

With a smiling face, Dubie winked at one of the hyenas.

"I never told Dubie anything about you," said Hero.

Chi watched Woozy closely, ready to stop him should he attack. Woozy was still seething with anger and showed no sign of cooling down. Chi knew it was time for him to step in. "Dubie, where did you get that information?"

"Well, honestly speaking, I heard that from Madingi," said Dubie calmly.

Dust blew up from the ground as Woozy exhaled.

"Did you or did you not tell Madingi a lie, Hero?"

Hero shook his head, stepping close to Chi in case Woozy lost his mind and tried to attack him. "No, I did not."

At this moment, Moabi arrived almost out of breath, his hands immediately dropping down to rest on his knees and drops of sweat falling on the ground. He had tried to tail Chi and Hero but could not keep up with their well-trained stamina and their breathtaking speed. He trailed behind by a kilometer or so. Fortunately, he saw them far in the distance, thanks to the scarcity of vegetation.

At first, he did not pay attention to the commotion. He thought they were just disappointed because Beelz was still on the loose. But when he stood up straight, he realized that there was a serious argument going on.

"Tell you what, Woozy, hold your breath," said Chi. "Let us go drink some water. When we get home, I promise you this: we will call Madingi and everyone involved. Then we will solve this problem. Believe me—I do understand how you feel, Woozy. Besides, we cannot defeat the enemy if we are fighting among ourselves." Chi took a step toward Woozy. "We agree?"

"Okay," said Woozy, nodding, but his eyes stayed on Hero. They all left for the water hole, with Hero bringing up the rear, praying that Woozy would not hurt him.

THE EXPULSION OF MOABI

Everyone was at the water hole, including the king. Moabi approached him with a big, easy smile, his hands in his pockets as if he had known the king for a long time. In recent days, the king had increasingly shown him kindness. However, this time, the king did not feel like smiling at all.

"Good evening, your majesty," said Moabi, sighing.

"How can I help you?" asked the king dismissively and rather rude.

Seeing the king in a dark mood, Moabi regretted approaching the king and thought about lying about what he actually wanted to say. Something is bothering him, he thought. "I would like to talk to you, if you don't mind, your majesty," said Moabi, bowing down to the king as usual.

"About what?" the king asked, his eyes rolling with agitation.

"Is it the right time to talk?" Moabi asked respectfully.

"What is it that you are talking about, young man?" asked the king.

"I have heard a lot about Angelix since I got here…"

The king's face darkened. "I do not want to hear anything about Angelix," the king bellowed, squinting his red eyes.

Moabi thought of his mother and mustered the courage to continue, "I understand she is very wise, and I think she can help me get home. So I am requesting that you allow me to go see her."

"What?" the king asked with a stern face. "Nobody disrespects me like that. You hear me? You must be ready to go now," said the king, huffing and puffing. "You think she is wiser than me?"

"I want to go home. Are you going to help me go home then?" said Moabi, losing composure.

The king's jagged upper teeth sank on his rubbery gray lower lip, which looked like a piece of a tar. All the animals were watching, eager to see what the king would do to his supposedly favored human being.

"Yes, I am going to help you get home. Where is your bag?" asked the king, struggling to swallow a lump of anger in his throat.

Moabi did not answer right away. Then, fearing the king's wrath, he opened his quivering mouth to speak. "On the bank, right there by the water hole."

"Go pick it up and leave this place right now. Choose any direction you want. I am watching you," the king bellowed.

Everyone watched Moabi as he shuffled among them, his bag dangling from his trembling left hand. The king stared at him as he walked along the river wall. "And don't come back here again!" he roared.

The pigs and wolves laughed. They actually laughed at the king, whose propensity for anger seemed to be taking a toll on him, dividing him against his kingdom, his own family, and now the human. Those who rejoiced had never admired the king's blooming relationship with Moabi. They mocked and laughed at the very human being who helped them to get water in the middle of a hostile drought. "Animal Eater," they secretly called him.

The king's last words thudded deep within Moabi. He felt like an outcast. He wished he could just vanish out of Vangoland and appear at his home. Tears formed quickly as he departed uncertain, and hopeless.

To some, such as Bizwax and Chi, the king's cruelty aroused compassion. To see Moabi walking away humiliated completely saddened them.

Immediately Zambi, the king's son, began to cry and said, "Please, Father, don't kick him out. He is a good person."

"He has to go!" bellowed the king angrily.

"That is wrong!" cried Zambi.

"What do you know about right and wrong? Go back over there to your mother!" the king shouted at Zambi.

Retreating and traumatized by his father's outburst, Zambi's old illness of banging his head on surfaces re-emerged with a vengeance. He ran to the river wall and started to pound his head against it. A couple of young lions tackled him and pinned him down as Queen Mambo paced back and forth in anguish. The fear that had long brewed in her was overpowered by concern for her son as she assertively addressed the king.

"I don't know why you had to talk to him like that," said the king's wife, "but I think it is high time we call for Angelix; this has become dangerous."

For a moment, King Tauza kept quiet, not even look-ing at his wife. Zambi's malady distressed him. He could feel the power of darkness weakening his joints. He looked at his wife's angry face, and then pride rose with-in him, strengthening his selfishness. "No, not Angelix," he said, shaking his head and stepping away from Queen Mambo.

The young buffalos and other animals were happy to hear Queen Mambo mentioning Angelix. They regrouped quickly, weighing whether to join the king's wife and de-mand the return of Angelix. But they reluctantly dispersed when the young lions advanced upon them. They were already warned, so they knew that this time they could really get into deep trouble.

"Who is going to pray for our son? Can you point to any-body here who can do that?" questioned Queen Mambo as Pinches buzzed above and landed not too far from the water hole where she listened to the conversation.

The air was thick with tension between the king and his wife. The king glanced at his wife from the corner of his eye, not saying a word; inwardly, he fumed. All of the animals remained quiet. It was rare to see the king and his wife in a sour confrontation. Whenever this happened, the animals would show them respect by not rejoicing in their woes. Besides, the king's guards, the young lions, would not tolerate any inappropriate behavior.

"Why are you so opposed to bringing Angelix back? Can't you see that everything is crumbling?" Queen Mambo growled in anger.

The king turned around and leaped, landing right in front of Queen Mambo, grinding his molars. "Don't ever talk to me like that!" he fumed. "I am the king and the only one. I make final decisions here. You understand that?"

Seeing the situation deteriorate, Queen Mambo reluctantly retreated. In a fading voice, she tearfully asked, "Are you going to let him die?"

"Who said he is dying? You?" exclaimed Tauza, nervously expectorating a cough from his throat.

Queen Mambo turned around and headed toward Zambi. He was quivering and sweating profusely. He looked fever-stricken and confused. The king ordered the young lions to accompany them to the compound.

"I will be there shortly," the king called after them, but Queen Mambo did not acknowledge him at all.

●　　●　　●

Moabi's trip was supposed to last exactly fourteen days. On the second day, Victoria received the news that her son had mysteriously disappeared in the hills while walking with other tourists. She was told that one tourist saw him lagging behind everyone else, and a few seconds later, he was nowhere to be seen.

The wildlife officers and some of the local people worked hand in hand, day and night, searching for Moabi. They traced some shoe prints that ran toward the female hill's cave but lost them where the snaky path turned into particles of rocks. The news distressed Victoria, who regretted that she had let him go. However, she refused to believe that something terrible had happened to her son, clinging to her faith that he would be spared from any danger. She couldn't wait for her sunshine to return.

● ● ●

With knees wobbling, Moabi headed east along the dormant river that had served as his path into the Animal Kingdom. Approaching the Movena tree, he quickly dismissed the idea of picking some fruits. He feared that he might be attacked if he tried to do so since he was no longer wanted in the kingdom. He stared at the tree as he passed by, appreciating that it had provided refuge in the days when he first arrived in Vangoland. He trudged through the cooling sand as darkness thickened into a young night.

• • •

Meanwhile, the king arrived at the compound with Chi. He knew that his wife would probably not want to see him, but he purposed in his heart that he would not aggravate the situation further. Rather, he would focus on the ailing Zambi. Not too far behind, the rest of the animals followed, flanked by the king's loyalists, the young lions.

Inside the hut, Zambi laid sprawled out on the dusty floor, his heartbeat faint. At his side, Queen Mambo sobbed bitterly. Her heart heaved with sorrow, and her mouth quivered as she whispered her son's name.

Sanza stood by the door, his face long and heavy with sadness. Normally, he would beam when he saw the king, but this time, things were different. He just shook his head. Tauza knew then that the situation had not improved.

"How is my son?" King Tauza inquired of his wife as he entered the hut "Is he asleep?"

Queen Mambo did not answer as the king knelt down and ran his tongue on Zambi's forehead.

"Are you going to let him die?" she questioned as she began to cry.

"I will never let my son die," said the king.

"I think you will because otherwise you would have done something immediately. Do you even love him?"

The king looked at his wife with livid eyes. "How dare you question my love for my son! You know I love him!" said the king, struggling to calm his temper.

"While you were busy doing nothing, I've been here with him, praying unceasingly. Yet, now, he is fading away!" She sobbed, tears trickling down her cheeks. "I don't even know if he is breathing now..."

With his paw, the king rummaged around on Zambi's chest. He couldn't feel a single pulse. He tried pressing his ear against Zambi's chest but couldn't hear a beat. But he had mounds of hair sticking out of his ears not to mention abundance of wax. He paced around, avoiding his wife's eyes. "It can't be," said the king, before bursting out of the hut.

The rest of the animals had just arrived in the compound. Most chattered about Zambi's sudden, violent illness and the expulsion of Moabi. For others, the unusually bright moon sparked interest.

The king's sudden departure left them open-mouthed. Never had they seen the king so erratic. Despite all the problems they had, the king never really succumbed to panic. He always maintained some level of composure.

"Boltex! Boltex!" the king bellowed, spit forcefully flying out of his mouth.

"Yes, my lord," said Boltex, the puma, as he hurried forth to meet the king.

"You know where Angelix is, right?" asked the king, whispering.

"Yes, my lord, I do know," Boltex replied.

"I want you to call her. Tell her that I said she is welcome to come back. Understand?" said the king.

"Yes, my lord, I will go right now."

"Tell her that my son is dying, and I need her right now to come and pray for him," the king added. "Hurry."

Boltex was arguably the fastest. Before the drought, all of the cats used to compete to determine who was the fastest, and for a long time, Speedo, the cheetah, was untouchable. The kingdom loved this event, which took place once a month. The winner would be rewarded with a dish full of cooked brown Movena twice a month. Besides, all winners gained the respect of others, which made them feel special. So Speedo was the sole beneficiary of this event for a long time, but that was before the rise of the young Boltex. When they had faced off in their last competition, Boltex decisively won the race. Since that time, Speedo pretended to like Boltex, but he would not train with him anymore.

•   •   •

Now, Boltex slid to a stop at Angelix's tree, barely halting before crashing into the trunk. "Angelix, Angelix! King

Tauza said you are to come back, and you must be there right away because his son is dying!"

Angelix stepped outside her nest onto a branch. She rolled her eyes and looked down. "Tell him he must come and talk to me himself if he truly wants me back." Then she slipped back into her nest.

In a short time, Boltex was before the king. "My lord, she demanded that you come and talk to her."

The king dashed into the hut and took a sharp look at his son. "I will be back."

"It's too late," the king's wife muttered sorrowfully as the king sped out.

• • •

Angelix was sitting on an outstretched branch when the king came running and puffing. The moon was full and brilliant among the scintillating stars. Angelix's eyes glinted, her wings glistened as she watched the king abruptly stopping and crumpling under the tree.

Once their eyes met, the king did not hesitate to speak. "I am so sorry, Angelix. Please forgive me, for I have been bad."

Angelix neither responded nor blinked.

"My son is dying. Please pray for him," cried the king.

"That's the only reason you are here, not because you have been disobedient; am I right?" Angelix asked.

"Please, Angelix, help," said the king.

"We were attacked by the giants of the North, drought came, our animals were killed by Beelz, and you scorned my advice. And now that your son is dying, you want my help. How dare you?" said Angelix.

"Angelix, now I see that I have been unaligned with the will of our Creator. Beelz deceived me. Please help."

"That is between you and the Creator," she said. "If I were you, I would run after that good human being that you did not blink to expel, and I would bring him back. This is a warning; if you refuse, it only shows that you are still full of pride. If you are not going to change, there is no way I can help you. But remember this, if you don't change, things will get worse, and you will be responsible for that before the Creator. Having said that, I am not going anywhere until you return with Moabi. I want to see him...alive. Hear me when I say this, I want to see the fruit of change in you. I will not be moved by mere words." Immediately after saying that, Angelix flew into her nest. But she popped her head out to say, "By the way, obedience is better than sacrifice." Then she slipped into the nest.

King Tauza stood there for a minute or so, confused. Following Angelix's instructions would demonstrate obedience and be the beginning of restoration. That much was plain and simple; he clearly comprehended that. It was up to him to obey. It was up to him to believe. Making the wrong decision would lead him the wrong way. Every bit of disobedience was connected to destruction. He had known those things in the first place, but he had allowed pride to take root. Now, he had no other choice.

He felt light on the inside, as if a heavy burden had been removed. Then he roared at once. His voice came rolling like thunder in the distance, and everyone at the compound heard him. The king had different kinds of roars for calling some individuals, such as his wife, Zambi, or any of his personal assistants. He also had a distinct roar when he called the entire kingdom. This time, however, he was calling exclusively for Sanza. Sanza burst through the gate, and in a short time, he was standing by the king.

"We must go now," said the king. "We must bring Moabi back."

"I am with you, my king," Sanza said, enthusiastically whipping his tail.

The king set a fast pace. Sanza, the loyal servant, followed suit. As they ripped across the plain, a strong echo could be heard as if mighty soldiers were speedily charging against their foes. They surged past the Movena tree, leaped over the riverbank, and landed in the river with a splash of sand. Leaping forth, their paws punched the riverbed, sending grains of sand in the air. Before amputation, the king used to be the fastest lion in the entire kingdom. Now running in the river was exhausting. Slowly, he came to a stop. Then they walked side by side as they approached the big rock in the middle of the river.

●　●　●

Moabi was walking along the river wall when Beelz slithered quietly into the river. It wasn't a coincidence. Beelz knew that Moabi was coming his way.

After the king expelled Moabi, Pinches flew back to Beelz with the news. It was good news then because King Tauza did not want to see Angelix, but what pleased Beelz the most was that Moabi's involvement in the kingdom did not spark her.

If he disappears from Vangoland, I will have missed the greatest opportunity of my life, Beelz thought. Now more than ever, he wanted to capture the human. His venom could only kill one animal at a time, and going through the compound wall delivering venom had caused injuries all over his body. He had bruises, bleeding wounds, and scabs. *Unlike my venom, which could kill only one animal at a time, Moabi's ear lobe would be big. I could poison the king and some of those lions they call loyalists*, Beelz thought, smiling. If he was successful in capturing Moabi, his partner in crime who lived in the compound would get the human poison and do the rest of the job. "I can take over by tomorrow if things go well," Beelz whispered to himself.

Once Moabi was in his sight, Beelz hissed and flicked his tongue, charging. As Moabi caught sight of him, he gasped with panic, and stumbled backwards to the ground. Beelz hated human beings, so he was ready to attack. When he was young, he would listen to his parents tell stories about how human beings hated snakes more than any other animal. They would add that a human being's first instinct was to kill a snake upon seeing it. Although they were talking about human beings in their world, particularly the giants, but Beelz assumed they were much the same.

Retreating, Moabi slid his backpack strap down his right arm into his hand, his eyes on the tongue-flicking Beelz. He was ready to defend himself with the bag. If Beelz jumped, he thought he could crush his head with it. He considered throwing it at the snake, but if he missed, he would not be able to pick it up for another try. He suspected that Beelz was not the type of snake to be easily defeated by someone fighting with a bag. He probably needed a real weapon. Beelz had been to war; he knew the art of fighting.

While Beelz contemplated his next move and the weight of the bag, Pinches landed on his head. "The king is coming to rescue Moabi. If he manages, Angelix will go back to the kingdom. If you kill Moabi, she would never go back."

"Tauza went to see Angelix?" Beelz asked.

"Yes. Your best chance is now." With that, Pinches flew away as Beelz coiled his lengthy body, his head hovering on top, preparing to catapult onto his foe.

Just as Beelz was about to spring and strike, King Tauza and Sanza surfaced where the river curved. Thinking quickly, Beelz slithered over the bank and disappeared into the luminosity of the night. Moabi wondered if he had scared the snake with his frightened look and threatening backpack. While still amazed that he'd both encountered and been spared by the vicious snake, he heard huffing and mutterings behind him. Slowly he turned his head. And there, the two lions advanced side by side.

Moabi stood still, wondering if he'd dodged one fate to be met with another fatal one. With his peripheral vision, he saw shaggy manes swoosh past him on both sides. As they skidded to a stop and turned around—presumably to attack, he prayed that they would have mercy upon him.

Instead they sat, Sanza slightly behind the weary king. Moabi locked eyes with the king.

"I am glad I found you," said the king humbly.

The words astounded Moabi. He was not expecting that. He had expected the worst. First, the snake did not strike him, and now, the lion was saying he was happy to see him. It was a bit confusing. It dawned on him that the snake slithered away when he saw the beasts advancing. *That snake must have been Beelz*, he thought.

"Now we have to go back together to the compound because Angelix wants to see you there," said the king.

Moabi's heart leaped at once with joy. "Angelix?" The sincerity in the king's eye loosened the grip of Moabi's fear. For a moment, he thought he was dreaming. He couldn't believe the way things had turned out. He never thought this great king would come running after him.

"We have to go now, Moabi," urged the king as he thought about his son.

At first, King Tauza planned to rush back to the compound to attend Zambi, leaving Sanza to escort Moabi. But then he changed his mind. "Sanza, I think you should go before us and call everyone to the meeting place," he said, omitting the reason for the meeting. If something happened to Moabi while he was with Sanza, Angelix might not pray for his son. He wanted to bring Moabi to the compound safely.

Moabi looked at the king's paw from the corner of his eye. It was bigger than his face. "With one swipe, it would kill me," he said under his breath. He wasn't scared, but he wasn't comfortable either. He felt weird walking side by side with this majestic beast. He felt somehow safe, yet vulnerable. It was quiet until the king asked Moabi if he was excited about meeting Angelix.

"It would be my pleasure to meet her."

"I should not have kept you from her. It was selfish of me," admitted the king.

"Hopefully, she can help me get home," Moabi replied, suppressing his shock at King Tauza's sudden humility. "I have heard a lot of good things about her, that she has been to many worlds. Maybe she can help me."

"Hopefully," said the king softly.

"Do you mind if I ask what changed your mind? Why did you come for me?"

"Angelix would pray for him. She would not return to the compound unless I brought you back," said the king.

"I'm sorry to hear about Zambi, King Tauza, but the fact she knows who I am gives me hope - for both of us," Moabi said reassuringly.

"You must be homesick."

"Very much so," Moabi sighed.

"Yours must be a better world compared to ours," said the king as they passed by an old, dry, leafless tree.

"Maybe it could be if evil was not rampant," said Moabi, shaking his head. "I worry about my mother every single minute, and I worry about evil people like terrorists."

"What is going on with your mother?" the king asked.

"She is fighting a terrible disease; she could die from it. I was not supposed to have taken this long," Moabi said in a low tone.

The king slowly turned his head to look at Moabi. Upon seeing the distressed face, he stopped. "I hope your mother gets better."

"Thank you. I hope so too."

The king was about to tell him about Zambi's condition when a swarm of bees buzzed above them and launched an attack. Moabi tried to shield his eyes. With every sting, he jumped and yelped in pain.

By the fallen trunk, Beelz watched with gleaming eyes, hoping to seize an opportunity to attack. Several bees landed on the king, inflicting a barrage of stings and driving him into a thorny bush.

"Blast these bees; they're everywhere!" cried the king.

"This is for Beelz!" declared Pinches, as she rounded up the swarm to retreat.

Everyone had been wondering about these bees, and now the truth was revealed; they were Beelz's little buddies.

"Tell your evil friend that I am going to cut his head off when I catch him," bellowed the king. But then he was only speaking to the bush; the bees had vanished.

"Did one of the bees saying something about Beelz?" Moabi asked the king.

"I do not have time to discuss Beelz right now. We have to go," said the king hastily, his face swelling fast. He felt as if the bees were still stinging, and he could hear them buzzing even though they were not around.

"I understand that you don't want to talk about him, but I think I just saw him," said Moabi.

"You saw him? When?" asked the king.

"He was trying to attack me, but upon seeing you and Sanza coming, he slithered away."

"Are you sure it was Beelz? Describe him!"

Moabi described the shady snake, and the description matched Beelz's.

"I am glad we saved your life because if he was able to kill you, I would be in deep trouble right now," the king conceded.

"Thank you for rescuing me," said Moabi.

• • •

The moon was almost in the middle of the sky, and the stars were twinkling all over as the animals of the kingdom waited for the king at the meeting place. The mood was rather somber, mostly because some had already fallen asleep and some were preoccupied with the rumors that Angelix would soon show up. However,

Madingi and some of her friends denounced the idea as bogus.

They hoped that the relationship between Angelix and the king would continue to be nasty and irreparable. They knew that if Angelix came back, the king might become powerful again, allowing him to rule even longer. What they wanted was a new leader, a non-lion; they would be elated if Madingi could become the next leader. Madingi did a very good job at selling her vision to her friends. They had made it their own.

When the king finally entered the compound's gate, they all stood up. Moabi walked steadily toward the animals while the king sprinted to his hut. His wife was lying outside the splintered door, totally distraught. As she turned her head slightly to look at the king, a tear fell from her eye.

"Don't even dare to say anything," Queen Mambo said, shaking her head before burying it between her front legs.

The king knew then that nothing had changed. He would be adding salt to the wound if he asked whether Angelix had shown up to pray for their son. Queen Mambo's posture appeared to say it all.

He entered the hut, hopeless. "He has not moved at all," he muttered as he stared at his son, whose head was partially illuminated by a beam of moonlight. "I thought Angelix was going to help me."

Just then, Angelix flew over the compound with wings outstretched. She landed on the rooftop, and a cheer erupted. Many left the meeting place and surrounded the hut. In a short time, the air was filled with boisterous melodious sounds. For the first time in a long time, their sweetest and most darling animal was there, and her presence lifted their spirits. At least the majority felt that way. Madingi and her allies remained mere spectators while others exploded with the spirit of joy. Even Moabi stood up, clapping and smiling. He felt sure that this great dove would be able to help him get home.

• • •

Inside the hut, the king stood listening to the intensifying chant. At first he thought the animals were revolting against him, and since he was in the hut, it would be easy for them to catch and slay him. He actually thought his wife had conspired with the young lions and rallied everyone against him.

The thumping of paws and hooves, as if besieging the hut, kept him on his toes. The ends of his mane stood up. He looked up, searching for a position—not to escape; he would die fighting—but he wanted to be ready to attack. If he could get on top of the roof, he could not only defend himself, but he could put up a fierce fight. *I must go through the roof now*, he thought.

He could see the shining moon through the skylight. Back and forth, he paced, grunting and bracing himself to spring up to the tattered roof. That was when he saw a head of a bird poking in, partially blocking the tranquil moon.

Outside, he could now hear the animals chanting the name "Angelix!" The young buffalos started to sing the song that they'd recently composed in secret. It quickly resonated as many voices joined in.

We want Angelix,
The Creator's messenger,
Whose ways are far removed from vaunt.
Her ethereal presence a pleasure.

We want Angelix,
So the spirit of evil will cease
With her, the future is bright.
For there will be rain and peace.

We want Angelix!
Let King Tauza hear and obey,
For obedience is the tunnel of blessing.
The curse shall be broken today!

King Tauza realized that the hullabaloo outside was ignited by the return of Angelix. Although he thought Angelix might be too late to save his son, a peaceful feeling was now brewing inside him—not because he was relieved that there was no revolt against him, but because he knew he had made the right decision by aligning with the truth. That was the reason Angelix had returned.

All along, though, he knew he had been evading the truth and needed to repent, but since he was utterly deceived, his pride was compounded. In the end, it held him hostage.

Even if it meant the death of his son, the king hoped Angelix's presence could heal not only his wounds, but also those of others in the kingdom. He hoped that the divisions among the animals would cease, and that the life- threatening drought would be lifted.

Angelix descended through the gap in the roof, flapping her wings in the dusty moonshine, and landed softly beside Zambi's body.

•   •   •

Outside, a hush came over the crowd as the young lions growled, demanding that the celebration stop. Only a few pigs whined, insisting that they were not causing any trouble.

Angelix began to take steps around Zambi. The king stepped back toward the door, nervous.

"I am not sure if he is dead or still alive," said the king.

"Do you mind waiting for me outside so I can pray for him? I will let you know the situation," said Angelix, interrupting the king. Perhaps she was not happy about the king's nervousness or lack of faith.

"Of course, of course," said the king, turning around and getting out of the hut, his shoulders drooping with humility.

"What is happening?" Queen Mambo asked, emerging from the circle of young lions guarding her.

"Angelix said she would let us know the truth about Zambi's situation," said the king.

"You want to know the truth? He is dead, that is the truth!" she said angrily.

"That is not helping!" growled King Tauza, stepping away from her.

Sanza and the young lions herded the animals to the court, especially the rambunctious group of young buffalos, hyenas, and wolves. They calmed down slightly when the lions assured them that soon the king would welcome Angelix. Many expected him to announce the death of Zambi.

• • •

Inside the hut, Angelix prayed for Zambi with a soft voice. Melodic glossolalia punctuated the prayer. "We believe that you are our Creator, and therefore, you can fix anything that you have created. Knowing that, and by your life-giving power, we command that the disease leave him right now and never come back."

Zambi remained still without giving any sign of springing to life.

If there would be a miracle, the king expected it to happen instantly. He would like to see his son walking again and the long-departed smile to grace his wife's face.

Angelix finally exited the hut. She halted about three feet from the open door, her face expressionless. When the animals saw her, a spirited cheer arose from the meeting place.

Reluctantly, the king approached her, limping and squinting his eyes, "Anything?"

"Like I promised, I prayed. There is really nothing I can do. I am not the Creator." She looked up into the king's eyes. His chin was touching the ground so he could be as close as possible to her since the cheers were so loud. "Your son is in a deep state of coma."

The king shook his head. "What is that?"

"Coma is a deep and often prolonged state of unconsciousness. Only our Creator has the power to wake him up."

"Okay," said the king with a low voice. Trembling, a weak smile wrinkled the corners of his eyes.

"Having said that, let us look ahead into the future. We cannot have a bright future if we are clouded by unforgiveness, and so I suggest that we start off with the forgiveness meeting, shall we?" Angelix said, stepping toward the meeting place amid rapturous cheers.

"Thank you, Angelix, the most high messenger of our God. I will forever cherish your advice," said the king, whispering to Angelix.

"I hope so," Angelix said, nodding.

The wolves and the pigs were flabbergasted as the king and Angelix strode side by side like old friends.

Under the blue, luminescent sky with its dazzling stars and perfect moon, most animals sat quietly, waiting eagerly to hear from the king. When he rose, he eyed his wife as he normally would do, but she avoided his gaze.

She couldn't pretend to be okay while her only son's life hung in the balance. Heaving, she left the meeting and slumped by the doorpost. There, tears fell on her knuckles.

All of a sudden, she screamed, startling her fellow animals. Their eyes widened; their ears pricked. She was now hollering and jumping in front of the open door. They thought she had gone insane.

"She's gone crazy," said one wolf.

"Zambi! Zambi!" she cried.

Upon hearing the name of his son, the king sprang up. In two mighty leaps, he landed by the door. When he saw that his son was alive and seemingly well, he stood on his rear legs and roared rapturously. He locked eyes with his wife, whose eyes glowed, and together they laughed jubilantly like parents of Moabi's world when their children have just won a competition. By now, the rest of the animals had figured out the reason for the royal zeal.

Zambi staggered through the doorway, looking feeble and trembling. The king nuzzled up alongside him and his mother supported him on the other side so that he found himself sandwiched between his two favorite animals. Zambi felt their warm love. They felt the connection. After a few minutes, Queen Mambo began to lovingly caress Zambi's fur, her rough tongue scraping off dark-brown flakes that became soupy in her mouth. King Tauza followed suit and soon Zambi was invigorated from head to toe.

THE FORGIVENESS MEETING

The king cried out with a spirited voice, "Let us all welcome Angelix home!"

Jubilant gasps bubbled from the crowd as some sobbed with joy. Moabi was moved by the amalgam of neighs, nickers, squeaks, chirrups, creaks, roars, songs, chuckles, tweets, clucks, and howls. There were yelps of foxes, chortles of kangaroos, trumpeting of elephants, the rumble of hippos, laughs of hyenas, screeching of eagles, bleating of goats and so on. Some of the noises, especially from small animals, could not be distinguished because of their high pitches. They danced, and pounded the ground rhythmically. The young buffaloes performed a fascinating slam dance. Hero performed a thrilling Terpsichore song, embellished by the ululation of elephants flicking their tongues up and down so fast so that one could hardly notice its movement. A sweet polished utterance of various notes emanated with excellence and grandeur unheard of in the human world.

Moabi stood there enthralled, astonished by the magic in the elephants 'mouths. The celebration went on for hours, until the meeting between King Tauza and Angelix ended. Then the king summoned all of the animals to convene under the big tree.

Sanza could not have been happier that the king had chosen to chair the forgiveness meeting. After acknowledging the leadership, he started off by calling a few names, summoning those animals to occupy the front row. They were Hero, Dumie, Dubie, and Woozy. Poised, Angelix occupied her old spot by the king. Those in the leadership sat facing the rest of the animals. Way in the back, Moabi sat quietly on a branch protruding from the compound wall, his bag in between his legs. He wondered whether he would be able to see Angelix after the meeting. Although he felt a special bond with these animals, home was where his heart was.

"I would like the young man to come up front and sit with us here," announced King Tauza sticking out his neck so he could see Moabi.

When everyone was situated, Angelix started the meeting with a prayer, asking for mutual understanding, that all would be transparent, that all would come to the truth and reconcile. She asked that wisdom and peace would rescue precious souls out of the cesspool of selfishness. Afterwards, she addressed the them, "Thank you for your warm welcome. I want to let you know that I truly love you all. Having said that, I want to make it plain that we are not here to accuse and strain anyone but to facilitate the peace process among us. Some of us have allowed egotism to be etched in our hearts, and unforgiveness has made deep wounds. Hear me: forgiveness opens the door for blessings. Forgiveness is freedom. Thank you." As she sat down, the compound remained quiet, and it was time for King Tauza to speak.

"First of all, I would like to say this: it was not easy for me to go and talk with Angelix." He paused, tears brimming in his eyes. "Although the condition of my son was the catalyst, it was high time for me to break through the prison of pride and approach her so we can reconcile. The vision of our land has never been so clear and bright that we ought to live in a peaceful and prosperous Vangoland. This will not come to pass if we do not obey our Creator. It certainly will not come to pass if we hold on to grudges and unforgiveness or harbor evil within us. I have already asked for forgiveness from Angelix, but as your leader, I want to do this again, this time before you." He looked at Angelix. "Forgive me for my disobedience, Angelix. I was totally wrong not to listen to you."

Angelix stood. "You are forgiven," she said solemnly.

"Thank you, Angelix," the king said. "I also ask you all to forgive me for causing Angelix to stay away from you." He panned his eyes across the animals.

"I know Angelix means a lot to you," the king said.

A few animals, particularly the lions and the king's inner circle, responded with loud voices, "You are forgiven, my king."

The rest just murmured and marveled at the turn of events. As for Madingi, she looked disgusted by what was going on. The last thing she wanted to see was the king becoming popular again.

As Madingi dealt with her demons, the king set his eyes on Hero. He regretted treating him harshly without considering the fact that he was hurt by his mother's death. He probably would not have run away if the king had shown some empathy. That would have made a huge difference, especially coming from the king.

Hero was also full of guilt. This peace and reconciliation process had come at the right time. He also needed redemption. There were many whose eyes could be opened and whose hearts could be healed. For others, it was an opportunity to rid themselves of malice.

"I was harsh and mean when I asked Hero about the death of his mother," said the king, earnestly, his brimming with tears. "I might have caused him to rebel."

It was quiet, and all eyes were on the remorseful king. They had not seen this humble side of the king in a long time—the one who took responsibility rather than placing blame. This was the king they had cherished in the past; this was the king of their Creator not the king of the dark and stony heart, the incessantly fear-mongering monster he had become.

As King Tauza looked at him, Hero's legs wobbled. He was overwhelmed as emotion billowed inside of him. He, too, choked back tears. He was not expecting the king to apologize to him. Chi comforted him with a soft pat on his back.

"Would you please forgive me, Hero?"

"Yes, my lord, I...I forgive you, but I must confess my sins now. I do not even think I deserve any good things right now," said Hero, casting his eyes down as the words struggled passed the lump in his throat. "I was wrong to run away from the kingdom, unspeakable for dwelling with the evil Beelz, dreadful for pinning Sanza on the roof, and for doing other bad things." He paused and looked at the king.

"I myself forgive you, and I urge the rest of the family to forgive you. You have changed, and everyone can attest to that," said the king. Although the king believed that

Hero had changed, there were still some doubters, espe-cially among the young buffalos, pigs, and wolves, who dismissed Hero's apologies as mere acting.

"Thank you, my lord, please allow me to confess to two of your noble animals, Sanza and Woozy."

"You may," said the king.

Hero turned to Sanza. "What I have done to you was terrible, Sanza. I apologize from the bottom of my heart, and I ask for forgiveness."

"I have already forgiven you," said Sanza, shrugging his shoulders. "You don't have to apologize for that."

"Thank you," Hero said.

"You are welcome," said Sanza. Seeing Hero's change of heart, he even felt renewed hope that the hare might help him with the tic situation under his tail after all.

"Woozy, I deeply and sincerely express my apology to you."

Woozy frowned, biting his lower lip, and did not utter a word. He shook his hefty head, perhaps in refusal, as Hero continued.

"The truth of the matter, though, is that I never stroked your nose and never heard you snoring at all. I just joked with Beelz, the snake, that I did that, but I never told any-body." He paused as some animals groaned, growled, and rasped.

Woozy snarled, fuming.

"Liar! Liar!" a wolf shouted from the back.

Another screamed, "He sleeps with the enemy! I would not trust him!"

"What really puzzles me," Hero said, with a glimmer of sincerity in his eyes, "is that Dubie says he heard Madingi talking about it. I did not tell Madingi anything; she must have heard it from Beelz."

Without wasting time, the king's eyes panned to Dubie. "Is it true, Dubie, that you heard that from Madingi?"

Dubie rose to his feet, cleared his throat, and swallowed some spittle. "Yes, my lord. The other night, I overheard Madingi and her friends laughing about how Hero stroked Woozy's vibrating nose while he guarded the water hole. She panicked as soon as she saw me, and tried to switch the conversation. But, by then, everyone was laughing like hyenas. I thought it would be best for me to tell Woozy about the rumors. I admit that I was a bit jealous that Madingi could tell jokes like I do." He paused, introspective, before confessing, "I got carried away and ended up telling Woozy the joke in front of others. Like Hero, I admit that I was wrong. Therefore, I ask that you to forgive me, Woozy," he said, a nervous smile lingering at the corners of his mouth. "I didn't really mean to offend you."

"What do you say about that, Woozy?" inquired the king.

Woozy panned his head to Dubie, huffed, and said in a deep voice, "I forgive him, my king. But I want to hear from Madingi."

"Thank you, Woozy," said Dubie, with a toothy smile.

The confessions shifted to Madingi whose barrel-like nose sucked in dust helplessly as she dreaded her turn.

"Quickly tell us your side, Madingi. Where did you hear that Hero stroked Woozy?" the king asked softly.

Madingi sneezed before answering and a green booger flew out of her nose, shooting right through the gaps in Dubie's teeth. Dubie jumped up and drove out the salty chunk with a violent cough.

The resulting laughter gave her a few more moments to compose herself.

Madingi had to tell the truth or at least a believable lie. Her eyes lit up as an answer came to her and she spoke confidently. "Well, while this might sound shocking, the one who brought the words to my ears is no longer with us." She paused. "Zingi, the elephant, told me, and indeed I did recite what he told me to some of my friends, knowing that they would never go out of their way to humiliate Woozy and make me a devil. Unfortunately, Dubie was spying on us and told Woozy in a reckless manner. All I was doing was simply sharing what I believed to be true," the pig said. "I wish I invented the truth. By the way, I was going to tell Woozy someday, but I was still carefully planning how to go about it. Hero is notorious and mischievous, so I would not let him off the hook because he might be the one who told Zingi. On that note, I rest my case." She abruptly sat down, making the sound of a deflating balloon as she sucked mucus.

"Ohooo!" Madingi's friends reacted, pleased with her slick defense. The majority of animals were dismayed; they couldn't connect Zingi with Beelz. Zingi's obedience was far from the boundaries of evil.

Excellence and truth were his delight. But even if Madingi was not telling the truth, they couldn't prove it because Zingi was deceased. However, if she was telling the truth, that raised a question. Somebody could still be liable for telling Zingi because it was inconceivable that Zingi and Beelz could share a space. In that case, Madingi's suggestion that Hero could still be the culprit made sense.

Hero stood up without being asked to. "I swear by my dead mother that I never told Zingi anything."

"Can I say something?" asked Angelix, blinking her eyes.

"Of course you may," said the king.

"What is done in the darkness comes to light," said Angelix. "Digging for the answer could be a waste of time."

They had to move on. While there was abundant doubt as to whether Madingi was telling the truth, reconciliation between Hero and Woozy was more important. Woozy still had to make up his mind.

"Angelix, do you have a word for these two?" the king asked.

"Yes, I do," Angelix nodded and quietly flapped her wings. "Woozy, I want you to listen to me. It is for your own benefit to truly forgive Hero, not just say it, and I am not talking about forgetting. Forgiveness is freeing yourself, and if you do not, the poison of bitterness will take root in you. It could lead to depression and perhaps to a deadly disease, or it could even lead to Self-destruction. Right now we have an enemy out there trying to deprive us of joy and seeking to divide us. We must come together as one to defeat the enemy."

Tears began to roll down Woozy's flat bony cheeks as Angelix's words resonated in his heart.

"You do not want to hold onto bitterness, do you?" Angelix asked.

"No," Woozy answered, shaking his head.

"Now, Hero, I would like you to apologize again to Woozy, if you would," said Angelix.

Hero cleared his throat with a cough. "Woozy, I apologize. I was wrong by telling Beelz a lie. Please forgive me."

With tears trickling down his face, Woozy opened his mouth to acknowledge Hero's words. "I forgive you, Hero."

"Thank you, Woozy," Hero said, stepping closer to Woozy.

Woozy reached down and softly clamped Hero's body with his neck in an embrace. It was clear that they both felt the power of reconciliation through forgiveness. Encouraged, Hero addressed the others.

"I would also like to express my sincere apologies to the entire family for being an outlaw. I was deceived. Please forgive me," said Hero, looking around.

After the emotional forgiveness between Woozy and Hero, others were moved with compassion, "You are forgiven!" they shouted.

"This is good. Here is what we are all going to do to solidify this process," King Tauza said. "If you feel convicted and want to apologize to a fellow animal, feel free to do so. Remember that forgiving each other allows the love of our Creator to flow among us, which allows our souls to heal from the past," the king said, sighing. Full of bliss, the king swished his meaty tail. His mane swayed as he panned the crowd, then set his eyes on Moabi.

Moabi watched the king take a step toward him and wondered what he was going to say. The king's mouth was stretched in a smile that unveiled uneven incisors that were sharp enough to cut anything in their path. Nevertheless, he couldn't resist the infectious smile of the king of Vangoland. A grin spread across his face, dimpling his boyish cheeks. He nodded repeatedly as the king uttered his apology, asking to be forgiven.

His face saddened as he imagined how a forgiveness ceremony might heal the bitter relationship his mother had with her mother, his grandmother.

It was on a windy night in Sacramento, California, when after an intense argument, his intoxicated grandmother snapped and shot his mother in the foot. Since then, the mother and daughter had not spoken. Moabi had not seen his grandmother since he was seven. Despite the deep rift in their relationship, he had hoped that one day there could be a reunion.

Just when he thought things couldn't get any more hopeful in Vangoland, Angelix landed between him and the king. It was the moment Moabi had been hoping for, the moment when he could ask Angelix if she could help him get home. Surprised, the king glanced at Angelix then to Moabi. A knowing smile illuminated his face, and without saying a word, the king slipped into the spirited crowd.

Angelix tilted her head up to Moabi; her misty eyes sparkled as if to say, "*Here I am.*" Her beak was smooth like a polished horn. The first thing Moabi noticed were the multicolored circles around her shining eyes that appeared like rings of the planet Saturn.

"I thank you for helping the animals," said Angelix, her head tilted up to Moabi's face.

"You are welcome. I've heard a lot of good things about you, and I can see why Moabi," said, bubbling with excitement yet nervous.

"Well, it is the Creator, your God, working through me. Every good thing that I exhibit or do comes from God," said Angelix.

"My God?" asked Moabi, surprised.

"The same God who created everything in your world is the same God who created everything here and all the worlds. There is only one God. We have power over evil if we trust in him."

Angelix's words were profound; the power they carried was the essence of love. Moabi could feel the love. She is wonderful, he thought. He wanted to believe her, and he could feel the knot of disbelief in God melting.

The healing of the king's son was his turning point, and Angelix's wonderful words cemented the conviction. He realized that his hope in Angelix was hope in God because if Angelix was to help him, that help would come from God.

"I can now say I believe there is a Creator who created everything. Without shame, I believe in him," Moabi conceded as tears filled his eyes.

"Good for you, for without faith in God, there is no hope," Angelix said.

"I need your help, Angelix, my mother is sick, and she needs me. Please let our Creator use you to help me go home."

"I will be happy to help, but first we must make sure Beelz is indeed defeated," Angelix said. "Don't lose hope."

"But...how long will it take to defeat him?" asked Moabi.

Angelix stepped closer, widening her eyes. "If you really need my help, then you will have to wait. I can't just drop my duty and leave everything in darkness. As long as we are still under evil's threat, I can't go anywhere."

"Okay," Moabi said, shaking his head and afraid of provoking Angelix.

"I believe there are many mothers, fathers, and children who need help, and so if you would just be patient, you and I can help them. Besides, are you going through these events and not finish your story? Maybe your story, our story can inspire your world."

Moabi grinned. "How do you know I am writing a story?"

"You have been living in our world, and you expect me not to know about you?" asked Angelix before fluttering away and leaving Moabi to think about—and perhaps embrace what he just heard.

Meanwhile, the whole compound bustled with activity. The animals mingled, looking for others they had wronged. There was neither hesitation nor haste but deliberateness. In this moment, they selflessly realized how much they missed each other and longed for unity. Many felt the prison walls of divisions that had marred them for such a long time disintegrate in their minds. Yet the hearts of some, such as Madingi and her followers, hardened. They just froze as if they were statues.

As various animals thronged Angelix, expressing their love for her and how much they had missed her, she shed sweet tears of gratitude. After a few minutes, Angelix asked them to draw back and sit down so they could conclude the splendiferous night. She flew onto the platform. "I would like to congratulate King Tauza for his leadership, for his willingness to change, and for ushering in the forgiveness meeting. Now together, we will work for the common good of our beloved kingdom. I thank everyone for their cooperation as we allow healing to take root in our hearts," Angelix said. "Together, we must make sure that Beelz, the snake, does not prevail over us—"

"We don't want his tail! We want his head!" the king bellowed, his temper stirred at the thought of the villainous Beelz.

Many were stirred up, and in few seconds or so, they started to chant boisterously, "We don't want his tail! We want his head!" Even Zambi had become exuberant, joining the chant. Waiting for the chant to subside, Angelix stood quietly on the platform.

Moabi found himself repeating the same words they were uttering, lifting his heels up and down, gradually assimilating into the synergy. He was not sure whether King Tauza's words meant that Beelz must be beheaded or captured dead or alive. Pondering this, he also thought about the "tail" as a metaphor for Beelz's followers and the "head" as Beelz himself.

At the same time, the chant began to take on a vicious tone. Moabi was rather disturbed when the lions became ferocious, clamping their jagged teeth together and shaking their heads vigorously to illustrate how they would cut Beelz's head off. That convinced Moabi that they would definitely behead him if they caught him.

Angelix stood patiently, waiting for the madness to quell. She thought about the king's reckless words. He still needs to grow. He *could have chosen the right words,* she thought. Sensing her disappointment, King Tauza called for the animals' attention.

"Okay, okay, let us all listen to Angelix as she finishes," the king roared. "I apologize for that, Angelix. I got too excited."

"You are forgiven," Angelix said, slowly turning around to look the king in the eye. She was shaking her head, yet smiling. The king could tell that Angelix's nice gesture meant that he can't be that sloppy.

Angelix continued with her speech. "This is the time we must completely detest malice. When we do that, the blessings of our Creator will shower us, and we will no longer labor hopelessly. Instead, we will enjoy the fruit of love." She paused. "If we don't stay away from darkness, where some of us are right now, we will find ourselves moving in the same direction that Beelz took. Beelz used to be a very nice Vangolian, but he chose to take the route of selfishness and destruction. But now he has reached a point of no return. So I warn everyone who harbors self-ishness to get rid of it and only allow love to propagate your hearts and minds. Otherwise you will face the same fate as Beelz. We must become vessels of light, not of darkness, because the Creator will not tolerate darkness. With light, the future is bright." Again she paused, allow-ing her words to resonate among them. "We want light more than the head of Beelz, because without the light in us, we cannot overcome the forces of evil."

A loud cheer of approval thundered across the meet-ing place.

"Since the wee hours are upon us, let us now go back to our sleeping spots for a sweet sleep, knowing that a brighter future is at the tips of our toes, believing that our Creator is on our side and evil forces are already defeated! Thank you, and may the Creator bless all of us."

They all dispersed to their respective places. In a very short time, most were snoring. In the middle of the com-pound, Moabi slumbered restlessly against a tree trunk.

DON'T LET THE DEVIL ESCAPE

Pinches, the queen bee, had been delivering and gathering messages to and from Madingi, the pig. She would come and land on the little branch that was twisted awry next to Madingi's spot. Early in the morning, right the reconciliation gathering, she came and relayed the message that Beelz would be coming to deliver poison.

"Tonight? Did you say tonight?" inquired Madingi, whispering.

The queen bee rolled her eyes. "Yes, he is coming, and he wants you to be prepared. He wants you to place the same stick you used last time at the entrance of the secret passage."

"Okay, I will be ready," said Madingi, her heart pounding.

Immediately, the queen bee hummed over the compound into the young day.

Madingi did not expect that news, especially after the emotional event that had just taken place. Nevertheless, she'd made up her mind to do it. Both she and Beelz had agreed that waiting too long could wreck their plan. Although she was not as deep in the darkness as Beelz, she was in deep enough to kill without remorse—deep enough to disguise the darkness in her.

$$\bullet \quad \bullet \quad \bullet$$

The full moon crawled up the sky in the east, glittering and illuminating everything. Beelz had stopped in the middle of the river because he thought he had heard some noises. But after some time, he uncoiled to resume his sinister journey. Confident, careful, and determined, he slithered over patches of grass and soil. At times, he would disappear inside the sere grass of the silent wood.

Finally, he arrived at the back of the compound in the stillness of the night. He searched for Madingi's wooden locator. It was smooth and slender, splitting into two at one end, which made it look like the letter Y. It was placed upward, leaning against the thorny tangles of the wall and barely touching the ground.

Beelz pushed hard through tangles of thorns and bushes, running into obstacle after obstacle. In the old passage, at least he could see some specks of light whenever there was moonlight. Not this one; it was as dark as a dungeon. "I hope Madingi did not trick me," he mumbled. He felt his skin peeling off and the thrust of sharp sticks and thorns. Then he tasted blood in his mouth. At one point, he couldn't move at all. He was stuck between sticks and had hard time breathing. But something kept him going; he was willing to do anything to replace King Tauza's rule with his. Whatever it took, he was prepared to do.

• • •

Madingi had been waiting for a long time, and she started to doze off, her head hitting the ground a couple of times before she totally fell asleep. As usual, she snored, sounding like a trumpet.

A strong vision appeared to her in a dream. In this dream, Beelz had four sharp horns protruding from his head and straight red whiskers sticking out from the sides of his mouth. His eyes glowed with fire. Suddenly, he sprang forth and wrapped his entire body around her.

"Why did you do that?" Beelz accused her.

"Do what?" Madingi asked, cringing and scared.

"Why did you tell them?" demanded Beelz.

245

Beelz tightened his body around Madingi.

"Don't kill me, please, Beelz. I don't want to die, please. I've never mentioned you!" Beelz's mouth was wide open, about to devour her. Then she saw Angelix sitting on top of the compound's wall, dripping water, as if it was raining. She woke from the dream suddenly with urine trickling down her thighs. She began to pace around. "I am not doing this anymore," she muttered. "He is too scandalous." Shaken and now skeptical, she rushed to grab a splintered piece of wood she saw earlier on behind the king's hut. She vowed to defend herself should the dream become a reality. She desperately hoped Beelz had changed his mind and was not coming.

• • •

As Beelz struggled through the wall, making slow progress, Lazzi, the wild dog, barked. He smelled a snake.

Beelz stopped moving.

Hero jumped up and rushed to where Lazzi was. A few other animals had assembled to investigate. Even the king emerged from his hut to address the small commotion. He looked approvingly at Moabi and Hero, who had hopped to his side. "You are showing good team work," he said. "Keep up the good work."

"Thank you," Hero said.

With nothing coming of Lazzi's alarm, the animals went back to sleep, and it was quiet again. Hero kept his eyes open, sensing that evil was at hand. He remembered his mother telling him not to live by fear. That night, even though he was restless, he felt fearless.

Through thick stems and excruciating pain, a window finally opened up for Beelz. A sigh of relief rejuvenated him. "There is hope!" he marveled. He panned his eyes across the compound and could not see anyone moving around. Most of the animals were snoring. The bigger the animal, the louder the snore.

In the middle of the compound by the big tree, a hunk of wood was slowly burning. Beelz could see the hot yellowish-white petals of flames blazing, releasing minute bursts of embers. There had never been a time when there was no fire burning all night long, except when it was raining. To the kingdom, fire was a symbol of vigor and power. About six feet beyond the fire, Moabi's face glowed. Above him, on the tree, Angelix rested in her newly woven nest.

Slithering close to the wall, Beelz made his way to Madingi's secluded resting area. "Wake up. I am here," Beelz whispered.

Madingi felt like her heart had just jumped out of her rib cage. She trembled, adrenaline shooting through her. She looked around and could not see anyone moving in the open space. Slowly, she turned her head toward Beelz. As soon as her eyes landed on him, she started to relive the dream, terror filling her heart. She stood there frozen for a good minute, staring at Beelz.

"Where is the wooden container?" Whispered Beelz.

Madingi rolled her eyes down and grabbed the wooden container between her hooves. Because of her discontent and nervousness, her teeth slammed hard on the wooden cork, cutting it. She trembled in the snare of fear.

"Hurry up! Hurry, Madingi. We do not have much time," Beelz hissed impatiently.

Madingi opened her mouth, and the container plummeted down, followed by a piece of a cork. The other half was stuck in the neck of the container. Panicking, she snatched the container with her teeth and with her tongue, she felt the cork yet it was impossible for her to yank it out. Butterflies crawled in her stomach, and the flurry of fear overwhelmed her. She stopped moving her jaws and stared at Beelz with scared eyes.

Beelz's glossy eyes instantly turned hazel red. "What? You broke the cork?" He sensed that the plan was going sour. *Madingi might have defected, he thought.*

"I can't yank the rest of the cork out," Madingi said, trembling.

"Do me a favor, Madingi. Just cut the whole neck off," Beelz ordered. "Be quick, Madingi. We are still doing well." Beelz tried to calm down. All the time, he was staring at Madingi without even blinking.

The dream flashed in Madingi's mind again, and she felt resentment filling her heart. Beelz's eyes looked exactly the way they had looked in the dream. Nerves took control as she grappled with the container and started to chew the neck.

Not able to sleep, mainly because of vibrating noises rumbling out of the noses and mouths of hyenas, he decided to walk around. As soon as he approached Madingi's spot, he heard a soft humming noise. He stopped abruptly and listened attentively. He noticed that Madingi was in an awkward posture. Her scabby front knees were on the ground, and she was grappling with a wooden container. *There must be something wrong with he*r, Moabi muttered. Along the wall, he took slow steps forward. Lazzi barked again. They ignored him.

Meanwhile, nervousness distracted Madingi, causing her to look side to side. When she saw Moabi approaching, she froze.

Beelz flicked his tongue.

Madingi tried to drop the container, but its neck was stuck in her upper teeth, protruding from her mouth. Madingi tried to grab the wooden stick with her shaky paw. Before she could lift it up, Beelz stretched forth and bit her, shooting venom between her eyes. As if someone was pulling her by the tail, she fell back. Quickly, Beelz retreated into the wall. Moabi rushed over as Madingi attempted to get up, but she only went in circles before finally crashing to the ground, her eyes lifeless.

Moabi cried out, "He is here! Beelz is here!" He continued to scream as he stared through the thorny wall that revealed Beelz's path.

With all of its fortifications, Beelz struggled to find his way back though the wall. Half of his body was squeezed and crammed into the tiny passage. It was almost impossible for him to move backward. His life was at stake. He knew if they caught him they would be merciless.

Alerted to the call, several animals jumped out of their sleep and sprinted to Madingi's spot.

"There he is! He bit Madingi!" shrieked Moabi, jumping up and down and pointing to the wall, which emitted the sound of a creature scurrying through it, snapping branches and rustling woven switches.

When King Tauza heard the news, he burst forth out of his hut. Queen Mambo and Zambi followed, scrambling through the tattered door. With just a few leaps, the king landed at the scene, which was literally behind his hut.

"King Tauza, there he is!" Moabi pointed at the wall, more excited than frightened. "He is trapped! He can't get out!"

Although the moon was shining bright as day, the king's aging eyes still could not see a whole lot. Chi brought a burning stick from the fire and held it close to the wall so the king could see. Through the thistles, thorns, and branches, King Tauza could see glimmering hints of Beelz's luminescent skin.

The king smiled, excited. He had been praying for this moment. "I see him! We've got him!" the king exclaimed. "Our Creator answers prayers!" He smiled. "Dumie, Speedo, and Woozy, summon your teams, and go outside and make sure he does not escape," the king ordered.

Meanwhile Madingi was now surrounded by a group of mourners—mainly the pigs, some hyenas, and several wolves. Their faces wore a mixture of sadness and shock. They would miss her underground leadership, secret meetings, and disguised strategic recruiting. But she had not told them one thing—the thing that perhaps would have kept them far away from her. She never told them that she and Beelz were partners. They just knew that she had a dream to become the leader of the whole kingdom. Her underground message resonated with them because she had promised that she would have an inclusive leadership style that was totally different from King Tauza's. She had also promised that she would co-rule with others and that she would not stay in power for a long time so that others could have the opportunity to lead, too. They liked that a lot.

"Take her over there, please," the king ordered. The pigs and some of Madingi's friends cried out bitterly as they pulled her body away.

"What is that in her mouth?" the king asked, examining her thoroughly. With his paw, he pulled out the container. He put it up to his nose but removed it quickly. "Do you know what this is?" he asked the pigs.

They looked at each other, confused and unable to utter a word, yet still sobbing.

"Go, go, go—you will answer me later," the king bellowed. As the king turned around, he faced Moabi, who appeared to have been waiting for him. "You have a question?"

"I think we should toss fire in there," Moabi said confidently, locking his eyes on the king.

"So you want to burn my compound, huh?" the king said angrily. "Do you know how long it took us to build this?"

Moabi looked down and shook his head.

"No, I do not think so. That is why it is easy for you to say such a thing."

Angelix landed in between them and said, "Let us do it, my king."

The king watched Angelix as she flew over the compound. "Chi, toss that fire in there!" The king shouted so that those who were on the other side could hear. "Be watchful on that side! Don't let him escape!"

Chi tossed the fire into the compound wall, and all eyes stared as dry wood and thorns blazed.

Beelz knew he was in deep trouble. All he could do was to hope for a miracle. A ball of reddish flames engulfed the area where he was trapped.

Moabi moved back toward the gate because of the smoke, knowing it could spark his asthma. However, he was reluctant to do so because he wanted to witness everything that was happening.

Absorbing the heat and inhaling smoke, Beelz's fatty skin began to blister. He felt like he was being broiled. The fire roared emitting heat and pushing the animals back. A dark plume rose, casting darkness over the moon as Beelz desperately contemplated his next move.

Many already suspected that he had perished in the fire. Dumie began to sing a victory song, his velvety voice inviting others to join in.

Beelz so slick 'n' sly
Today he must die.
He rebelled, spurning,
Now his soul yearns, burning.

Queen Mambo and Zambi headed slowly toward the gate, sad to see the wall being consumed and worried that their hut might catch fire. Queen Mambo loved to be inside of it, relaxing and pampering Zambi or having a lovely conversation with the king.

Suddenly, Beelz catapulted like a rocket out of the blazing wall, catching everyone off guard. Alas, he had made up his mind that he would not give up. He landed in the middle of the compound, skidding toward Zambi.

"Watch out, Zambi! Watch out!" Moabi warned from the middle of the gate. When Zambi turned around, he saw the blazing Beelz coming straight toward him.

Beelz was about two feet from Zambi when Chi intercepted him, his nails piercing Beelz's back, but the tiger could not hold on. Beelz flew through the air, missing Zambi by a few inches. When he realized that he could not kill Zambi, Beelz quickly turned around, lunging toward Chi, his tail flaming.

Chi gripped the ground tightly with his rear feet; his front paws elevated in the air, ready for his opponent. Beelz quickly lowered his head and dived under Chi. Chi tumbled over him as Beelz narrowly missed his belly.

Chi's hind nails caught Beelz on his lower back and raked him almost to the end of his tail.

Quickly Beelz coiled up, his head hissing above his body and viciously flicking his tongue. A cloud of smoke spiraled up from scraped and partly burned burned body. Although he was injured and advanced in years, his moves were like those of a young serpent.

Completely coiled and rolling like a smoldering tire loosed from a speeding car, Beelz launched forth again. Before Chi knew it, Beelz was tightening his tail around his neck and dragging him down. As Beelz tightened his grip, Chi screamed in the thin voice of one suffocating. After grappling with Beelz's meaty, slippery body, Chi finally managed to get a grip on him, sinking his claws into Beelz's flesh as he pried him loose.

In growing pain, Beelz lost control over Chi's neck but managed to wrap himself once around both of Chi's rear legs, tipping him over. Chi managed to free his legs as he landed on his back. He quickly grabbed Beelz by the neck as the snake lunged at his head. It was now a face-to-face encounter, with Beelz on top, exerting more power against Chi's robust legs.

With a swoop of his tail, Beelz flung dirt into Chi's eyes. Chi pawed at his face and flung the snake into a group of hyenas who were enjoying the fight. They ran away, fearing and opening a gap for Beelz to escape.

Chi sprang up, blinking his watering eyes as Beelz slithered his way out of the compound at high speed. Suddenly, Hero tumbled over him, brandishing his sword. Spinning the sword with his front paws, Hero seemed to confuse and daze the snake. He looked like a zombie, his face deranged and his body mutilated. The young lions moved quickly to surround them. Hero pressed a button on the hilt of his sword, extending the blade. He pounced toward Beelz, but the snake rolled aside and Hero's sword pierced the ground.

Hero pressed the button again, and the blade retracted from the ground. Beelz swayed back. Hero continued to advance and lunge at Beelz with his long sword. Dodging, Beelz swayed side to side. Hero sprang up into the air and drew his long blade down on Beelz. Beelz rolled backward, swaying to the side, but this time he was too slow. Hero caught him, sinking the blade into his flesh and pinning Beelz to the ground. A roar broke from the circle.

Hero jumped onto the handle of the sword and rocked his body, exerting as much weight as he could. He looked up at the king, and the king smiled back at him. He looked down to his opponent. There was no sign of resistance.

Even Zambi was impressed and he cheered, starting a chant of Hero's name.

As black slimy fluid welled from Beelz's rubbery mouth. Hero jumped off the sword and bowed down before the king and his wife.

"Good job, Hero," the king congratulated him.

"Thank you, my king," said Hero.

"How did you do that?" asked Zambi.

Smiling, Hero stretched his paw to give the young lion a high five. "I worked hard at that, Zambi." He then rose and found Chi slumped on the ground and being comforted by Magexie, the leopard.

"Are you okay?" Hero asked Chi.

Chi smiled and nodded. I am fine. Well done Hero. "You passed the test."

"Well, thank you. You are my teacher," said Hero, a tear rolling down his whiskery cheeks.

Moabi took in the surreal scene of the animals celebrating the death of the enemy as the compound wall burned in the night. The king's wife wept as embers fell on the hut. They watched as it caught fire.

"Sometimes you have to lose things you value in order to gain the right thing," the king explained to his wife.

Queen Mambo just shook her head in disbelief. "Our belongings are in there. Our Movena harvest is in there. Our memories are in there. Everything," she cried out.

"Do not worry about that. Our Creator will provide," said the king. "Old things are wiped out as new, better things come."

BEELZ'S GREAT GETAWAY

The morning was already bright and the compound wall still burning when the king summoned Sanza. He rushed to the king at once.

"Listen Sanza, I want you to hold Beelz at his ends and throw him into the fire."

"Please don't throw him with my sword," Hero cried out, pacing around.

"Sanza, pull out Hero's sword before you throw Beelz's body into the fire," said the king with a deep voice.

Sanza approached Beelz and began pulling the sword that had pinned the snake to the earth. Alas, he had no more than lifted it a few inches before the snake sprang up from his possum act and darted away, the sword retracting in length and bouncing along with him. A cloud of dust rose as the sword scratched the ground in what Moabi would later call, "Beelz's Great Getaway."

The blade had pierced Beelz's tissues but not his soul. A snake like Beelz would not die easily; he would die hard. He would fight to the bitter end. What did they expect, especially from Beelz? He was the devil of devils. He had escaped death many a time. They were all wrong to think that he was already dead.

"Get him! Get him!" shouted the king, spit flying out of his mouth like he was a mad dog. Everyone woke from bewilderment and dashed like slingshots after Beelz. The king and his family followed.

"Let's go get him, Father!" Zambi said enthusiastically, He felt this was the time for him to do something significant. Although he was happy for Hero, he was a bit jealous.

The king looked at his wife, and she nodded. "Follow them, son." This was the first time his father had urged him to step up and take part in the weightier responsibilities of the kingdom.

Hooves and paws pounded the earth, creating a rhythm that sounded like a drum circle. This time they were all in accord. Even the pigs and wolves followed. Boltex, the puma, was at the forefront, running like the wind but came to a tumbling halt when a long thorn pierced his paw. He watched Speedo, the cheetah, fly by as he writhed in pain. Behind Speedo, Chi, and Hero followed at a constant pace. Surprisingly, Zambi was right behind them.

"Look who is behind!" cried Hero.

"Well, it is time for him to step up. Otherwise, he will be a sloppy king. It is time!" shouted Chi.

Ahead of them, a tall tree stood before the slithering Beelz. Speedo closed in on him. Speedo increased his speed, hoping to catch Beelz before he could climb the tree. Beelz went straight for the tree. As soon as he was an inch from the bark, he shifted his head to the side, and the bulk of his body swiped against the trunk. Speedo failed to stop and hit the tree with his forehead, blacking out.

Beelz continued across the Vango River. Some of those who saw Speedo's tragedy stopped to attend to him as a scary lump swelled quickly on his forehead. Chi and Hero stayed the course.

Beelz moved with incredible speed and could have opened up a big lead if the sword did not hold him back. It was still stuck in his flesh opposing his slithery movement. It also made it easy for them to follow because it left scratch marks on the ground. It was late morning as Beelz transitioned from the arid area into the salt pan. Extending at least fifteen kilometers, the salt pan shone like the sea. It was bumpy and rough in some places, but otherwise, reasonably smooth. At the very end of it, stood Mount Fear.

The protruding sword continued to hamper Beelz's momentum but not his resolve. He pressed on, even when the salt rubbed into his wounds, causing excruciating pain. He hissed and screamed, wishing he could jump out of his worn-out skin. Hero and Chi ran steadily side by side and wondered if Beelz would ever give up. They assumed that at some point he would turn aside to avoid Mount Fear and its great dangers. In the long run, they expected him to fall apart. Alas, they were wrong. Beelz was not afraid of Mount Fear; he had been to the very top of it.

●　　●　　●

After been kicked out of Vangoland, Beelz did not hesitate to climb Mount Fear. He didn't doubt his ability to persuade the evil, greatly feared monster that together they should invade the kingdom. The more he contemplated the thought, the more confident he had become. He believed the notion that a true winner would always take risks. *The*

dragon will be on my side, and we will wipe them all out,
Beelz would swear to himself, convinced.

• • •

While Chi and Hero, thought Beelz was doomed on
Mount Fear, Beelz was equally convinced that as long as
he kept fleeing toward the mountain, the animals would
eventually stop chasing him because they were afraid
of Mount Fear. He was shocked when they pursued him
aggressively. Now his aim was to get to the mountaintop
as quickly as possible so he could rally his beloved dragon
and annihilate them all.

Meanwhile, Clips, the eagle, glided above him, strategically low. If I were as strong as the flying dragons, I would
just snatch him, she thought. The animals that could see
her knew where Beelz was at any point in time. But as the
pursuit lengthened, she got tinier and tinier for those who
couldn't cope with high-speed chasing.

• • •

Far behind everyone, before the river, Moabi hobbled
to a nearby tree, not too far from the bank. The tree

had dry branches with thorns pointing everywhere. He began to vent negative words, condemning his right shoe for allowing thorns to pierce his foot. When he tried to remove the shoe the way he normally would, the pain became so severe that he felt the throbs in his heart. He had to untie the shoe, remove the laces, carefully open the shoe wide, close his eyes, hold the shoe down, breathe in, and quickly pull. Of the three long thorns that had stabbed him, one was still stuck in his foot, its base covered by a bloody smudge. He was frustrated by the delay and eager to help the animals catch Beelz. "Why do I have to go through this?" he muttered.

His head was between his knees as he pondered how to remove the thorn when Angelix landed on a thorny branch that hung low, right above him.

"Are you okay?" Angelix asked.

Moabi sighed. "I have a thorn in my foot, Angelix. I am trying to take it out so I can follow the rest."

"If I were you, I would not bother to go anywhere but just wait for everyone to get back," said Angelix, not looking at Moabi but staring across the river.

"But, Angelix, I need to see how everything is unfolding so I will be able to put it in my book," Moabi said, looking at Angelix's blinking eyes.

"Why would you want to aggravate your wounds by walking a long distance when you could just wait? I mean, you can always get the information from someone else," said Angelix.

"First hand observation is better than getting information," said Moabi.

"I am just trying to help. I am not telling you what to do. That was just a suggestion," said Angelix.

Before Moabi could respond, a drop of blood landed on his arm. "You are bleeding, Angelix!" cried Moabi. "Your blood just dropped on me."

"Oh my goodness, I am so sorry," Angelix said, her eyes wide.

"That's okay. I am already bleeding from my own wounds. It can't be any worse to have the blood of a dove falling on me," said Moabi, looking back at his arm again. Something very strange was unfolding. The blood was penetrating his arm. He looked at this strange activity with awe, his mouth wide open, and his eyes widening. Then he looked up, trying to seek understanding from Angelix.

Angelix remained speechless, squinting her eyes as if figuring something out.

Suddenly, when Moabi thought it couldn't get any weirder, a gray mist, more like a fine cloud, began to emanate from the place where the blood sank in. It hovered an inch above his arm but without spreading all over. Flabbergasted, Moabi remained quiet.

"Oh my goodness, I think I have a glimpse of what might be taking place here," said Angelix, rolling her eyes to the heavens.

"What is it? Angelix, tell me please," said Moabi, staggering to his feet, his eyes still glued to his arm.

"I must ask my Creator about this, but I do not think that will hurt you."

All of a sudden, the cloud condensed into clear drops and then quickly dried up.

"I have to go now. Take rest," said Angelix, flapping her wings and soaring to the east.

Moabi watched her in breathless wonder. While he was still in confusion, Bizwax arrived, slamming her head on the ground.

"Wow, what happened to your foot?" Bizwax asked.

"Stabbed by thorns and one is still stuck in there; it's very painful. Maybe you can yank it out for me, Biz."

"I am toothless," said Bizwax, showing him a red hollow mouth.

Moabi laughed.

"Is that funny?"

"I am sorry, Biz. I didn't know you don't have teeth," said Moabi, still laughing.

"Whatever. But anyway, Clips is pretty good at yanking out things like that."

"Okay, I guess I will wait for her."

Now that Moabi knew that Beelz had been driven away, he decided to go to his old place, under the Movena tree, where there was nice, cool shade. He tried to invite Bizwax, but she declined, citing that animals were prohibited to loiter under the Movena tree. Instead, she decided to hang out on the bank and wait for others to come back.

• • •

The king and his wife finally caught up with the tired animals, the majority of whom were now just dragging their legs. When they saw that the king and his wife were determined, they felt courageous and kept up with them at least for a little while. The king's intention was to make sure that they drove Beelz to the evil mountain, for he was convinced that the evil would not spare him if he dared to go up.

• • •

Beelz was now in the area of the salt pan where the salt layer was very solid, causing the sword to incline and draw back. That reduced the rate of friction, allowing him to dash smoothly despite his partially corroded belly. He turned his head without yielding, and he could see Hero and Chi far away dwindling in size. Before him, Mount Fear was getting closer and bigger. He grinned.

By this time, many of the animals had sustained blisters on their feet. As they continued, the blisters burst, and salt escalated the pain. This caused some of the animals to take just one step at a time. Some who lacked wisdom licked at the salt, and that resulted in extreme thirst, which only further reduced their strength.

Up front, Hero was starting to show signs of fatigue and trailed Chi at least half a body length.

"C'mon, Hero! We have to get him before he climbs up," Chi urged as he increased the pace.

"I am with you," Hero said, gasping for air.

Speedo was back on the chase after his worrisome black-out and his friends' multiple attempts to resuscitate him. But he was now running like the wind despite the swollen forehead and his stiffening neck. He passed many animals, receiving cheers. "Go get him, Speedo!" some shouted.

• • •

Meanwhile, Beelz arrived at the foothills of Mount Fear, where a pond full of crystal clear water was tempting. White stones of the same height formed its perfect wall. Amazingly, there was no stream flowing into this pond. It was surely a mystery; although, it was possible that the water could be streaming from underneath the mountain and surfacing in the pond.

Although Beelz was thirsty and salty, he did not even stop to smell the water. As he snaked up the hill, a bent branch from a fallen tree blocked the sword, extending the tear in his body several inches. A pain sliced through his heart as he helplessly rolled down until his fall was blocked by a huge stone before the pond.

• • •

When the king realized that Chi and Hero would not be able to catch Beelz, he ordered Sanza to send a roar and a message so they would not go up the mountain. Sanza could roar more loudly than the king or any other lion. If there was a competition for roaring, Sanza would definitely win gold.

Sanza thundered, relaying the message. "Stop, stop, the king forbids you to climb the mountain."

Chi and Hero waited. Hated it.

• • •

After a long struggle to climb the steep slope, the ailing Beelz stopped to catch his breath on the edge. He looked down and could see Chi, Hero, King Tauza, Queen Mambo, Zambi, Sanza, Speedo and a couple of lions at the end of the salt pan by the pond. Trickling into this group, one by one, were animals walking in a straight line that stretched at least from the belly of the salt pan. From Beelz's vantage point, those forming the line looked tiny, and he could not tell who was who.

• • •

Now the king spoke what he had been thinking. "I do not want to entertain the thought that Beelz is partnering with Mount Fear's evil forces, but I am afraid because it might be true. On the other hand, I want to believe that the Creator is driving him to his demise. Let us hope so."

Not wanting to turn back after coming so close to catching Beelz, Hero spoke up bravely. "My king, why don't Chi and I follow him? You are right, he could be working with the evil forces, but since we trust in the Creator, who hates evil, I believe He will protect us."

The lions booed Hero because he did not make sense to them at all. They could not see how he and Chi could climb Mount Fear.

"Hero, we have lived to know about the evil on this mountain. Stop dreaming," the king said, irritated. Hero dropped his eyes to the ground, embarrassed.

One of the hyenas, Ross, who had been sniffing around the place and not paying attention to the king, turned around and saw the pond full of water. He smiled, licking the crust from the corners of his mouth. He quietly stepped forward. "There is water here, my lord!" Ross shouted.

All eyes turned. Ross was notorious for being a pure, pathological liar. He was small in stature and had a reputation for teaching others how to practice the art of lying. Madingi had recruited him into her camp, and they had gotten along quite well.

He screamed again, "My king, I am not lying! There is water here!"

As soon as he realized they weren't taking him seriously, he plunged his crusty mouth into the water and tasted something he had never tasted before: it was extremely bitter. Red, purulent sores began to cover his entire mouth, inside and outside. Inside, his intestines churned. With shame and fear, he turned around to face the others.

They allowed him into the semicircle they'd formed around the king. They were shocked and speechless. Even the pigs and other hyenas who normally would have burst into laughter at seeing Ross afflicted but this really shocked everyone, sparking empathy.

"I want to apologize for disrespecting you, my lord," cried Ross, tears mixing with mucus underneath his nose.

"What happened to your mouth?" asked the king, shaking his head.

"The water over there is poison," he said, sobbing and in growing pain.

"Well, that is what you get when you do not listen," exclaimed the king harshly, taking steps toward the pond. "Come, show me."

Nervously, they all followed the king and the stricken Ross.

"Hero, do you now believe that this mountain is evil? Look what happened to Ross. This is a sign that you cannot go up. Beelz will never return." Agitated, the king panned his eyes to face Hero. "If you want to disrespect me like Ross, go ahead. Hero, I am sure that you will never return," the king said with a husky voice.

"Not me, my king. I see the danger and will not climb the mountain if you order me not to!" said Hero, cringing back with humility.

Angelix flew in, flapping her wings before the agitated king. "My king, I just got the impeccable word from our Creator."

The king sat on his tail, bit his lower lip, and looked Angelix in the eye. Everyone was eager to hear Angelix's heavenly message.

"Okay, okay, Angelix, say it. I would like to hear what the Creator is saying," said the king.

Casting her marble eyes toward heaven before opening her old, elegant beak, Angelix said, "My king, with much respect, the impeccable word from above is that you should let Hero and Chi go after him."

"Will they come back?" inquired the king.

"I do not know. That is all I received," answered Angelix.

The king remembered that he had agreed never to question what Angelix told him. He coughed, clearing his throat as he turned to face Hero and Chi.

Chi eyed his young protégé who seemed to be worried now, despite his earlier request to follow Beelz all the way.

"You can go. Go well, and make sure you bring his head back with you. We will be waiting for you," the king said.

CROSSING THE
THRESHOLD

Hero and Chi sprang toward the mountain. The
king and the rest of the group watched as they

disappeared behind rocks and trees. The smear of blood all on the slope made it easier for Chi and Hero to track Beelz; although, the steepness of the grade hampered their progress. It was a real challenge for Hero. His developing muscles shuddered. Chi nudged him with his forehead, sustaining him and preventing him from slipping or tumbling down the mountain. Hero had never climbed a mountain, but Chi had. He used to leisurely climb the mountains that ran on the sides of his original place.

• • •

Beelz was struggling to climb a smooth, vertical slope. After a long stretch of tireless swaying and pushing hard, he emerged at the top of the slope, where he coiled like a fire hose. He told himself that what did not kill him would make him stronger. As maimed and mangled as he was, he assured himself that he would become very powerful indeed.

At the sound of tumbling rocks, Beelz looked down the slope. He saw Chi and Hero below. It was taking Chi and Hero a long time because they were climbing in a zigzag pattern, which was a safe way to climb a slope but Beelz knew it was draining their energy.

• • •

Chi and Hero huffed and puffed.

"Whatever you do, don't look down, Hero, because if you do, that would be your end," Chi warned.

"Believe me, I am focused," replied Hero with a trembling voice.

"Stay focused then," emphasized Chi.

Beelz hissed, unrolling seamlessly toward a tree standing above the edge of the slope. He climbed the tree and inched along a branch projecting toward the slope. He could see Hero and Chi clearly now as they neared the edge of the slope.

Chi gave Hero the last push. Hero sprang over the edge.

"Step back, Hero, so I can jump over there," cried Chi, whose hind legs precariously gripped the slope and front legs held onto the edge. Hero retreated way back to give space for Chi so he could land without obstruction. As Chi sprang onto the edge, Beelz elastically catapulted over Hero, whipping Chi on the head. Chi lost his footing and slid down the slope, gathering momentum with no hope of regaining a grip. Hero looked on in horror, helpless.

With Hero and Chi caught off-guard, Beelz dashed away, disappearing behind a big dark-brown stone that sat loosely on top of a small one. Hero wondered why the snake did not try to attack him, but he also knew that Beelz could be devising a strategy. He hoped he would not strike him from the back.

Below, Chi had plummeted down onto a tree with thick, clustered branches. It was a fall that looked impossible to survive. Up on the mountain, Hero was left shaken and in a dilemma. He was unsure whether he should try to rescue Chi or continue to pursue Beelz. He couldn't carry Chi—he could barely climb the mountain. Assuming Chi was alive, he would surely need to go down the mountain to find help. Chasing Beelz without Chi would be perilous. Nevertheless, he considered what Angelix had told King Tauza: "The impeccable word from above is that you should let Hero and Chi go after him."

Beelz scrambled forth, staining stones with drips of blood. His pain was appeased by the belief that he had eliminated one of his toughest enemies. Certain that Bubbles would join him, once again he vowed that he would go back and annihilate them all.

Hero followed, staying out of sight as he followed Beelz's bloody trail. He stopped a short time to catch his breath and marvel at the sunset. The stunning sight reminded him of the long way he'd come and yet that he was far from being able to rest.

• • •

Up ahead, Beelz entered the cave. As soon as he showed up, Ozca, the fish, dashed under water, hating the very sight of him. Beelz slithered by Ozca without saying a word. He turned right and entered a compartment where Bubble's thick, leathery tale protruded. Beelz swayed over the large tail. The compartment was dark and almost perfectly oval. A crack above the compartment allowed light to spill through, revealing Bubbles' glossy, iridescent scales.

Inside the compartment, an argument ensued—one that was clearly unbalanced. Bubbles was loud and rather harsh, and Beelz kept saying, "Calm down. Calm down. It is going to be okay."

THE KINGDOM HEADS BACK

At the bottom of the mountain, the king become impatient, for the animals had been waiting for a long time. Eventually, he stood up in the middle of the fatigued group. "We have to go back now because it is getting too late. We shall all go to the well to drink some water, and hopefully Chi and Hero will be okay. Is there anything you want to say, Angelix?" He looked down to Angelix, whose chest was resting on the ground in front of Dumie and Sanza.

"Not at all," said Angelix.

Ross was suffering. His entire head was covered with red sores. White slimy mucus began to foam out of his mouth. All of a sudden, he collapsed and began convuls-ing. While everyone watched in horror, he became still, and there was no sign of breathing. Fearing contagious-ness, the king warned that no one should touch Ross. After a few minutes, the horizon light totally fading, they pronounced him dead.

As the animals rose from the foothill to go back to the compound, a black owl with green marble eyes and white legs enigmatically landed before them. This was the sec-ond time the bird had appeared. The first was the day be-fore Beelz launched an attack on them. Those who saw it said the owl landed on the tip of the king's hut and imme-diately took off toward the east. Now, as they took a close look at this inscrutable bird, it took off toward the east as it had done before, and their eyes went with it. They stared as it soared, dwindling then vanishing into the ap-proaching black blanket of a storm that immediately sent a chill down their spines.

"Look, the storm! The storm is coming!" one of the hyenas cried out loud, dismayed.

"Let us get out of here," ordered the king.

THE GHOSTLY FACES
AND THE CAVE

Darkness loomed over the mountain by the time Hero arrived at a flat area covered with fine, gray soil. A boot made of zebra skin caught his eye. He trotted quietly to it. Suddenly, six ghoulish human faces with stringy necks floated up from soil and loomed above him. Their faces were smeared with a white substance, revealing hollow eye sockets that glowed like fire.

The faces began to groan and shriek like demons. Shocked, Hero trembled, stumbling back. He fell down on the boot as if a powerful force had swept him to the ground. The faces scowled at him as a deep blue slime dripped from their toothless mouths. Realizing that keeping quiet was not going to help him, he shouted as they kept on approaching him. "I am not scared of you! Get away from me!" he said with authority.

The ghosts began to laugh hilariously but they retreated. With confidence, Hero ordered them to stop shrieking. They stopped at once.

"Where do you think you are going?" one of the ghosts asked.

Hero was startled by the words, but maintained composure. "It sounds like you already know where I am going, so back off," Hero commanded.

They laughed again, and one of them said, "If they killed us, what do you think you can do?"

"I'm talking to ghosts!" marveled Hero.

"We are trying to warn you. You should go back."

"Did you see a big snake passing by here?" asked Hero ignoring the warning; he hadn't traveled so far to lose courage.

"Yes we did," one of the ghosts giggled, bouncing around.

"He was mutilated, and a spear stuck out of his back. Did you do that?"one of them asked, chuckling, then bursting into wild laughter.

"It wasn't a spear; it was my sword," Hero proclaimed. As soon as they erupted in a fresh wave of laughter, the moon surfaced at the top of the mountain, filling the atmosphere with light. The ghosts disappeared in the twinkling of an eye before he could ask who killed them.

Whoa, they can't be in light, Hero thought to himself.

Advancing, he spotted more weathered, shrunken leather boots scattered around. But what puzzled him was the manner in which they were strewn, each the same distance from the next. They stood upright, except for one, which lay on its side, a slimy, substance oozing down its side evidence that it had just been knocked down. Hero had no doubt that Beelz had knocked it down. Without wasting time to examine it further, he trotted up the gradual slope that led to the tip of the mountain.

Hero arrived at the next flat area. Facing him was a huge circular rock, almost conical at its tip. There was a dark entrance in the middle. Amazed, he stepped forward and immediately noticed drawings on either side of the entrance. At a close proximity, strange characters were written under them. It appeared that a sharp tool had been used to execute the work and then a red substance had been applied on top, making the drawing pop out.

Intrigued by this, he examined every drawing. The first painting revealed a giant man aiming a bow and arrow at an animal that looked like an antelope. The next painting showed the arrow traveling. The third showed the arrow striking an antelope, and last depicted the man carrying the animal on his shoulders.

Hero returned to the dark entrance. As he looked back to see whether someone was behind him, a feeling of unease threatened to overtake him, but he quickly shrugged it off. "I am a winner, and I shall overcome." He looked down and noticed tracks from Beelz marking the ground.

Hero trotted back to the shrunken leather boots. Among the many things he'd learned from Master Chi was how to make fire. He grabbed a thin, hard stick approximately his length and a decaying slab of wood wide enough for the stick to spin on. He placed the wide wood flat on the ground and piled lots of dry grass on it. Then he rolled the stick between his paws so that it spun at a high speed, creating friction. Without high friction, the fire would never catch. He knew that, and he knew the trick quite well.

Soon, there was a glow at the friction point. He flicked grass toward it with his rear left paw. Eventually, sparks began to fall on the grass, igniting flames. He threw a couple of sticks on top to bolster the fire. Then he checked all the boots, found one free of slime, and tossed it on the fire too. After it caught fire, he drove a stick into it. Then, he hopped back to the cave, carrying his makeshift torch, and found himself in a tunnel.

●　●　●

The tunnel was approximately one and a half meters in height, and to his amazement, the floor was paved. He took a deep breath. This is different, I did not expect this, he thought. He stopped and listened. Beelz is always in a nice place, he muttered.

In the distance, he could see smears of Beelz's blood on the wall. He slowed down at the curve. The flaming boot dropped to the ground as the wooden stick charred. However, light spread around the bend in the tunnel.

When he rounded the curve, he was puzzled to see a totally different and stunning world. The moon was casting a bluish light into a spacious, lavishly designed cave. The cave was conical; the opening at the top was round and a lot smaller than the floor space. Hero stopped abruptly. Straight ahead, he could see a pool of shimmering water. He stepped back, taking a deep breath. Then, after making up his mind, he stepped forward into the exquisite space.

On the left side of the pond, where the light was dim, a bow and arrow hung on an iron hook that protruded from the wall. Lowering his eyes, he saw Ozca, the fish, with his head propped on the edge of the pond. Ozca looked engrossed in his thoughts. He could be listening to something, Hero thought. After a while, Hero could actually hear the heated conversation coming out of the compartment to the right, Beelz suppressed.

• • •

Bubbles, the dragon was yelling, "How many times must I tell you this?"

"They are right at the bottom of the mountain, I swear," begged Beelz.

"No, I refuse," said Bubbles, the dragon. "I told you I can't attack, right? Do you remember what I told you about the storm?"

"Yes, I remember that, my Bubbles," answered Beelz in a subdued tone.

"So why try me, then?"

"All I am saying is that they are not far. They are just down the hill. This is a great opportunity for us."

"The only reason you even call me 'my Bubbles' is that you want my favor. When are you going to quit being an opportunist, Beelz? You are gone most of the time, and when you show up, you want me to do something for you.

You are too busy trying to take over Vangoland, and you forget that we are about to have a baby."

Beelz sighed. "I know, I—"

"Ozca prophesied that the baby will be hatched today," Bubbles interrupted.

"You know I love you, Bubbles," Beelz whined, "Nothing shall separate us. I am not doing this just for myself. It is for us and the baby." He paused to allow the words to sink in. "Bubbles, we are just a step away from taking over. I burned the entire compound." He paused for few seconds and took a deep breath because of the pain. "Isssshooohow."

"What's wrong?" yelled Bubbles.

"I have wounds all over, and I have a sword stuck in my back," cried Beelz.

"You have a what?"

"Let us go to the light so you can pull it out," Beelz requested.

Ozca dropped under water as soon as he heard those large bodies shuffling out of the dark. They unfolded into the pond area.

Hero stepped back into the darkness of the tunnel.

"This is ridiculous. They did this?" Bubbles shook her hefty head fiercely.

"Yes...ooh," Beelz cried in pain. "Are you ready?" Beelz shut his eyes and said, "Yes."

Bubbles quickly yanked the sword out, and Beelz moaned. The sword fell into the pond, grazing Ozca on his back.

"They are going to pay for this. This is serious and cruel, Beelz," said Bubbles angrily.

THE KINGDOM AND
THE STORM

The wall facing the cave's entrance glittered with the black bees swarming around their hive, while the silver beetles nested above them. The black bees' zone was divided into two. The upper zone was for queens and the newly born. The lower zone was populated with workers and drones. They were smaller in size, and their bite could cause severe swelling. Honey trickled down the wall like a slimy fountain, pooling in a round, stony basin from which Bubbles fed.

Jack, a silver bug, dislodged himself from the upper zone and flew over to his boss, Bubbles.

"Listen," Bubbles said, "Tauza and his kingdom are right at the bottom of the mountain. Look what they did to Beelz. So I want you to annihilate them all. Do not miss the king and his son. Even if they've left, go after them," Bubbles ordered.

Jack and his company of silver beetles burst out of the cave, zooming.

Hero pressed himself flat to the wall as the colony buzzed above him, sending a chill down his spine. Some flew through smoke from the burned boot and dropped dead right on the spot.

They can't handle smoke, Hero thought.

• • •

King Tauza and those who were with him were now in the middle of the salt pan, trudging homeward. The pigs and the wolves trotted lazily behind, chatting about the tragedy that befell Ross. Some of them complained bitterly. They could not understand why they had to go all the way to Mount Fear just to follow Beelz, only to come back spent. "We did not have to go this far. This was ridiculous," one of the pigs lamented disrespectfully.

All of a sudden, a swarm of beetles landed on the stragglers, biting them everywhere and chewing their ears. They screamed helplessly. The rest of the animals turned around to see why the pigs and the wolves were crying. With her sharp eyesight, Clips could see what was harassing them. "My king, they are being attacked by silver beetles," Clips cried.

Several victims ran and jumped around, while others rolled on the ground, trying to avoid being stung.

"Let's move on and catch up with the king," ordered Jack, the silver bug.

The beetles rose, leaving the pigs and the wolves and headed for the rest of the animals.

As Jack and company zoomed in on the king and the rest of the animals, the black storm from the east thundered, approaching. When lightning struck again, it revealed its crimson fury. In the darkness between lightning bolts, the silver beetles attacked fiercely. Until something miraculous happened. The storm thrashed the beetles to the ground. Some fell on the animals like hail, dead, as the storm moved quickly over them. The animals were amazed. Then the real hail began to fall. The animals swallowed hail pellets to quench their thirst. Next, rain started pouring down.

They congregated together among the bushes rejoicing. They had been praying for this moment to come. Their hearts blossomed with happiness.

After some time, the rain slowed to a drizzle, allowing them to proceed. Some of the young animals had never seen hail or rain before, so they splashed in puddles as they sprang about. The older ones sloshed around. Then they all crossed the Vango River, the young ones frolicking in the wet sand.

MOABI'S DREAM

Moabi had crawled into the trunk cave. Immediately he fell asleep and a troubling dream came upon him. In his dream, he could see his mother, bedridden, eyes closed, and sunken into a shrinking bony face. Her arm hung down on the side of the bed as his cousin Gloria sat mournfully on the nearby chair, a tear trickling down her cheek.

As the dream progressed, the bedroom atmosphere transformed into a strange place with high stony walls. In this place of high walls, a little dragon began to crawl in circles. Moabi watched it growing and becoming pugnacious. A sharp horn protruded from its broadening skull. Green eyeballs jutted out. They looked hard and glistened like marbles. The monster dragon breathed green fire from its mouth and from its barrel-like nostrils.

Moabi could now see Chi struggling, pinned to the ground by its mammoth foot. From the dragon's right foot, Hero was caught within the claws and hanging about four feet from the ground, screaming. Then he heard the dragon bellow, "It won't take long for you two stupid animals to die. When I am done with you, down the mountain I will go and consume everything with fire, including your white dove!"

That was when Moabi woke up, sweating profusely and gasping for air. Like a frog, he leaped out of the tree cave and burst through the dripping branches into the drizzle. He felt light as a feather, like he had just finished weight lifting. When he walked, it was as if wind was pushing him. His adrenalin was shooting, his heart thumping. The dream was not fading away. He knew he had to do something. The last time he had such a vivid dream, elements of it had happened.

Despite the thorn in his foot, he started running toward the river where the animals gathered. Ironically, running eased the pain in his foot. The smell of rain reminded him of home, especially that very first rain marking the end of summer. When he arrived at the gathering, Moabi located the king. "Where is Chi and Hero?" he asked, looking around and hoping to see them.

"They followed Beelz up on the mountain," the King answered. "Why are you asking?"

"I think they are in trouble. We have to go and help them now! I just had a dream, and they are in danger. There was a dragon on the verge of killing them. The scariest part it that it kept growing. If it cannot be stopped now, it could come and consume all of us with its fire. We must take this very seriously, King Tauza!"

"We can't climb that mountain," the king said, shaking his head. "It is an evil mountain, cursed. Even if your dream was true, we can't climb the mountain without the approval of Angelix."

"Okay. Where is Angelix?" Moabi asked.

"She is around somewhere," said the King, distracted by his own thoughts.

When Moabi could not find Angelix anywhere, a strange feeling of aggressiveness overwhelmed him. He had never felt like that before. Without saying a word to the king, he took off fast.

•   •   •

In a very short time, Moabi had crossed the wet sandy river. He ran as fast as he could, on the cooled salt plain. He could feel his heart racing in his chest, but amazingly he wasn't winded or tired. In fact, he was amazed by his own speed and endurance. It must be the *blood of Angelix*! he thought.

As he climbed the mountain, Moabi kept on thinking that he would meet the dragon, having already devoured Chi and Hero. If it had not done that yet, he wondered where the three of them could be. In his dream, it was a walled area. It could be on the other side of the mountain, which meant that the chances of stopping the monster were little to none. Besides, he did not really know how he would rescue Chi and Hero, let alone stop a dragon. All he knew was that he would do something. "God will be with me," he assured himself.

The moon was shining over the quiescent mountainside. As he climbed on, heaving and sweating, Moabi noticed the wiggling smear of blood. Beelz went over here, he thought. Dust puffed through his fingers as he pulled himself onto the flat place, which was entirely covered by a very fine clay soil. He stood up, appreciating the cool whistling wind that that cooled him as it played in his face. A few steps further, boulder sat as though it was rolled to this area for a purpose. The place smelled like a dog, dead for days. Approaching the boulder, he was shocked to see old boots scattered nearby. "What happened to the owners of these boots?" He said out loud to himself as he pinched his nose to block the smell.

A slimy green substance was still oozing out of the boot made with zebra leather that Beelz had knocked over. While wondering if there was a connection between the old boots and the perfect boulder, something creepy diverted his attention. He heard a voice coming from behind. Petrified, he turned around. Nothing. *Perhaps it was just the wind*, he thought. Thoughts of doubt mush-roomed, briefly clouding him with confusion.

Just as he was starting to doubt whether he could pre-vail, Angelix flew over him and landed on the boulder.

"Angelix!" Moabi exclaimed, surprised and turning around to face her. "What are you doing here?"

"I am astonished by your courage, having the nerve to climb this mountain," said Angelix.

"I was looking for you and could not find you any-where..." Moabi began.

"I was in prayer at that time, and I heard from the king that you had a dream and wanted to help Chi and Hero," said Angelix.

"A bad and vivid dream; I was compelled to do some-thing immediately. See, I am convinced the dream is true. If I can't stop what I saw in the dream, I might never be able to see my mother again. You told me that you would not be able to help me if the kingdom is still threatened by evil. Not only that, but in the dream, there was a ferocious dragon and it promised it would not spare even you!" Moabi said, his voice cracking and thinning. "I don't even know how I would stop this monster can be stopped..." he lamented.

"From what I saw when I was in prayer, all I can tell you is that we must not be deterred by a spirit of fear; we have to go forth boldly," Angelix proclaimed, eyes glistening.

"What you saw?" Moabi asked in a surprise tone.

"I don't understand that."

"While praying, I had a vision. In my vision, you were dreaming, and I could see what you were dreaming about.

Then after your dream was over, I saw you and me climbing the mountain, and we entered an area where there was a total darkness," said Angelix, "and my vision dissipated."

"That confirms that my dream is true, and I am doing the right thing then, right?" Moabi asked enthusiastically.

"Well, I am not here to stop you. We are in this together," said Angelix.

"Really?" said Moabi, brightening up.

"Let's talk as we move," Angelix said, turning around and making a jump forth.

"Please! This place stinks," said Moabi.

"All my visions and dreams are true," said Angelix. "Every time I see myself in a vision at a particular place, I know I am supposed to be there and doing what I was doing in that vision. From there I just open my heart to receive divine direction. Once, I went to another world, watched thousands of people perishing, and could not do a thing. Sometimes I can't prevent evil when it comes. My assignment however was to save an important piece of information that was needed for the betterment of that world and ours. I am just a creature and not omnipotent by any means. Right now my assignment is to travel with you through that dark entrance, and I don't know what is going to happen on the way or on the other side."

"At least you have wings to fly away," said Moabi, taking a deep breath.

"You shouldn't think negatively against evil," said Angelix.

Moabi stopped and looked at the contusions on his hands, and his mind dug the pain from his thorn- inflicted foot. A sense of vulnerability overwhelmed him, filling his eyes with tears. Then he looked at the glowing moon that seemed to smile at him. After awhile, he took a deep breath as he looked down to Angelix.

"Be courageous. I suspect the entrance for this cave is not too far from where we are at," said Angelix as she flew toward the face of the cave.

CLIMAX

Up in the cave, against the dark wall, Hero had just watched Bubbles licking Beelz all over his body, sympathetically tending to his wounds. Every time Bubbles ran her tongue over Beelz's wounds, Beelz twisted and cringed in pain. Now they lay side by side, waiting for Jack, the silver bug, to return with good news.

"I wonder what is taking them so long," Bubbles mumbled. "I hope everything is okay with them."

"They will be okay. There are lots of animals down there, you know. You told them to annihilate them all, so it will take some time," said Beelz.

"Silver beetles are fast. Trust me. It would not take them a long time to do their job. But anyway, I know they will be okay," Bubbles reassured herself.

After assessing the situation thoroughly, Hero tiptoed along the wall in the semidarkness and arrived on the other side of the pond without being noticed. He smoothly slid into the pond. Then he swiftly pulled the sword from the bloodied water. Ozca darted to the surface, but then he plopped back underwater. Hearing the splash, Bubbles turned toward the pond.

"Ozca!" cried Bubbles, seeing that the water had turned red and realizing what she had done.

Although Hero could not swim, he was able to propel himself to the wall. He raised only his nose to the surface so he could breathe while holding the edge with his left front paw and the sword with his right.

There was no answer from the pond except the popping of effervescence.

"Ozca, where are you?"

No answer.

"Since when did you become deaf?" Bubbles fumed, swaying to the pond.

As soon as her head hovered past the edge of the pond, the sword went through her throat. Leaping back, she roared in pain. Hero emerged from the pond with streams of water rolling down from his head. He split his sword into two and held the two blades high.

Bubbles did not waste time. She leaped up, attacking, her mouth wide open to swallow her foe. But she was too slow for Hero. Hero easily stepped aside, and she fell hard into the water, forcing Ozca to the bottom of the pond. Struggling, she gathered her heavy self, her short, chunky legs scraping the edge of the pond. With his sword, Hero gestured to her to come as if he had no fear of the fierce, enormous creature.

Bubbles yelled at the remaining silver beetles on the wall for help. "Get off of that wall and get him!"

The beetles dislodged quickly from the upper zone of the honeyed wall. Hero was ready, flipping and spinning the two blades. As soon as the beetles were upon him, he pressed the buttons on the handles of the blades. The blades emitted a spectrum of bright light about fifty centimeters in diameter around each blade. Blue rays struck like lightning from the middle of the spectrums. Little did the beetles know that those rays contained electromagnetic fields. As they haphazardly entered the beams, they fell to the ground like pieces of zinc. Within minutes, they were all over the place, lifeless.

Beelz slid into the darkness by the entrance. He was sad because he needed the beetles for his plan to rule all territories from Mount Fear to the animal compound. He hoped Jack and company had accomplished their mission. He watched Bubbles as she slipped on slain beetles and rolled on her side.

"Beelz, where are you? Look what you did. This is a mess!" Bubbles cried out.

There was no answer.

"Beelz! Beelz, where are you? Are you hiding?" Bubbles bellowed. She looked over at the chuckling Hero. "What are you laughing at, you...?" She swayed forth, launching another attack.

Hero darted away, and Bubbles crashed into the cave wall. But she managed to whip Hero with her massive tail, sending him crashing against the statue of the king of the giants. One of the blades flew from his left paw, stabbing the hiding Beelz in the back.

"Aaaaashi!" Beelz cried, trying to suppress his reaction, but, he could not handle more pain. Both Bubbles and Hero heard his cry.

"That's what you get, you stupid liar!" Bubbles screamed. "Come out and help me!"

"I can't move," Beelz cried out.

"I am tired of you! You brought your mess in here, and you can't even clean it up! I am through with you, Beelz," said Bubbles as she took another huge leap to crush Hero.

Hero pressed a button on the blade handle, and a single robust blue laser collided with Bubbles. She retreated in excruciating pain. Her roar exploded through the mountaintop, reverberating so far that even the animal kingdom could hear her. As her flesh bubbled, she crashed into the wall of the cave, dislodging a boulder that struck her head, pinning it to the ground where she lay motionless and silent.

Beelz averted his eyes. He had no time to come to her aid; there was another left to be resolved: defeating Hero.

Maybe I can lure Hero to yank this blade from my back, and then I can easily kill him. Yeah, that would work, he encouraged himself. But his thought was interrupted when suddenly Chi appeared in the middle of the entrance.

Chi was completely puzzled by the flames scattered everywhere as though the cave was a war zone. He wondered if Hero had survived. *And if he did, where is he?* Chi asked himself. He carefully scanned around, contemplating a move, not realizing that Beelz was just a few feet away from him, hiding in the dark.

As soon as Beelz saw the opportunity, he knew he could not waste time. He had to deal with Chi quickly because it would be hard for him to defeat the two at once.

Chi carefully stepped into the precarious atmosphere. It was quiet except for the crackling of fire.

Without vacillating, Beelz sprang from behind and wrapped himself around Chi from neck to rear legs. But Chi was swift with a defensive maneuver. His right paw grabbed Beelz's neck, pushing his head away. Beelz resisted, his tongue flickering only inches away from Chi's forehead. The pressure he applied on Chi caused Hero's blade to fall off. Chi rolled into the light as Beelz threatened to suffocate him. Beelz laughed and declared, "This time you are going to die."

Chi fought back, scraping Beelz's body with his claws, yet shaking tremendously as his strength weakened. Beelz's tongue kept on flickering closer and closer. Chi darted his head from side to side, avoiding Beelz's poisonous saliva. Although Chi was evading Beelz's fangs, the fall had cracked his ribs and reduced his strength. It appeared that Beelz had the upper hand.

Hero climbed a tall, slender rock—the statue of the king of the giants, which was on the left side of the honey wall. He struggled to balance himself on its head and fell down when he extended his leg trying to snatch the bow and arrow that hung on the wall. He scrambled back up and this time managing to grab the bow and arrow. But as soon as he sat on top of the sculpture to take a good aim at Beelz, a little monster with short legs like Bubbles' stumbled out of the dark compartment. He was slimy and appeared dazed. Hero was shocked and wondered if there were more of these kinds of creatures, but he had to deal with the situation at hand.

Beelz was just an inch away from biting Chi when Hero unleashed the arrow. Ozca watched from the pond as the arrow whizzed through the air and pierced Beelz's head from the side. Chi could feel Beelz's body getting heavier and loosening as he took his final breath.

Hero dropped the bow and stood on the rock with his front legs in the air. "Victory!" he shouted. He jumped down, grinning at Ozca as he strolled by the pond.

Hero brushed Chi's neck with his little pad. "Are you okay?"

Tears glittered in Chi's tired eyes. "Once again, you have saved my life, Hero."

"You taught me how to fight and inspired me with your wisdom. Now I know why The Creator sent you to Vangoland."

Chi smiled, regaining strength. "There you go."

"Now, I saw what looked like a young dragon, and there may be more of them," said Hero as he yanked his blade and the arrow out of Beelz's back.

THE REVELATION

Outside the cave, Angelix and Moabi discovered the entrance into the tunnel.

"Look, look, Angelix, smears of blood here," said Moabi pointing to the ground by the entrance. "Must be Beelz's."

"Only the brave will go in. I am going in," said Angelix.

"I hope this is not the grave for the brave, because I am going in too," Moabi said.

They ventured into the darkness, Angelix leading the way.

"It smells like death in this cave," Moabi said softly.

"Be of good courage," Angelix encouraged. "We talked about this already. Don't you want to go home?"

"Of course I do!"

"Well then where is your trust?"

"I guess in the Creator," said Moabi.

"Don't guess, believe in your heart."

"Got it. So how come you have never been to this place, Angelix?" Moabi asked.

"Because I was never assigned to come here. Okay, we have to keep quiet now and get going," said Angelix.

• • •

Curious whether there were any more dragon-babies, Hero trotted toward Bubbles' compartment. He pressed a button on the side of the sword handle. A pool of blue light illuminated the whole compartment. Right in the middle of the compartment, two equal halves of a green shell, the size of a very big watermelon, lay side by side, empty. Hero continued to search, but there was nothing to be found, other than the single shell. Taking in the opulence of Bubble's quarters, Hero shook his head in disbelief. *This place is so magnificent*, he thought to himself.

Finding no additional threats, he tiptoed out gingerly. Young Beelz—or Young Bubbles—was still in the same place, outside the compartment entrance, as if glued. The sharp horn protruding upward from its head was now visible. Its jaws were bulging, with budding fangs growing at an alarming rate, really stretching its mouth. From a couple of feet away, Chi looked at the little monster with distrust and contempt.

Chi glanced at Ozca. "You speak?"

"Yes," Ozca replied.

"My name is Chi, and my friend's is Hero."

"What's yours?"

"Ozca."

"How did you get to this place, Ozca?"

"Well, it is a long story to tell." Ozca tilted his head toward the sky, and tears welled in his eyes. "Human beings snatched us from the Vango River many, many years ago and brought us here. Amazingly, they did not roast us. I guess they just liked to watch us swimming around and also feeding on whatever they fed us. But as the time went by, the rest of my family died, and I am the only one left. After my family passed away, I was given the gift of prophecy—"

"Who gave it to you?" Chi interrupted.

"The very same day I was alone in this pond, I found four tiny precious rocks glittering at the bottom. Then I heard a voice, saying, 'Prophesy with those little stones, and you can also see visions through them.' That was it. I never heard that voice again. Since then, my stones have been helping me to see what is going on around this world."

"So what happened to the people who brought you here?" asked Hero.

"To tell you the truth, they started worshiping statues, like that stone that you stood on to shoot Beelz. I tried to warn them against it, but they never listened to me."

"So what happened to them? Talk to us, Ozca," said Hero.

"One day we were all relaxing when suddenly Bubbles, accompanied by swarms of silver beetles and black bees, actually, fell through the tip of this mountain and into this cave. That was an unforgettable dFay. There was a violent storm over the mountain, and it was as if it cast her and her legion down as lightening," Ozca shook his head. "These beetles started to whirl around, filling the whole place with a scary sound. I was so frightened. As the people scattered in panic, the beetles went after them. They were screaming in agony. As for me, I was left unscathed. Bubbles liked me right away." Ozca slid his head along the edge of the pond as he described the traumatic experience with a cracking voice. "By the way, I have good news for you."

Hero and Chi looked at each other and then looked back at Ozca.

"What is it?" asked Hero.

"Through my prophecy stones, I saw the silver beetles perish after they left this place."

"Really? How?" Hero asked, keeping one eye on the little monster.

"They were upon King Tauza and the rest of the kingdom when a massive storm destroyed them," Ozca explained.

"Well, indeed that is good news," said Chi hopeful. "Hey, Ozca, when did Beelz first come here?" asked Chi. "Do you know?"

"Oh," Ozca said, grinning. "I thought you knew."

"I wouldn't be asking," said Chi.

"That liar," said Ozca, sliding his head side to side on the edge of the pond. "I am glad he is gone. He crept in here a couple of years ago and seduced Bubbles. She was in love with him, so she let him stay here, but he was gone for the most part."

"Ozca, since you are a seer or whatever you call yourself, what is the future of this little monster?" asked Chi.

"Well, let us see." Ozca plopped back into the water, and when he resurfaced, he spit out three glistening diamonds. "I had four, but Beelz stole one of them. That diminished my prophetic abilities." He glanced at Hero before laying his eyes again on the precious stones.

Hero's heart started to beat like a drum. The precious stone his mother had given to him was still tucked under his tongue, and it was just like the ones Ozca pondered before them. His mother never told him where she obtained the shiny little stone. Embarrassment and confusion unsettled him. *Spitting out the little stone to compare it with those on the ground might reveal the truth about my mother's death,* he thought. The main reason he had decided to rise against evil was to find out who killed his mother. Hero glanced at Chi and then at Ozca. As soon as he opened his mouth, the stone fell on the ground. "That's it!" Ozca said excitedly.

The young dragon stirred, as if awakened from a daze and bedazzled by the four stones glittering on the ground. The young monster began to move back and forth, colors shifting iridescently like a chameleon.

"If you try something mischievous, your first day will be sorrowful," said Hero, pointing at the little monster with his blade. He panned his head to Ozca. "Do you know how the stone got to my mother?"

"Well, Beelz gave it to Madingi, the pig, to entice your mother with it."

"What?" said Hero, his eyes widening in shock. "To do what?"

"To kill some of the king's loyalists and eventually the king."

Hero began to pace around. "Tell me this, how did my mother die?"

"When your mother saw the stone, she asked Madingi where she got the stone. Madingi said it was a present from a mysterious, beautiful, sparkling creature that she believed was an angel. Your mother couldn't resist it. She was attracted to the stone instantly. As you know, the stone helped her to perform her magic brilliantly."

Tears started to stream from Hero's eyes. "So what happened after that, Ozca? I want to know the whole truth."

"One night, Madingi approached your mother and told her that the giver of the stone, the angel, would like to meet her in a nearby woods, the place that Madingi called 'the divine spot' because she claimed her prayers were answered there. Your mother was enthused by what she was hearing. She looked forward to meeting the angel who liked her so much. So she rose early in the morning, before anyone was awake, to go meet the angel." Ozca paused, coughing to clear his throat. "It was a very quiet morning, and as she walked, she could hear only the sound of her feet. She kept on stopping and looking back because she thought someone was following her. But soon she arrived at the divine spot."

Chi interrupted the story. "Stay right there, don't move," he shouted to the little monster, who seemed to be growing every second now.

The little monster stared at them with angry eyes.

"Continue, Ozca," said Chi.

"That morning, above the so-called divine spot, Beelz waited inside a hollow branch that curved down. Then cleared his throat so he could project easily with a different voice. He said: '*Madonzi, I am happy you could make it, sweetie. I knew you would anyway because this is very important to your life.*' Your mother jumped up at once. She looked up to trace where the voice was coming from but could not see a thing."

Chi ran a paw of comfort on Hero's back.

"And so," Ozca continued, "with a fake voice, Beelz said, *'Do not be afraid, Madonzi. Your life is about to blossom. Today I will only appear to you in voice, because I do not want to overwhelm you with my glory. But listen, sweetie, everything starts with words. If you can receive my words this morning, you will truly be blessed.'* Madonzi kept on watching in between the branches until something really shocking happened: a light leathery substance slid off the branch. Suddenly the voice paused," Ozca said, laughing.

"What's so funny? What happened next, Ozca?" Hero prodded.

"Beelz did not notice that his skin was peeling off when he forced himself inside the hollow branch, but upon realizing it, he quickly tried to cover. *The devil will: try to instill fear in you, Madonzi, but guess what? The devil is already defeated,'* Beelz said. Madonzi noticed that the voice was a little bit different this time. It was a little bit deeper." Ozca paused again, panning his eyes from Hero to Chi.

"He is evil," said Hero, dabbing at his eyes with furry paws and looking back at the dead Beelz.

"Your mother was not stupid at all, as you can attest, and so based on these two facts, she became suspicious. Without wasting any time, she dashed away. Not long after that, Beelz met with Madingi and plotted to kill your mother. That night, Beelz crept into the compound wall and spat the poison in a wooden container, Madingi holding it. Shortly after that, Madingi put the poison in your mother's food. That is how your mother died," Ozca said, sighing.

"So all those who died after Madonzi were killed by Beelz's poison?" Chi asked.

"Of course, and you know what? I am glad you two had the courage to end this terror by pursuing the truth," said Ozca, panning his eyes from Hero to Chi before looking again at his glittering stones.

"Thank you," said Hero, still wiping tears from his furry face.

"Back to the question about what is going to happen regarding this monster," Ozca said. "Wow. This creature is growing at an alarming rate," he said, looking at the little monster.

The dragon curled his tail like a whip. Multiple colors radiated from its head to tail. It was truly a combination of its parents. It had stocky, muscular legs and evil eyes. It yawned, revealing teeth that looked like broken bones.

Hero eyed Chi. "Maybe we can tie it up, then drag it to the kingdom. Maybe we can train it to be good."

"I do not think that is a good idea, Hero," said Chi, shaking his head.

Ozca skillfully licked and snapped each stone into his mouth. He shook his head and then spat them out on the ground again. After a careful assessment of each stone, he said, "I do not see any hope regarding this creature."

"Well, maybe it will be different, unlike its parents," said Hero.

"Whatever you decide to do, make sure you don't leave it here," said Ozca.

At this time, the little monster yawned again, this time emitting a rumbling yowl. They could see its reddish tonsils vibrate. Chi and Hero took a couple of precautionary steps back, but the creature whipped its tail in the air, spun around quickly and struck Hero and Chi across their faces. Ozca plopped back into the water. The little monster spiraled out of control now. It scooped up Hero's sword with its tail and tossed it away, leaving Chi and Hero vulnerable to its wrath.

Angelix and Moabi entered the cave and found the dragon swelling in size and scooping their friends up like rag dolls. Hero, who dangled from its lengthy right claws, caught a glimpse of the pair and motioned weakly with his ear toward to his sword.

"Get Hero's sword," Angelix whispered.

"Where is it?" Moabi asked.

"Behind them," Angelix said, gesturing with her head.

"But how will I get there?" Moabi asked.

"Walk quietly against the wall, then tiptoe to the sword."

"What if the monster sees me?" Moabi asked.

"If it sees you, I really don't know what will happen. Just focus; be courageous," Angelix said with a reassuring nod.

"Okay," Moabi said, biting his lower lip, his hands grappling with the wall, and his eyes on the agitated dragon. He walked with his back and hands pressed against the stony wall. It was as if he was walking on a very high tight rope and would die if he fell. Several feet from the wall, Hero's sword glistened in the moonlight. Moabi contemplated whether he could reach it undetected. The dragon stopped as if it sensed something. Then it growled with such deep reverberation that debris began to fall from the walls. Green flames suddenly billowed out of its mouth.

Moabi wanted desperately to run away but stayed in one place, shaking and praying that the dragon would not turn around. As soon as the dragon calmed down, Moabi proceeded cautiously toward the sword. Crouching down like a tiger, he crept away from the wall and snatched the sword without detection. Pointing the sword toward the dragon, he retreated to the dark wall.

"Leave them alone!" Moabi shouted. The moonlight vanished from above as dark clouds overtook the mountain. Thunder rumbled from the approaching storm and reverberated throughout the cave as if to punctuate his demand. Near the entrance, Angelix waited in the darkness, praying fervently.

The dragon turned and charged toward Moabi with a flaming roar. Moabi pressed and held down a button on the sword, releasing a red beam that enveloped then extinguished the flame. Amazed, he pressed the button again. This time, the beam pierced the dragon's eye, and it let out a deafening cry. As if the thunder and cries of her offspring had awakened some latent strength, Bubbles stirred from under the boulder.

"I said drop them!" Moabi shouted out as he pointed the sword towards the creature again, totally oblivious to Bubbles. Hurling the wearied animals into the pond, the dragon charged toward Moabi again. Moabi haphazardly pressed the two buttons at once and the lasers flew wild, colliding with the raging beast. Moabi dashed aside as it crashed into the wall. Slipping on fallen silver beetles, Moabi sprawled headlong toward the entrance while the sword slipped out of his grasp.

Realizing that her offspring was in danger, Bubbles reared up to defend the creature before Moabi could retrieve the sword. Dragging themselves out of the pond, Chi and Hero saw her steely eyes zero in on Moabi. "Moabi! Watch out!" they screamed in unison.

Moabi scooped Angelix into his arms protectively and scrambled to find firm footing. As Bubbles stepped into the center of the cave in front of the young dragon, thunder rumbled again. The black storm had fully descended on the mountain and lightning flashed down to the center of the cave. The young dragon, embracing its mother, clung to her side as Bubbles looked up, frightened by the storm. A deafening thunder shook the ground and a rotating funnel swept into the cave enveloping Bubbles and the young dragon. They swirled violently in the vortex as the funnel sucked them up into the clouds.

Suddenly, the storm was gone and the cave was silent. Hero and Chi limped towards the entrance of the cave. Angelix fluttered towards them with Moabi just behind her. They were all shocked by what just happened. It was surreal. They looked around, uncertain whether the threat would return. Ozca emerged from the pond, sliding his head over the edge. "They are not coming back," he said.

They all stepped toward Ozca, relieved by his words. Finally, they would be able to return home.

"Are you going to be okay when we leave Ozca?" Hero asked.

Ozca smiled. "I am absolutely okay. Please do not worry about me. I am going to enjoy this place alone. Look at this! It is peaceful and beautiful!"

"Well, we will be back then to make sure that you are okay," exclaimed Hero.

"Before you leave, you should consider that the animals might not believe what happened here," said Ozca.

"They will just have to believe it," Chi responded.

"Ozca is right," said Hero. "They all want to see before they can believe. Even the king said he wanted Beelz's head," Hero recalled.

"They should learn to believe, even when they don't see," Angelix sighed.

"I don't think the king was serious about wanting Beelz's head. Trust me—they will believe us," Chi said.

"Maybe Moabi can throw the head into his bag," said Hero, smiling and tilting his head to Moabi.

"Not in my bag, please," said Moabi, shaking his head, "I am not carrying dead snakes."

"Well, I guess I'll have to carry our trophy," said Hero. His sheath had two straps, each with a buckle at one end and a hook at the other end. Hero hopped to retrieve his sword and chopped off Beelz's head like it was a piece of wood.

Reluctantly, Moabi helped Hero drive the hook through Beelz's mouth.

"Now that that's done, I have something special for you," said Ozca, addressing Moabi, "I knew you were coming here."

"What is it?" Moabi asked, taking a step closer.

Ozca plopped into the water, and when he came out, he dropped a light grey stone, the size and shape of a lemon from his mouth letting it clank and roll toward Moabi like a grenade. Moabi stepped aside and watched it until it stopped on its own.

"What is that?" Hero asked inquisitively.

"It is the precious stone that the King of the Giants prized above all," Ozca replied.

Moabi picked up the stone and stepped into the moonlight, beaming with enthusiasm. He gasped as it caught the light of bright, full moon.

"Where did the king of the giants get this?" he inquired, looking at the gleaming stone.

"He chiseled it out of the wall of this cave, right there behind you," said Ozca.

"Wow. How did it end up in your pond?" Moabi asked, curious.

"It fell in here when the King was escaping Bubbles' wrath," explained Ozca. "It is my gift to you." Giving Moabi the stone appeased Ozca's guilt for encouraging Beelz to cut off his ear.

"Well, thank you," said Moabi softly. He knew the precious stone must be a diamond. It was truly a giant diamond, clear and colorless.

The sojourners stayed in the cave throughout the night listening to each other's stories. Ozca, as the oldest of them, had the most fascinating tales particularly about his life. Moabi talked about how the storm's lightning reminded him of the one that struck him when he was young. Hero told them about the wisdom his mother had imparted. Angelix spoke of her journeys to other worlds. Chi told of China. But the greatest story was the one they now shared, of the storm swooping in and carrying off Bubbles and the offspring.

FROM DEATH TO LIFE

Somewhere in the spiritual realm, Ross found himself standing on a string of blue light. Nervous, he looked down. The light divided the space below into two separate planes. Propelled by instinct, he began to move forward.

A majestic voice commanded, "Look to your right," making him to tremble in fear. Shaking, he panned his head to the right. The natural beauty of the place stunned him. All sorts of healthy animals were grazing, some relaxing peacefully in green pastures and some sipping water from the pure silver stream that snaked elegantly across this paradise. Then he noticed several animals that he knew. First he saw Zingi, the elephant, looking healthy and young. As reality began to sink in, Hero's mom, Madonzi, walked toward Zingi with amusement on her face. *I thought they died*, he thought.

"Now look to your left," the voice commanded.

Multitudes of screaming, tormented animals were confined within red-hot stony walls. Here, the snare of death was unending. Ross saw many animals he had never seen before. He saw bizarre animals with only one eye on their foreheads. They were not from Vangoland for sure. Some had hollow eye sockets. The majority were snakes intertwined like burnt spaghetti.

"Well, well, well, it is your choice," said the voice. "You have a chance to choose love."

Ross looked up for the voice only to be met with the sight of the stunning celestial sphere. He couldn't liken it to anything. Billions of colorful stars dazzled him as two glossy ribbons of rainbows formed a cross through a transparent golden globe perched in the center of the icy sky.

I guess it is the beauty that speaks, Ross thought.

"Which side would you like to live on, Ross?" asked the voice with an irresistible authority.

Ross was astonished that the voice knew him by name. "The right side," he answered without hesitation.

"Good. Now go back and live in love and tell others the truth and about what you saw," said the voice, fading away.

The rainbows dissolved into a gray, misty cloud that vanished into the icy sky. In the twinkling of an eye, Ross was standing on wet sand and did not know what happened to the sky. He looked around and saw Mount Fear behind him. He realized he was standing in the Vango River. He smiled in disbelief as the breeze swept across his face. His feet squelched in the sandy river. The power that had brought him back seemed to be present in him as he marched with vigor.

The rest of the animals were amazed and surprised when they saw him coming. But they were more shocked when they saw no signs of his wounds. He looked fresh; he was the new Ross. They all believed his story of the blue line and voice, and many were inspired to renew their faith in the truth.

GOING BACK HOME

Moabi, Angelix, Hero and Chi finally stepped out of the cave's tunnel. A cool morning breeze blew smoothly over the mountain. The sun eased its way up, progressively turning a sparkling yellow. Hummingbirds chirped beautiful tweets as they fluttered up and down. Rocks were still wet, for it had rained overnight.

Filled with joy, they stood on the cliff, watching the slope shimmering with a silver sheet of water. Waterfalls gushed, roaring down gorges, and in the distance, fog hovered over the salt pan. Without saying a word, Angelix took flight, ascending into the sky.

It took a long time to circumvent the slippery slopes. They wished they could fly like Angelix. Pulling Beelz's head had become a challenge for Hero. Most of the time, the head would roll to his side or over him, sometimes tripping him. At one point, Hero fell on his neck when a fallen branch trapped Beelz's head. Suppressing a laugh, Chi had to go back and help his young friend.

They finally arrived at the boggy foothills, where butterflies fluttered their silky wings. They sloshed along a pathway that led them by the bitter pond and slipped on slushy soil as they entered the fog covering the salt pan.

"Oops, it is slippery here," said Hero as he skidded and landed on his knees, hitting the ground with his chin and sliding further until he was stopped by the thickening mud. This time, Chi couldn't conceal his laughter. Even Moabi looked away to quell his.

"I am so sorry, Hero," Said Chi, chuckling.

"Sorry is just a sorry word. It does not help me, and I see you are enjoying this," said Hero.

All of a sudden, the fog began to ascend, and immediately the landscape was filled with light. They could not believe their eyes. The salt was swept away, and they found themselves standing on a golden road that seemed to have been rolled out especially for them. It stretched all the way to the end of the salt pan, and it was amazingly straight. "I think the people who used to live in this region were sophisticated," said Moabi.

"I would think so," Hero agreed.

"Perhaps it was the giants of the North travelling from the river to the mountain," Chi said.

On both sides of the golden road, blades of green grass were aggressively breaking the ground and spreading fast.

Within minutes, the scene was gold and green. They all felt the sun rejuvenating them as they walked in the fresh air.

As they arrived at the end of the golden road and stepped onto the muddy ground, they could see Vangonians family lined up along on the other side of the river. Several of them were jumping up and down in jubilation, welcoming the Vango River.

• • •

By the time Moabi, Chi, and Hero stepped into the river, the water was just swelling past Moabi's ankles. Every time he made a step, he could feel the current shuffling sand under his feet and his heels sinking.

"Listen, Chi, the whooshing sound. What's that?" Hero asked, erecting his ears.

"It sounds like the river is coming in full force," said Chi. "It must have rained a lot in the western mountains."

"Well then, we must hurry," Moabi added.

They were somewhere in the middle of the river when King Tauza roared, "Hurry, we are waiting for you! Be careful out there!"

At that point, the river began to swell even more, angrily turning brown. They could feel its mighty rush threatening to sweep them away. Quickly it turned murky and littered with wood and other objects it had accumulated along the way.

"How are we going to do this? I can't swim!" cried Hero as the water swept him against Chi. "Maybe we should go back."

"We are halfway. It would not make sense to go back. Hold on to my tail," Chi said.

Hero clutched Chi's tail.

"I'm not the strongest swimmer either," Moabi said nervously, gasping, as a stick whipped past over him. "This river has become violent now!"

"We have to push fast or we will not make it to the other side," cried Chi.

Soon, only their heads poked above the rushing water. With little skill, Moabi swam forth.

"Don't be afraid, Hero, we will get there," said Chi.

"I am with you," said Hero softly, his two upper teeth biting his lower lip.

On the shore, one of the wolves muttered mockingly, "They angered the gods of Mount Fear."

Sanza heard him and confronted him. "If I ever hear your stupid utterance again"—he pushed his face into the wolf's—"I will not hesitate to break your neck."

The wolf cringed at Sanza's strong words.

Clips continued to monitor Moabi, Chi, and Hero's situation from above. King Tauza worried that the swelling waves might sweep them away. Many feared the trio might not make it. However, there were those who believed that if God had delivered them from the snares of Mount Fear, certainly he would deliver them from the tumultuous river.

Sadness loomed on the riverbank. The king stayed in one place, with growing concern about the river. Where was Angelix? As everyone congregated around the king, Clips shouted from above, "I see Chi's head! Hero is clinging to his tail!"

"Where? Where?" shouted animals on the shore.

Magexie, the leopard, cried, and many others were touched by their perseverance. Several let out an exultant cheer. But where was Moabi?

As they approached the shore, the current tugged at Hero's holster. He could feel the sword threatening to come out of the sheath, but he needed both paws to hold on. First, his beloved sword would be gone, and second, the evidence, Beelz's head, would be gone. *To live is better than dying to protect the evidence*, Hero thought.

Just as the undertoe whipped away Hero's holster, Chi caught hold of a fallen tree trunk and jumped onto the shore, Hero still clutching to his tail. The animals cheered. For some wolves and pigs, the feeling was rather different—not because they wanted them dead, but because they knew Chi and Hero would be promoted above them. They were already jealous.

Moabi was still in the river. He was losing strength yet still fighting hard to push across the violent current. To King Tauza and those who really cared about Moabi, the celebration had to wait. The king, along with others, stomped the riverbank. On the Movena tree, which was about two hundred feet from the gathering, Angelix prayed for God's mercy.

Zambi, the young prince, spotted something glistening on the riverbank. He looked at it for a long time with suspicion.

While Moabi continued to plunge and tumble his right hand touched a long, hard object. He grabbed it, fumbling for a better grip. It felt like a rope. Even though the current threatened to sweep him away, he would not let go of his lifesaver.

That hard, long object he was holding turned out to be the root of Movena tree exposed by the eroding force of the water. Despite being pounded and thrashed, he began to pull himself forth on it. As he reeled himself in, he felt the root becoming thicker and firmer.

"There he is! There he is!"Angelix called from her perch. They all came rushing to witness Moabi's heroic emergence. A whopping uproar erupted upon seeing him. Tears glistened in Angelix's eyes as she sang some well-known notes.

The king knelt on the shore with his amputated leg, his other front paw pounding the mud. "You made it! You made it!"

While everyone embraced the exhausted Moabi, Zambi crept out of the celebration and checked on what he had seen earlier. It was Hero's sword, still attached to Beelz's head.

Hero was thankful to have his sword back. In the midst of all this, and out of nowhere, Gray, the mouse ran around deliriously as he avoided the jubilant paws and hoofs. He was trying to locate Hero, and when he finally found him, he didn't care about those paws and hoofs anymore. He zoomed toward his friend. Surprised, Hero dropped his sword, picked Gray and kissed him repeatedly on the mouth. "I thought you were dead Gray."

"When I woke up I thought I heard your voice. Couldn't find you. But then I was happy that I didn't have to see Beelz," exclaimed Gray.

Soon, Hero was running around with Gray on his back as the kingdom rejoiced that the evil Beelz was defeated. The celebration became louder and louder as they sang:

The agent of evil is no more
Thanks to our Creator we adore
Let the evergreen pasture blossom
For our Creator is awesome.
We shall forever live as family
And forever shall we live happily

No more deceiving skins.
For there are no more vessels of sin
Much love to Angelix of holy wings
And respect to Tauza, our mighty King
Out of light, new life begins
For Vangoland and all within

•　•　•

Now that the adrenalin of the adventure was subsiding, the thorn that had pierced his foot bothered Moabi. "This thorn!" he exclaimed, sitting down to inspect it. As he attempted in vain to find a way to extract it, Clips flew in, chirping.

"Bizwax said you got a thorn in your foot," said Clips, looking up at Moabi.

"Yes, and it is really throbbing now, Clips. Do you think you can help?" Moabi asked.

"Let me see," said Clips.

Moabi extended his foot. It was bruised and raised like a boil where the thorn was. With her sharp beak, Clips probed around the wound and scratched in the middle to see if there was puss.

"The thorn is deep," Clips said.

"So you can't help me?" Moabi asked.

"It is going to require an incision. If you are prepared for that, I can perform it. I did the same for Boltex, and he was screaming like a baby."

"Even if I scream, don't stop," Moabi said, taking a deep breath and squeezing his eyes shut.

He screamed and fist-pounded the ground as she pinched and clipped the flesh, but he felt almost nothing when she yanked out the thorn. He thanked her for her kindness. After that, his foot felt numb and walked toward the shore as light raindrops fell on his face.

THE DRIFTING OF THE LAND

It happened so fast that all the animals did not know what was happening. The turf they were standing on drifted away from the rest of the land. There was no rattling, rumbling, or any other extreme noise, except the whistling of the wind. Those on the drifting land, including the royal family and Moabi, crammed together, fearing the possibility of plunging into the river. A few animals fainted, and some trembled as the flood rocked the piece of land. They thought their ordeal was over, but it seemed as though another had begun.

Some pleaded the Creator to save them. Moabi quivered and vomited. "We've come so far, please save us,

God," he whispered. As if his God heard him, the rain stopped, but there was a giant, cotton-candy-like cloud accelerating toward them.

As the cloud hovered above, those who dared to look up could see Angelix's head leading the cloud, her body fully immersed in it and her eyes twinkling. As the cloud enveloped them, they couldn't hear each other anymore, as if the fogginess was absorbing their voices. They felt the tumultuousness of the island subside. They began to coast down the river smoothly, as though the land was a sled on ice.

Moabi could see the stoic stares on their faces, still confused. As for himself, for a brief moment, he experienced déjà vu, then he felt as though small insects were crawling on him. He looked down at the swelling veins in his hands, and he felt a strange power surging in them. He felt waves of warmth traveling through his body and a heavy drowsiness coming upon him, causing his eyelids to gradually shut. Suddenly, bolts of lightning flashed forth out from his knuckles, ripping through the cloud and sending the rest of animals into panic. They watched Moabi convulsing on the ground as if the lightning bolts were striking him.

"He must be struck!" the king exclaimed.

Angelix hovered over Moabi and flapped her wings. The electricity and convulsions subsided. However, Moabi remained unconscious.

• • •

A few minutes later, Moabi opened his eyes, dazed. But when he saw Angelix staring at him with a glorious smile glittering in her eyes, he felt the breath of grace quickening him. With her beak, Angelix tapped his forehead, and like a geyser, he jumped to his feet.

"What happened to you?"Angelix asked, smiling.

"I don't know. I remember being sort of entranced and the next thing I knew, I was walking in this beautiful place—an amazing place."

"Really? What was it like?" asked Angelix, smiling like she knew what he was talking about.

"I was walking in a tunnel of frozen rain, dust, clouds, lightning, and hail. It was all blended together like the colors of a marble. It was really amazing."

"Incredible. That is good news, Moabi. Those are attributes of the power that you now possess."

"The power that I possess? I don't understand that," said Moabi, perplexed.

"Yes. Remember the cloud emanating from your arm after my blood dripped on you?"

"Yes," said Moabi with eyes wide open.

"That is how you were able to get the power. See, not too long ago, you fell down because the power in you was reacting to the power in me," said Angelix, blinking and rolling his eyes. "Those bolts of lightning that flashed forth out of your knuckles are the evidence that the power has been unlocked."

"I am still confused," said Moabi.

"Moabi, I know that this was not your choice. Please allow me to explain this to you, Moabi," Angelix advised.

"Please do!" said Moabi with deep concern.

"Okay. When I was worshipping later that day, after I bled on you, the Creator revealed to me that when my blood comes in contact with human beings, it infuses them with power. I have special connections with human beings," she said, smiling. The Creator's word was loud and clear in my heart that what happened is not reversible."

"So what is going to happen to me now, Angelix? What am I going to do with this so-called power?" said Moabi with a concerned face.

"Use it," said Angelix.

"How?" Moabi asked.

"First of all, your thought system must be rooted in the Creator's love.

If not, you will not be able to apply or control the power. This is where the Creator's will comes in. Thus, you have to be led by his will. When your thoughts are aligned with his will, you will be able to take the right action."

"I don't understand," said Moabi, a smile visible at the corners of his mouth.

"Don't worry, soon you will understand. Now let's talk about other good news," said Angelix.

Moabi couldn't take his eyes off her, as she seemed to glow with a beautiful energy force. He had never seen her happier or more at peace.

"I like good news. Are you going to help me go home now?"

"We are taking you to your world."

"Really? Are we going there now?" inquired Moabi, rubbing his hands against each other. "That's what I have been waiting for."

"Yes, and I have a surprise for you," said Angelix.

"What is it?" Moabi asked quickly.

"For one, you were able to help us with the water hole during the drought season. Second, I applaud you for being bold in facing the king, who was in denial. You planted the seed of change in his heart. When I told him that I would not pray for his son until he brought you back safe, I was just watering the seed you had planted, and so I thank you for your courage. Your presence in our kingdom was needed, my friend, and I couldn't be more proud of you."

"Thank you for your kinds words, Angelix. At least my presence in Vangoland was not in vain," said Moabi, smiling.

"You are welcome. Now, for all these reasons, I am sending you home with a gift for your mother," Angelix said.

"What is it?" Moabi asked eagerly. He couldn't imagine anything grander than the stone he carried in his drenched backpack.

"Let me see your hand," she said.

Moabi raised a cupped hand to Angelix.

Angelix spread her toes, and a seed fell into his hand. It was dry and hard. It had a golden tone and looked much like a simple apricot seed. "This is the seed of a tree called Como from a world called Galala. Listen closely. When you get home, take this seed, break it carefully; make sure the powder in it is not wasted. There is also a second seed inside. Put it aside safely. I will tell you later what you ought to do with it. Pour the Como seed powder into a vessel and mix it with cold water. Give it to your mother while it is fresh. With that dose, she will be healed," directed Angelix.

Moabi felt like he could jump as joy overwhelmed him. "How much water?" he asked, like a small child given a candy or a cookie.

"It doesn't really matter. What matters is that you mix all the powder in the water, but she should drink the mixture immediately because it loses potency if exposed for a long time."

"Thank you, Angelix," Moabi appreciated, kissing the Como seed. "So what about the little seed inside that you said I should put aside?"

"Be careful with it. It is black, smooth, and small as a pear seed. It could easily slip away. Find a secret place by a river where you can plant it. In a year or so, it will start producing fruits. The powder inside each seed of a fruit will heal one person who suffers from disease. The seeds can become plants only when planted by you," Angelix explained.

Moabi thought about his grandmother's home in California that sat just on the other side of a levee. It was an ideal location, but unlikely because he did not have any relationship with her. "My only problem is the location," said Moabi softly.

"Well, don't worry about it. Just keep the little seed. It won't grow anywhere unless you plant it. But you could heal many people with it."

"Yes, I understand, Angelix. I really do. My grandmother has a big yard on the bank of the Sacramento River, but we have not talked in a long time," Moabi said. "But I'm excited about what you are telling me. My mother and I started an organization to fight cancer back home. But we've never cured anyone."

"You have the cure in your hand now," said Angelix, getting close to Moabi's face. "But I want to warn you, this is not going to be an easy task for you. There are those who will try to cut the tree or even kill you if they know about this."

"Wait a minute. Did you say kill me?" asked Moabi alarmed.

"Yes, because they will see you as an enemy since you will represent a threat to their profits. The emphatic devotion to money is the source of many immoral deeds."

Moabi scratched his head. He didn't like the idea of being killed, but taking a risk to save innumerable lives, he thought, would make him a hero. It was at least more honorable than letting fear hold him captive to an uncertain demise. "I want to help people."

"Very good. The other thing that you should remember is that the powder cannot be sold. You must give it freely, just like I gave it to you. Okay?"

"Got it," said Moabi.

Suddenly, Angelix fluttered away, up into the big cloud that was upon and both vanished.

"We are alive! We are alive!" some of the animals shouted, while most twitched their ears with eyes wide in awe. "This is not home," one lion lamented immediately.

"O-o-o-o this is beautiful!" cried one of the hyenas.

They all marveled at the shimmering river, the silver waves rolling along with their floating land. Behind them, they could see an island with a blue, black, and white flag mounted in the middle. It was the Sedudu Island in the middle of the Chobe River.

A little bit beyond the island, elephants sloshed out of the river as their young ones resisted the departure. Moabi smiled at this beautiful scenery. He could sense from the flag that he was back in Botswana—that he was in his own world.

Soon, Moabi began to see buildings behind tall trees on the bank. One of the buildings was a two-story house, and what he saw on its balcony startled him. A broad smile rippled his mouth. Then he exploded with a loud chortle, exhilarated. He turned around to face the stunned animals. "I am home! I am home! Look at the people! See?" he said as he pointed to the balcony. The animals watched him as he jumped around, some with stone faces, but the majority, including King Tauza beamed with easy smiles, happy to see him joyful.

The couple who was on the balcony rushed down to the riverbank, calling out to neighbors to come see. They were so fascinated that they rallied everyone to come and witness the sight. "Bunch of animals on a floating island!" they shouted as they ran.

When the land and the animals were adjacent to Mowana Lodge, Angelix landed on Moabi's shoulder and began to whisper in a soft voice.

"I hope the story you are going to write will affect your world in the most positive way."

Moabi nodded. "I hope to do a good job, Angelix."

"But remember, if you choose to do evil things, the power in you will leave," said Angelix, her eyes wide open.

"I am human and not perfect," said Moabi. "I don't even know if this power—"

"Making a mistake is different from being evil. You must always rise against evil," Angelix interrupted.

"I will try."

"Listen, Moabi, you will be fine, and you are going to do well. Just don't be evil," she reiterated.

"Okay," Moabi nodded. He could sense the seriousness, the encouragement, and the imperative nature of Angelix's words.

"The time has come for the rest of us to return to Vangoland. I hope to see you again, but can't promise I will. So, for now at least, goodbye Cloudman," said Angelix as the land slowly came to a stop, an inch from the shore.

Moabi chuckled at the title Angelix has bestowed upon him. "Thank you, Angelix." He couldn't imagine being called Cloudman. In fact, he thought it was hilarious. Then he turned around to face the rest of the animals. "Thank you all for allowing me to be part of your life. Experiencing your kingdom with you has taught me a great deal about life and I hope you feel the same way." He paused. "I want to thank King Tauza for his hospitality, and commend change of heart for the betterment of all." He stepped towards his friend, Bizwax, whose tears were now running into her toothless mouth.

"Don't forget about me," said Bizwax, putting her head on Moabi's muddy shoe.

"I won't. Thanks for everything, Biz. You have been a wonderful friend.

I wish nothing but the best for you."

Bizwax looked up and winked at him.

Chi and Hero gave him big smiles, and the king waved his amputated leg at him.

Moabi jumped onto the bank of the Chobe River, and he felt new energy with the realization that he had landed in his world. Onlookers murmured and pointed, but he did not bother to look at them, for his eyes were glued to his departing friends. Then he watched the land veering left and turning around in a slow semicircle, slightly rippling the water. He dabbed a tear at the corner of his eye, simultaneously waving at them.

Angelix perched next to Dumie, fluttered her wings. She asked him to sing "The Song of Life." For Dumie, this was an honor. As soon as Dumie elevated his voice in a song the animals all knew, they joined in.

Let us all sing the song of life
And not cringe at the devil's knife.

Vangoland, the land of our roots
Of our Creator we love
The one who gave us
The ever-fruitful tree

We give thanks to the Creator we love.
He loves us so much,
He sent us His dove,
So his wisdom can become our light,
For with the wisdom
We overcome plight.

Let the wisdom of our Creator be revered
As He delivers us from our fears
Through us, let His breath flow
In us, let His peace grow
For we all come from His heart,
Evil shall not tear our kingdom apart.

The people on the banks were charmed and captivated by the animals' exuberant performance—the supreme soprano of the wolves, the fine alto of the foxes, the breathtaking tenor of the majority and the smooth baritone of the lions.

Angelix flew over the crowd of people one more time as if saying goodbye as they watched the animals head toward Sedudu Island. Out of the sky, a fleece of cloud descended, completely covering them. Now, only the floating cloud could be seen. As soon as the cloud touched

Sedudu Island, the land, the cloud, and the animals all disappeared in the twinkling of an eye. The humans gasped at this phenomenon. For a long while after that, people continued to visit the place, promenading on the banks, hoping to see animals parading on a floating island.

THE COMO SEED

Moabi arrived home and found his mother bedridden. His cousin, Gloria, was by her bedside, clinging to hope. It was quiet; there was no TV or radio on. He kissed her pale cheek as he struggled in vain to hold back tears. Before Victoria could open her sunken eyes, Moabi rushed to the kitchen, grabbed a wooden nutcracker, and carefully cracked the Como seed. With caution, he extracted the glistening, inner seed and placed it carefully in an empty spice jar. He then emptied the powder into a cup of water, and stirred well. He brought the concoction to his mother.

"Is it really you, baby?" Victoria said in a low raspy voice.

"Yes, it's me, and I'm so glad you are awake, Mom. I brought you a special tea. It is going to make you feel better," said Moabi.

"Where did you get it?" asked Victoria, raising her head from the sweaty, spongy pillow.

"I brought it with me. Just drink it, and you will thank me," said Moabi. "This is medicine from the real healer."

"Who is this healer?" asked Victoria, struggling to sit up. She mustered a weak smile, but her eyes shone brightly to see her son who she'd worried about without end.

"Trust me—you would not know her. I'm sure you must have so many questions, and I promise I will explain everything. Please, Mom, take the medicine now," Moabi insisted. He and Gloria helped Victoria sit up and positioned the pillow between her back and the headboard.

She took a sip with Moabi holding the cup to her trembling lips. She began to drink steadily, without taking her eyes off of Moabi. "How is it?"

"Tastes good," she said her voice stronger, as if her throat was cleared, "I missed you! I am so glad you're home!"

"I love you, too, Mom, and I missed you terribly. I was so worried about you," said Moabi, kissing her on her forehead.

Within an hour, her strength was returning and she developed an appetite. By the evening, she amazed Gloria by rising from her bed to join her and Moabi at the dinner table. Then it was Victoria's turn to be amazed as Moabi led them in saying grace. The spirit of gratitude and wonder radiated palpably as Moabi recounted his adventures in Vangoland.

• • •

Although Moabi's journal and cameras were water damaged, Moabi's memories were vivid. He fashioned the stories of his adventures into a novel, Adventures In Vangoland: The Rise Against Evil. As Cloudman, he resolved to use his newly found powers to benefit not only the citizens of New York but around the world. He thought about Angelix often and all that she told him. With his mother thriving, he contemplated how he could carry out his responsibility to plant the como seed. Somehow he knew the diamond from Mount Fear would play a certain role in his journey.

ABOUT THE AUTHOR

A devoted husband and father, Sonny Walebowa is a native of Botswana. There, Sonny began writing stories and poetry in both English and his native language, Setswana. He moved to the United States in 1997 on a scholarship, earning a BFA in Film and Television

Production and later obtaining MA in Human Services and Executive Leadership.

After writing, directing, and producing shorts, commercials, music videos, and documentaries in the San Francisco Bay Area, Sonny moved to Los Angeles, where he worked at Arista Records in music marketing, sales, and A&R. He also worked in production, and film-distribution. He later returned to Northern California working as a web and TV broadcast editor and multimedia producer.

While authoring juvenile fiction and screenplays, Sonny previously self-published a biography on Nelson Mandela for the juvenile market, which includes a narrated CD. He also penned two books of poetry. Sonny loves travel and adventure.

Made in the USA
Columbia, SC
24 January 2018